I0460561

DarkSF is the Dark Chocolate of SF

If you love movies like *Blade Runner*, *Dark City*, and <u>Alien</u>, and love to read dark, cinematic novels of literary and poetic value, you will savor this one.

DarkSF is the Dark Chocolate of Science Fiction. So says John Argo, a pioneer in Internet publishing since 1996. The rich, nuanced texture and pacing of a *Blade Runner* or a *Chrysalis* is definitely not for everyone. But those who love a dark coffee with swirls of heavy cream, along with a good jazz lounge and some chromatic overload, will love DarkSF.

In fiction, think Frank Herbert's *Dune*, Thomas Pynchon's *The Crying of Lot 49*, William Golding's *Lord of the Flies*, Aldous Huxley's *Brave New World*, Ray Bradbury's *Fahrenheit 451*, George Orwell's *1984*, and so many more. See **www.darksf.com** for commentary and detail about all this.

So what's the core of DarkSF? It's not more violent or gruesome than many readers might think. It's filled with wonderful love stories amid all the adventure and chaos, out there in the galaxy or here on Earth in the strangest corners and darkest woods. It's not necessarily a horror story, although it may be as scary or bloody as the author wants to make it.

The core principle of DarkSF is its rich, glorious texture and poetic swirl of effects. Movies like *Blade Runner*, *Chrysalis*, *Dark City*, and *Alien* are frequently panned by readers who prefer fast food rather than a fine restaurant meal. DarkSF offers steak, violins, and red wine to connoisseurs.

This isn't milk chocolate for light weights. This is the dark chocolate of the science fiction genre. And come to think of it, virtually all great SF has this marvelous flavor. We call it Sense of Wonder with good reason. More info at **www.darksf.com**.

Nebula Express

A DarkSF Novel
by
John Argo

(from an older edition cover)

Clocktower Books
San Diego, California

Nebula Express by John Argo

Copyright 2004 by John Argo. All Rights Reserved.

You may not reproduce any part of this book for any purpose without the publisher's written permission.

Print editions available on line and in bookstores. E-book editions available from all major platforms.

Art Design: CTB/JTC

Photos: iStockphoto.

This novel is a work of fiction. Names, characters, places, and incidents are products of the author's imagination. Any resemblance to actual events or locales or persons, living or dead, is entirely coincidental.

About the DarkSF Series

DarkSF is the Dark Chocolate of Science Fiction.

It's not for everyone. However, most SF is Dark SF. Think of your favorite movies or novels in this genre, including *Blade Runner, Alien, Dark City, The Body Snatchers, Chrysalis, Fifth Element, Lord of the Flies, 1984, Brazil, The Time Machine*, and so many more. For a longer discussion of DarkSF, visit DarkSF.com, a dedicated website.

Think of it in an Aristotelian sense. Most literature is dark (tragic) versus comedy or melodrama. Long discussion to be had at www.darksf.com and across the author's webplex.

For a quick understanding, DarkSF is not necessarily more violent, gruesome, scary, or otherwise horror than most literature. The secret is not about any of those things but, as in *Blade Runner* or *Chrysalis*, it's the *atmosphere.* It's rich like a good espresso or dark chocolate: layered, nuanced, takes its time, not just another wham-bam-thankyou-ma'am fast-and-easy food snack that's not literature but melodrama. If that's not your cup of espresso, please do move on; no hard feelings. If you love a rich, creamy read, a dark mouthful of the mysterious night side, a luxurious stretch of jazz and poetry with your oeuvre, this is your cuppa dark brew— and a rich, dark chocolate bar besides.

Dark SF Novels by John Argo

Nebula Express
Monopol City
Doom Spore
Streamliners
This Shoal of Space
Strange Doors (Anthology)
Robinson Crusoe 1,000,000 A.D.

Empire of Time SF by John Argo

Moon Berry Wine
Lantern Road
Time Train
Runners: Escape from Prison Planet
Mars The Divine
Pioneers
Cosmopolis (2017)
Night Songs At Um (short)
Harps (short)

Visit www.johntcullen.com for more information. John Argo is a pseudonym of John T. Cullen, a San Diego author.

John (birth name Jean-Thomas Cullen) is the author of more than forty books of fiction and nonfiction. He has been publishing online since 1996. The hub of his webplex is www.metrowebplex.com.

Chapter 1

The engineer's eyes radiated terror as he ran along the slowly revolving inner surface of the cargo liner *Neptune Express*. Close behind him, fast bare feet skittered on steel decks. The engineer heard the sinister fluting breaths of his pursuers. They preferred moving in darkness, so he avoided shadowy corners.

He ran hard through alternate stripes of shadow and wan light. The light around him was sickly dim, while in the distance brighter yellowish smears glowed. Brown and amber shadows drowned in a spattering of rusty water. His gasps left puffs of vapor. He smelled rust and decay, mud and mushrooms, as he ran through the echoing holds. The brightness of WorkPod01 drew all too slowly near. Several times, he paused weakly and doubled over. He held the heavy black gun in both hands, and took several deep breaths before he lurched on.

"Come on, you bastards," he taunted them, and his voice echoed harshly. The air in the vast holds was breathable, though it smelled flat and metallic. In places, the metal joints had separated like tissue in rusty layers, and between those sheets grew angry red and white fungus whose acidic powders burned the skin if you touched it.

The engineer looked back and spotted a grayish figure moving between shadows, from a stack of barrels, across a glittering metal floor wet like chrome, to some other black void. The engineer fired twice, and the powerful therm gun sizzled in his hand. The hot ray streaking from its barrel crackled across the air in two short bursts. The air glowed bluish, and not too far away something screamed. The scream was near-human, coming from a throat made for gulping meat rather than talking or singing. As the mudman died, thrashing on the cold wet ground inside the cargo ship, others of its kind made that strange, low, haunting flute-like noise. Whatever they were communicating among one another, the running man shuddered at its ominous sound.

He fired off one more round for good measure, though it depleted the charge in his gun and moved his desperate situation another step closer to impossible. How long before they got to him? The mudmen never failed to track down their prey.

"I'll take a few more of you with me!" he called out over his shoulder as he ran in the direction of WorkPod01. Already he could see the bright lights there, among the windows overlooking the vast cavities of the holds meant to carry people and goods between Earth, the Moon, and the colonies in the Solar System. He could hear the music, the laughter, the conversation of his own kind, and he knew he would be among them in a matter of minutes--if the gray, stitched, red-eyed shapes rising on the heights behind him did not get him first. The mudmen had neither speech nor art, but they had a strange and horrible music of their kind. They formed their mouths into small cones and emitted a deep breathing sound, like a boy blowing air over the mouth of a bottle. The quietly unnerving, nightmarish sound traveled far in the otherwise still, fetid air. Like the hunting sounds by which predators communicated with one another back on Earth-the coyote or the hyena laughing and warbling on a hill under the full moon, the wolf howling on a snow field--likewise, the mudmen whooshed and fluted and murmured among each other. Sometimes when a distant light flashed just so, the engineer could make out the ruby gleam at the back of their eyeballs. He had no idea how these creatures had come to infest the ship. He only knew they were hunting him like rats tracking down a mouse. He must reach the crew of unsuspecting technicians in WorkPod01 to warn them.

And so he ran on, already bleeding from his encounters with the mudmen. He alternately ran and staggered, hid and waited, then ran some more. His jumpsuit was torn and scorched. His hair was dirty, his face sooty, his scratches oozing. Slowly, the enormous mile-diameter drum of the ship turned as he ran. A stain of brown light with yellowish highlights slanted down among the girders and steel framework to light his path. Already he could see the narrow ladder stretching endlessly up, out of the darkness into the relative brightness above, into dazzlingly bluish white light. Behind the locked and sealed portal leading into WorkPod01 were a crew of eight technicians. They would just now be getting ready to emerge for their day's work. It would be their only day's work, as the running man well knew.

The running man threw himself at the cool steel ladder and started climbing. His clothing hung in rags and his breathing steamed about him, as did the sweat on his back. He felt the scratch of a claw on his heel and looked down. He saw two melon-shaped heads bobbing together, and yellowed horn-fangs reaching after him. Rabbit-mad eyes neither quite red nor quite blue in color, but wide open, stared hungrily after him, and he could almost make out a greenish-yellow smile in each cadaver-gray face. He kicked at their reaching hands and climbed all the faster. "Here," he said, pulling out the gun and firing straight down so he singed his own trouser leg and smelled scorched cloth, "here's a good one for you. Take this back to your queen and your hive." He fired twice more and did not look down to see what he had done. His hands were sweaty. The gun slid away, clattering, and fell down into the spattered mess at the base of the ladder. Trembling, he could struggle to keep his slick hands from slipping from the bare steel as he climbed hand over hand as rapidly as he could. He heard strains of innocent music and laughter above and couldn't help but laugh for joy at the thought of being with his own kind in a few minutes, though he knew better.

Chapter 2

Cargo vessel F.E.S. *Neptune Express* (Federal Earth Ship, 50kTn, 16 parallel main ion-drive power plants housed in external silvered nacelles) was one year outbound from and halfway through her two-year journey to Neptune's moon Triton, when an emergency beacon began to send distress signals back to the Colfirio Inter-Planetary Exploratory Corporation base station on Luna.

A meteorite the size of a golf ball had torn through the outer skin and exploded, vaporizing important elements of the ship's delicate cargo maintenance systems. The ship carried nearly one million individual seed units for trees, vegetables, and other living matter along with growth matrix, soil, hydroponics, shelters, converters, and supplies to be deployed on a major new research station approximately 29 AU from the sun and 81 AU from the heliopause.

The stock, matrix, and growth supplies were vital to the survival of 7,000 colonists on Triton engaged in mining, research, and support activities. Without the successful transport of these materials, the colony would begin starving and suffocating within one earth year. The next mission would not reach Triton for five earth years, so the success of the *Neptune Express* mission was nonnegotiable.

The ship had been designed with redundant systems, and was staffed by crews of highly competent maintenance and repair experts. These dedicated engineers were often all that stood between life and death in the infinite and lonely void. With the ship halfway to her target, rescue was out of the question. She was leaking atmosphere. Water and other fluids were boiling away from torn conduits. Without skilled and immediate intervention, the ship would begin to implode silently and irrevocably one section at a time within a few earth days.

Acting heroically, and with some injuries and loss of life, repair crews stabilized the ship and kept her on course. They worked around the near-catastrophic impact point. They sealed off gaping holes, rerouted torn conduits, reconnected loose and dangerously sparking conductor cables, and guided the automatic systems through self-test and reoperability routines. With the crisis resolved, there was nothing more to be done but to keep a close watch on all operating systems and subsystems, patch any new leaks, repair any further damage, and pray for the rest of the flight to be uneventful. This required periodic excursions to the far reaches of the huge ship by the surviving highly trained and dedicated maintenance staff.

Chapter 3

Section Leader Ridge had a feeling of *déjà vu* as he looked up from his digital writing pad at the main table in the crew mess in WorkPod01. Ridge was a slim, wiry man with dark hair, strongly angular facial features, and large inquisitive dark eyes. Rock music boomed from a speaker on one side, while holographic movies played in two or three corners, one woman lifted weights, another woman slept in a sling mat under an artificial sun-and-wind machine, and two men played chess over a tiny table. The table was littered with digital writing tablets, holographs of loved ones back home on Earth, and a hundred other little personal items that eight long-haul space mariners tended to accumulate around them in their everyday life. Last night had been Asian, and in the middle of the table were piled half-empty food containers that smelled faintly of miso soup, sweet and sour shrimp and beef, eggs tofu garnished with seaweed, sukiyaki, and a dozen other ethnic dishes. Ridge had to admit: the Corporation took good care of the crew's culinary and other personal needs, as best that could be done two billion kilometers from home port on Luna.

Mahaffey, a welding tech 1, belched loudly in a corner. He watched a holographic remake of a Hitchcock suspense film. "Are you looking at that food again?" Mahaffey said in a booming voice. He was a long, slender man of African descent, and Ridge always found it amazing how Mahaffey could be comfortable wrapping himself into a ball in his white composite chair with those long stocking-footed legs protruding.

"I just glanced at the boxes," Ridge said. "Isn't it Lantz's turn to clean house?"

"Guilty as charged," said the athletic redheaded woman who was just then pumping iron in another corner--Lantz, a metallurgy tech 1, which Ridge thought of as a fancy term for welder, although lots of times the welding was delicate micro, nano, and even smaller stuff requiring world class microscopes and tools so small a sneeze would blow one's whole toolkit from here to the asteroids and back.

"It's E.S.P.," Mahaffey declaimed without looking away from his holo. "If anyone even thinks about food, I start getting gas." Mahaffey was a metallurgy tech 1 and as a much a competitor as a colleague of Lantz. Like everyone on board, they were a careful match made by expert Corporate social scientists interested in keeping peace aboard these long hauls. One did this with lots of work, a little play, and no stray emotional crosscurrents except a little vinegary banter.

"I'm still full from last night," Ridge agreed. He flicked his stylus idly around his nose while struggling with the words in a report. Other section leaders he'd known could simply dictate verbally and the tablets output text, but Ridge was too self-conscious about his own writing to let it flow like that. Briefly, he thought about the other sections in the vast ship. What were they doing in WorkPod02? 05? 69? There were something like forty self-contained workstations like their own, each manned by eight technicians capable of handling any emergency or maintenance task whether mechanical, electrical, or biological-or any combination thereof. "Hey, Mahaffey," Ridge said, "don't we have intramurals coming up soon?"

"Yeah, we have a round of volleyball due," the long dark-skinned young man said, folding large hands on a flat stomach. "When we get the large holds on front and stern emptied out on the return trip, we can play baseball in them under the lights, just like home."

Lantz chimed in: "Just like home, but no honey and no kids."

"You're not married," Mahaffey bantered back idly.

Sweat dribbled from Lantz's tightly braided golden-red hair and ran down her plain, healthy, freckled features. "Speak for yourself, Moses. I have one kid and when I get back he'll never have to play alone again."

Ridge chuckled to himself and tried to focus on his work while the others chattered playfully. "Tonight will be Greek night," he reminded them, as if rubbing it in. "Work hard today. Burn off the carbs."

"Cruel master," Lantz jibed. "Who else here besides me pumps iron? Nobody. If I don't do this, I can work all day and still be as wide as I am tall."

"Which is not very," Tomson said. He was a shorter, older dark-skinned biotech, EMT, usually called Doc. He was the best biomedical tech in the service, but Ridge and most of the others thought Tomson had developed a sour streak and should have retired long ago. How many million-dollar jobs did a person need to retire rich, before he or she was too old to enjoy a beach house on the Med or a villa in the Rockies?

"Says who?" Lantz said, stopping to towel her dripping face. She wore black and blue tights under a flowery torso garment. She also wore a white headband and a wide blonde-leather kidney belt.

Tomson grinned from his chess game. "Says a hundred bucks I have in my pocket. You want to bet I can't lose ten pounds faster than you can with all that sweating and puffing?" Tomson's quiet chess partner was Yu, a Bio-Engineer 1 who specialized in servomech wetware but could expertly handle any sort of halfway intelligent motile artificial tool.

Lantz puffed loudly as she hopped to her feet after finishing her sets. "Exhale and you'll lose ten pounds of hot air."

Brenna came out of her module and slapped palms with Lantz. Lantz headed off to the shower, while Brenna took Lantz's place on the exercise complex. Brenna was the tallest of the four women in WorkPod01, towering inches above Lantz, Jerez, and Mughali. The latter, an Electrical and Mechanical Engineer 1 from Mumbai, who was still asleep in her personal module, was despite the name a practicing Hindu with a red dot of *kumkum* powder on her forehead.

As he watched Brenna walk by, Ridge felt a strange skip in his heart. He felt a special affection for her that he believed she somehow returned, although these things were not supposed to happen. Like every person on the ship, whether in this workpod or any other, Ridge and Brenna had their own loved ones back on Earth or Luna. Ridge was from San Diego, where his wife Dorothy and their two children lived in the sunny seaside community of Imperial Beach. Brenna had a husband, Ricardo, and a little boy and girl, back on Earth in Buenos Aires. She was originally of Cuban-German extraction, having grown up in New England, but had married an Argentine airline pilot and moved to the Villa Santiago de Liniers, Buenos Aires to be a school teacher. Ricardo and she were very much in love. Ricardo came from a wealthy family of building contractors, but they had fallen on hard times. Ricardo and Brenna had decided he should retire from flying and go it from scratch in a new business as a cyber engineer, using his copious college and family connections. They had decided that one four-year haul around the planets would set them up for life. With an extended family including lots of aunts, the hardness on the children would pass and they'd benefit for the rest of their lives. Like most persons on board including Ridge, Brenna communicated daily with her family back home. Ridge's situation was much more straightforward. He'd graduated *summa cum laude* from the University of California at San Diego, done six years as an Air Force engineering officer, married a Miss San Diego (Dorothy) just out of junior college, and planned to do four full tours before retiring as a wealthy man. This was his third tour. He was in mid-career. Standard practice was to get a year at full pay and half time, usually consulting, which was very cushy, and they'd moved from the more military oriented Imperial Beach to the more upscale Mission Hills overlooking the bay. Despite all that, Ridge felt a chemistry with her (ironic, because as they had kiddingly observed, she was a Chemical Engineer 1) that made them feel exceptionally close, even when they were simply near each other, without even looking at each other or speaking. It was a potentially dangerous matter, and they let a little go a long way, spending very little time directly or alone together. By common practice, a person's single-room room ("cube") was off-limits to all others, so individuals rarely visited each other at such a personal level. Instead, the workpods were spacious and designed to offer optimal elbowroom and the illusion of far more room than there was.

Brenna sat in her stirrups, rowing. She was an attractive woman with rich dark-amber hair and deep blue eyes. She had pleasantly proportioned features that conveyed a delicate balance of strength and softness. She was disciplined, but kind. Ridge watched for a moment as she moved forward and backward in the soft light. Tiny golden hairs glowed on her long pale arms with their wiry upper-arm muscles. Other than being tall, she was generally unremarkable in stature, with smallish breasts and a tendency toward a beanpole straightness rather than much curvature, so he wondered what it was about her that made his heart beat this way, and his thinking grow fuzzy, and his fingers tremble just a bit. She glanced up at him as she rowed, and smiled faintly, with her eyes glowing briefly, deep blue, like a forest pond amid the tangle of her hair. Ridge nodded and turned away, feeling a flush in his cheeks.

A shudder or a creak or the faintest of groans or something passed like a wave through the room. That would be WorkPod01 starting to move on its tracks, heading toward the area where repairs were needed.

Mughali, wearing an ornately decorated mustard sari of silk over her red tights, came from her cube to wash a few items of clothing in the laundry sink. "Looks like it's going to be a busy day," Mughali said in her lilting Universal Anglo. One of those laughing, happy, impromptu conversations about nothing and everything instantly ensued among the crewmembers. Ridge smiled to himself. He saw Mughali at the sink; Tomson and Yu playing chess; Lantz whistling as she swept from the showers in to her cube, wearing her carrot hair in a turban and a fluffy white robe over her newly exercised musculature; Brenna rowing away; Mahaffey curled up in front of his movie with his stocking feet outthrust; and now Jerez, the other woman, a Cyber-Engineer 2, emerged from her cube.

Each of the eight members of WorkPod01 had a round tunnel to crawl through, leading to the quiet and privacy of his or her personal space. Each cube was 20 feet to a side, and arranged as each person saw fit. Typically, it resembled a college dorm room with holos and a thousand little personal mementos attached to neutral beige walls, plus lounging space, a small collection of light recreational drugs approved by the home corporation, enough holofilms to last hundreds of hours, and access to a world's library. One could slide shut what Yu referred to as a moon door made of translucent plast, and be alone.

Jerez emerged from her moon door to find something cold to drink in the kitchen. Jerez was a slender, dark-haired woman of Filipino-Spanish extraction, who'd grown up in Singapore but married a Norwegian and had holos of her several blond children alongside a smiling Oslo businessman who, but for his buckteeth and daffy smile, might have been a Viking in some earlier age.

"Section Leader Ridge, are you there?" said the voice of Captain Venable.

Ridge ran his hand across the wall, and a cube of light flicked on. There was the image of the ship's handsome, graying captain who was from Paris and vaguely resembled Cary Grant. "How are you doing, Sir?" He added apologetically. "I'm working on my report about yesterday's repairs. I'll have those to you before we walk out the door today."

"No hurry," Venable said. "I'll take your report for both days if you want to pass that to me later this evening."

"I'll be tired," Ridge said. "I'd rather not fall behind."

"A sensible policy," Venable said. "Are you ready to go out?"

Ridge shrugged. "Sure, we all are."

"How are the crew taking the work?"

"You mean the disaster?"

Venable nodded. "Just a little concerned. I know you're all professionals but this was a close call for all of us."

Ridge nodded. "I think we are all calm and self-assured, Captain. No panic, nothing like that." He winked. "Your leadership, Sir, is exceptional, of course."

Venable winked back. "Flattery will get you everywhere, Ridge." Venable was an easy-going, confident captain of many years' experience on the Luna-Neptune run. His home was in

Miami, where his wife still lived, although his two daughters had grown up, moved away, and married. Though only visible from the chest up, with a bland background in his office in the Bridge Command Post (CP) area forward, as opposed to WorkPod01's location amidships, he looked tanned and fit as always. His bluish-white uniform shirt looked well tailored and crisply ironed, and his little color-garden of decorations sat snugly above his shirt pocket. On his shoulders were four gold stars on a black epaulet, in contrast to Ridge's humble one black bar on a collar tab. In matters of rank and service, the gulf between the two men was vast, but both were graduate cyber-engineers and that made them colleagues and equals on some level. Venable said: "I'll speak to the group again when you are assembled and ready to move out for the day's work."

"Thank you, Sir. I hope by then to have this..." (Ridge made a show of gritting his teeth and preparing to toss his digital tablet into the screen where Venable's image glowed) "...Damned piece of scribbling finished and out of my hair."

Venable chuckled. "There are all sorts of artificial writing systems available on the market if you wouldn't be so damned stubborn, Ridge. Do things the easy way." He signed off, and the screen beside Ridge went blank.

Behind him, during that conversation, the dynamic of banter and conversation had whirled about some unseen axis. The crew one by one disappeared into their cubes. They soon stepped back out of their moon doors, fastening up the tabs on their jumpsuits. In normal working conditions, everyone wore white work suits or jumpsuits with orange trim on the shoulders for safety and visibility. Depending on their occupational specialty, their collar tabs might be tan (bio) or light blue (cyber) or gray (chemical, only Brenna in this workpod), and so forth. Ridge was the only one with a black collar and a black bar edged in white.

Brenna emerged from the shower and sat briefly beside him, drying her hair. She wore a thick, fluffy blue *frotte* robe and toweled her hair with a white towel. "Am I bothering you?"

"You're never bothering me. You're taking me away from this report thing that I hate."

"I'll write them for you."

"You're kidding. You'll do that for me?"

"You look so helpless."

"Gee, thanks. I didn't know it showed." He sat back in his chair, folding his hands over the flat of his belly. "Talk to home?" It was a standard question. There was no weather here to make small talk about. Calling home was the big event in everyone's daily life.

She nodded. "Ricardo bought a new car."

"What kind?"

"He didn't say."

"Did he look sad?"

She laughed. "No." She had a lovely way of rolling her eyes and smiling so that her teeth glowed and there was warmth tumbling all around her. And all around Ridge, who did not wish she would go away.

"Well, then it must not be too expensive, and it must be a nice car."

She nodded. "I would imagine that's what it is." Her features grew faintly more serious. "How are Dorothy and the kids?"

Ridge thought for a second. "Oh hell. I need to call home, don't I? This report has kept me so busy. Dorothy was fine, when last we spoke. My son and daughter are fine." He added. "In school, doing well." He added. "My girl plays goalie on her soccer team, and my boy is in Cub Scouts."

She leaned her head to one side and toweled in her ear. Then she repeated the procedure on the other side, turning her head that way. Her dark hair lay glossy and wet and tousled against the perfect shape of her head. She had a wide, tall forehead that made her look intelligent, he found as he studied her skin. She had fine, clear skin, without any particular scars or deformations, although her nose had a strong frontal edge and a nice knobby bridge. She saw him staring at her and looked away. As she did so, she twirled the towel and did a dervish thing from the waist up to form a huge fluffy turban in one smooth, practiced motion from having done it many times over many years. He smiled, thinking about all those little habits each person acquired over a lifetime and how they made everyone unique. He wondered again why she made him feel warm and energetic, and why he wasn't frightened since he had a wife at home who would not like to know the truth of such a diversion in his affections. What could he say to her? He placed his hands on his knees, preparing for her to leave and himself to get busy with other things. Should he say, we've got to stop meeting like this? How did one not have small talk with a person on a space ship a billion klicks from home? And what had they really ever done together but sit close, over cups of hot steaming tea in the lounge among all the other crew, and talk softly together about their own wives and children? She had never been to San Diego, but he had filled her with tales of strolling with Dorothy and the children along the sandy paths on Fiesta Island or among the goldfish ponds and botanical gardens of Balboa Park. Likewise, she had told stories of walking with Ricardo and their children along the Plaza de Mayo, on the breezy Avenida Emilio Castro in Liniers, on the beach near Cantilo in Belgrano, or motoring north for the weekend though Pueyrredon. In a sense, all cities and families, all lives and desires, had a universality that made them at once unique and interesting to tell about, yet interchangeable like clothing; or so Ridge had once remarked, and she had laughed that sensual, throaty laugh of hers while throwing her head back aglow with fond teasing. You are too much, amigo. So she had said, still dripping from the fountain of laughter, and he had said with much pretense of wisdom: Better too much than not enough, carissima.

She rose, pressing her turban between her palms, and said: "I'll write your report for you later when we get back. Just leave it there on the table for me."

"Thanks." He rose. "You're a life saver."

"You are a life worth saving," she said, walking to the privacy and secrecy of her cube in long, languid strides. She left him a sultry afterglance, a mix of innocence and hidden meaning he could not fathom.

Within an hour, Ridge stood by the portal and the others were beginning to form up in a casual line facing the video screen in the bulkhead beside the exit. On the other side of that dark, riveted metal door was a steel grid platform, and beyond that the vast belly of the cargo ship *Neptune Express*.

Ridge had an uneasy sense in remembering the meteorite impact. No surprise--the wounds and the shock were still fresh, and six plain white coffins sat in a special holding room far away in the stern of the ship, with Federal Earth flags draped over them--mute testimony to the frantic and chaotic days spent saving *Neptune Express* just recently. Once you lived through something like that, it took a long time to sleep well again and not to jump at the slightest tremor or noise. Then again, people were resilient. They joked. They fought. They talked. They started healing immediately. In space, you had to. There was no choice.

Since Brenna had made his day by relieving him of his report writing agony, Ridge spent some leisure time, first in his personal cube, then at the main crew table eating breakfast.

First he shaved and showered. The showers were in a common area, but each person had a reserved and private bath cubicle. (The potty facilities were also individual and private, located in another area of the workpod, and each crewmember had a virtual library in theirs.) For a good ten minutes in the shower, Ridge stood in the steamy atmosphere while needles of hot water exercised his skin. He changed the showerheads several times, settling finally on a nice steady stream. He used the special milled lavender soap he and Dorothy had picked up on a tour through Provençe, along with sunflower kitchen towels. He'd shaved using a new gold-plated four-blade razor and some very foamy cream, which worked fine as long as no stray suds escaped from the steamy confines of the shower. He changed from hot water to hot air and let the stimulating breeze dry him off. Grabbing a fluffy robe from a dispenser, he wrapped himself up and strode back, through his moon door (named after those round moon gates built into classical Chinese gardens and palaces) into the comfort of his personal cube. He felt much better.

He turned on the wall screen and dialed up San Diego. Familiar scenes of beaches, palm trees, botanical gardens, workaday streets, shopping centers, and freeways flashed by. Dorothy's face appeared on the screen, looking a bit formal since she'd had a makeover just to create this video reply. "Hello. I can't answer my personal comdeck just now, maybe because I'm in the garden or busy with the kids or out shopping, but if you will leave a message I will return your com as soon as possible. Thanks, and have a lovely day."

"Honey," Ridge said, "sorry I missed you today. Give the kids each a big hug for me, and a kiss, and maybe I'll have a chance to catch you after we get back from our work detail if I'm not too tired. You know how it is. Long hours, no sleep, and I'm too beat to even fall into the shower. Love you. Bye." These messages were always awkward, though he could tolerate them a lot better than writing reports.

With an hour to kill, and knowing the long exhausting shift ahead outside the workpod, Ridge crept into bed--a fancy sort of sleeping bag on a large upper bunk. He snuggled in to get comfortable, thinking it ironic that the living quarters were called the workpod, while the work was done anywhere but in here; although, one might allow, the entire lower floor consisted of specialty workshops for welding, brazing, chemical analysis-almost a mobile factory, so to speak. Closer to home though: in the cube, below the bunk where he now lay, was his desk, his thinking area, his place to speak recordings for home, read poems sent by his two small children, watch holovids directly on the desktop of Dorothy relating neighborhood gossip. Sometimes she would shoot him an hour or so of just plain day to day, moment to moment footage, like the mailman ringing, the children tramping through on a rainy day and getting yelled at, the golden retriever romping from couch to love seat and around all the living room furniture in one big circle while Dorothy, predictably, doubled over in a mix of laughter and yelling. These were the truly relaxing and wonderful moments of his day. What a miracle, that the tiny moments of life in a San Diego suburb could be beamed across such vast distances to such a tiny dot in space. Ridge had not slept well last night for some reason, and now his body hungrily sopped up the extra hour of sleep, like a plant soaking up a good watering.

As he drifted off, he looked forward to spending a little time, maybe a half hour, talking with Dorothy and watching the kids, all with a delay of several hours, of course. He and Dorothy couldn't directly talk because of the delay, but sent each other loving little messages. The pix of the kids were usually a few hours old. The time of day on board *Neptune Express* was synchronized with that in San Diego, but this time delay threw it all off. Dorothy liked to transmit early, so he tended to be watching early morning footage. He could just put it all together in his head, from the senses and from memory. He could imagine that the dew was still wet on the grass, and maybe the street lights were still lit against a dark blue sky, and the morning breeze smelled fresh with the faint distant undertones of ocean and desert, not to mention eucalyptus and jasmine wafting up from the canyons, and maybe a touch of anise, a scent of citrus blossoms, and of course always that noxious hint of hydrocarbons not burned well from a passing mail truck.

Daydreaming of Dorothy and his little son and daughter, he dozed off. Distantly, he thought he heard laughter from a card game in the galley. He felt regular little tremors as the workpod moved on its axis, as it crept along on greased mirror-like steel surfaces. What luck, he thought again, to be alive, when they could all have died if a slightly larger object had struck the ship.

As he dozed off, he could imagine what sorts of dreams the others might have. Lantz might dream of running along the deep, mysterious green rainforest trails around the Olympic Peninsula, her home. Mughali might dream of shopping for clothing in the fashionable Marais in Paris, where her parents had moved, in this cosmopolitan and global world. Yu probably thought of his family, who lived in a planned development on Chongde Lu near Huaihai Park. Tomson, on the other hand, most likely had stormy thoughts of a crowded neighborhood in Sand City in old Philadelphia, a blues joint, a good pizza, and a brisk whiskey before bed. What did Jerez think of...sleepily, he lost track and thought of Brenna strolling arm in arm with Ricardo on the Plaza Dorrego in Colegiales, Buenos Aires, or perhaps sharing a half-pint of Italian-style *cerveza tirada* while watching *tango* dancers and listening to sensuous but melancholy *bandonéon* music. Why did he somehow feel he belonged there with her? He almost sobbed with frustration at the impossibility of it. Why have these dark thoughts? Why have these forbidden fantasies? In his dreams, as he lay on his back savoring the quiet and comfort of his cubicle, Ridge forced his thoughts in another direction. He made himself think about how he would take Dorothy and the children up onto the breezy bluffs of Cabrillo Point, high above San Diego bay and North Island, with the sandy and sparkling Coronado far below, and the red conical roofs of the Victorian-era Hotel Del, and beyond that the high-rise condo hives of wealthy Mexican economic refugees along the Silver Strand.

Feeling rested and refreshed, Ridge woke about an hour later. He could still feel occasional gentle rocking motions as WorkPod01 traversed forward under pressure of its inner worm gears all packed with grease and silicon. He put that off--work would begin in the dimness, far from the sun, inside the vast hangar-like structures of the ship, and that was what they got paid to do, and do well. He washed his face at the sink, dried himself with a towel, donned fresh underwear, and changed from his robe back into his jump suit.

Out in the lounge area, a loud card game was in progress as the staff sat in their jumpsuits ready to go. They looked stiff and bulky in web gear with back and front packs containing water, oxygen, and tools. The place was cheery with laughter, the aromas of brewing coffee and tea, the sweetness of pastries, and the occasional exhilarating whiff of stimtube. The conversation was a customary desultory mix of cross-talk, some of it revolving around salaries. They were all paid well, on standard sliding scales, and everyone pretty much knew what everyone made, base, but of course the company strung them all along with various bonuses and nobody actually revealed what he or she really had waiting in their bank account back on Earth. Whatever it was, it had to be comfortable and the envy of Earthside labor, or these people wouldn't risk life and sanity out here in the eternal silence, so Ridge thought as he wandered through.

Ridge fixed himself a little breakfast in the galley and sat at the table. Someone had cleaned away last night's Asian detritus and the empty containers sat in an autowash incubator ready to get cleaned and processed for reuse as Greek or Tejano or Hawaiian or Belgian or whatever was the next culinary adventure. Ridge blocked out the general noise as he sat reading Homer's *The Odyssey* and slurping milk and cereal from a bowl. In artificial gravity, one could slurp from a bowl, albeit cautiously. A loose loop of sugared, cinnamoned, toasted wheat could float away in the low gravity ten feet above the baseline floor, get into a vent, and seriously hog up the whole show if it found its way into just the right--or wrong, Ridge supposed-- tube or hole or whatever. As he read, he idly plashed a finger in the liquid that pooled around his cereal bowl. A milk container stood like a little tower nearby, still beaded with condensation from the fridge. Like much else on board the markings on the cereal box and milk carton were cheery, subdued, and functional without the excessive clamor of commercial advertising. There was, however, a small caricature of a smiling cow on the milk carton, and pictures of happy children with red cheeks on the cereal box.

A red light began to silently wink on and off, high up in the dark struts that resembled faux ceiling beams. The ship was loaded with psychological tricks to put walls of comfort between the interplanetary travelers and their natural fears, their loneliness, the constant nearness of disaster and death. For one thing, the ship maintained a natural cycle of days and nights in exact concordance with that at the travelers' most recent stay on Earth--the northern temperate zone space center near San Diego, where Colfirio had its global headquarters. Next, although the ship was a cylinder ten U.S. football fields long and one football field in diameter, with huge amounts of empty air space inside, one normally never saw any long vistas. There were tight spaces for coziness, wider spaces for communal but still cozy activity, and of course the huge warehouses for cargo. Most of the time, by day, you were surrounded by glassy and light-reflective surfaces reminiscent of the semi-arid mesas and canyons inland from San Diego. Dry, fresh breezes maintained the illusion further. By night, one tended not to see ceilings and far spaces, which stayed in shadows and countered any feelings of claustrophobia. In short, the ship was state of the art, first lulling the body with unspoken cues that it was in a familiar and safe place on earth. In so doing, the ship cued the subconscious into believing this information. Finally, this lulled the conscious mind into forgetting where its owner really was--on a fragile dust mote floating far from home.

Two images seemed to creep out at one from nowhere, at odd moments, unexpectedly, on a wall monitor here or there.

One was the white and blue wispy globe of Earth with its cratered olivine Moon. The other image was that of another disconcertingly blue planet with wispy clouds, albeit four times the diameter of the home world, and choked with liquid methane: Neptune, named after the ancient Roman sea god. In that second picture, one tended to be looking over a greenish-glassy landscape pimpled like a melon's skin: Triton, Neptune's largest moon. That image came from Triton Base, the orbiting space station from which workers could rise or fall above Triton. As the image of Earth got smaller, the image of Neptune got larger.

As always, the ship performed miracles in managing its artificial gravity, spinning on its axis, and it was sometimes hard to remember one was deep in the solar system like a grain of sand in the ocean.

There was a definite shudder now. The workpod was moving slowly on its axis, heading through the vastness inside the ship toward the next trouble spot the crew must fix, resulting from the recent meteorite impact. The images of Earth and Neptune had not appreciably changed in size, but that was an illusion of the human eye and the ship's technology, for the ship was rushing along faster than a bullet shot from a rifle. All banter stopped for a moment, and the crew of WorkPod01 looked up.

"Good morning, ladies and gentlemen." A face appeared on the view screen, that of Captain Venable in his command module far away on the other side of the ship. The captain had a classic face, filled with a mix of severity and understanding. The colors were bad, and he looked a bit washed out. Ridge always thought it was the low sunlight this far out, but they had batteries charged up to the point of smelling and foaming, so it had to be just a few bad wires someplace. He'd thought about putting in a work order, just as a mercy thing, because the imperfect reception annoyed his engineering nature, but then he always dismissed the thought. Why volunteer for things, when it could only lead to complications and unexpected consequences?

"Good morning," the Captain said. He appeared to glance at a wall clock near his desk. "Still early." He smiled, like a friend who knew each of them personally, and each of the crew had met Venable at least once or twice. "I'm sure you are ready for a long, hard work day," the Captain said, "and I want to be sure to thank you for your great work in saving and restoring the ship thus far, and to tell you how much I look forward to our being completely back on line and in good shape as we approach our target planetary system."

Ridge nodded to himself, picturing: elevator-style, a dark blob amid lengthy dark and copper-colored shadows, the entire workpod would be moving toward the next trouble spot. On its upper side (up and down being artificial but necessary concepts here) WorkPod01 was a rather luxurious living area for eight. On its lower side, it contained a complete workshop. In a few hours, the entire pod could traverse huge industrial segments of the yawning interior of the ship. It was good this way. You could drive your home to your work, unlike uncomfortably commuting for hours between home and a job in the teeming and smoky industrial centers of Earth.

"Again," the Captain said, as he sat with his big, gnarled hands folded on his glass desktop, "thank you for your heroic and decisive action in saving the ship a few weeks back, and for staying on top of things so that we can make it safely to Triton for repairs. In the meantime, we have new secondary explosive damage in the outer cargo pods in Level..." (he paused, put on reading lenses, and consulted the gleaming readouts in his desk surface) "...61. That's where you will need to apply your next set of workarounds. I'm expecting..." (again he paused and waited while his desk computed data and spat out results) "...that you will need just two days to restore power and then splice together the cabling on 61A through 61L. It does get a little trickier. The shaft you're on is impacted all the way up to Ring 98, where we had a major blowout. WorkPod07 and WorkPod10 were unable to get close enough to make repairs..."

Ridge spoke up, helping the Old Man. "Sir, I believe those pods are more chemostatically oriented. We have the complete systech kit on our station for the repairs I think we'll need to make."

"Thank you, Senior Lead. You are absolutely right." The Old Man grinned feebly. "At least, I feel reassured to hear you say so."

Laughter rumbled through WorkPod01.

"We'll make you proud of us," Ridge boomed. He winked at Lantz and Mughali.

"Set your chronometers," the Captain said. "Thirty-six hours max, and I expect you'll return for an equal rest period. Insurance regulations, you understand."

Ridge spoke for everyone else. "That sounds good to all of us, Sir. Let someone else carry the load while we rest."

"That's right. Division of labor." The Captain looked pleased. "Thanks again, and best of luck. See you all back here safely at the end of your shift." Captain Venable signed off.

Tomson gave his usual supercilious look, and Lantz regarded Tomson with faint displeasure. Yun gave a thumbs-up sign demonstrating his equanimity, while the pragmatic Jerez quietly helped herself to a slice of bread, which she started buttering.

"All right," Ridge said as he carried his cereal dish to the sink, and tucked his Homeric classic on a shelf under the table for later reference. "Let's clean up so we return to a clean home." It seemed childish, but they had to be reminded sometimes not to act like a bunch of toddlers. It was all part of the human condition.

Just then there was a pounding on the door.

"What's that?" Tomson said, frowning. As EMT and sergeant at arms, as well as Bones or Doc, whatever epithet best clung to his strong shoulders at that moment, he was the first to push the others aside and stride to the portal. The gate was not quite ready to open, but he pulled aside the stiff canvas drapes covering a wide, narrow window in one door, and several persons cried out in shock and anguish.

A nightmarish and violent scene-a desperate scene without rhyme or explanation-was taking place before their eyes.

A man was outside the door, pounding on the glass window with the palms of his hands so that the door shook. The man was screaming, but his words sounded muffled and incoherent. His eyes were wide with terror and pain, and he seemed to be throwing himself against the door repeatedly.

"My God," a woman cried out-Jerez.

"We have to help him," someone said, but another person said: "No, don't open the door, he looks crazy." Another person said: "He looks berserk. He's scaring the shazzam out of me."

Ridge and Tomson exchanged glances. Tomson reached up in a small box above the door and pulled out a handgun. He looked at Ridge and shook his head. "Keep the door closed until we know what's going on."

"Anyone know that guy?" Tomson said.

There was a murmur of negation, a collective gasp of horror.

"I'm for that," Ridge said. Tomson tossed him a gun, and he caught it deftly while picking up a hand-phone from the wall. Pressing the buttons 3-3-3, he attempted to connect directly to Venable's CP while crew shrieked and nervously laughed all around him. The desperate man kept pounding on the window, but more feebly. He was leaving bloody palm prints now. It was getting hard to see through the reddish gore. "Hello, Captain?" Ridge was puzzled. "Sir? We are having an emergency of some sort." Instead of the Captain, he only heard static as if the line had been severed. "Sir, we need to know if something is going on out there."

There was a general shriek, and the techs inside fell back as the man suddenly appeared to be attacked from behind. He looked over his shoulder and made a face of sheer terror. Just one more time he looked into the window through the haze of his own dripping blood and gore. His eyes were wide and his mouth was open as if he were yelling-a warning of some kind, Ridge thought-and then gray shapes flashed by, tearing him away. It was all over in a second or two. Ridge did not get a good look at the man's attackers, and he was sure nobody else had. The window was just that gory and dirty by now. They had a single fleeting glimpse of the man being torn away backward, his eyes rolling up in his head, his arms twisted behind him. Grayish shapes, maybe men in pressure suits, briefly appeared on either side of his receding figure, and then he was gone.

The techs and engineers stood frozen in shock and disbelief, looking at the smeared window. Ridge hung the phone back up. "Nobody home," he told Tomson.

"What do you want to do, Ridge?" Tomson asked.

Ridge stepped forward. "We will go out as an armed work party. The work has to get done. There is no choice. The ship needs to be repaired, and we are on a tight schedule."

"That's pretty scary," several people protested.

Lantz asked in a kind of lamely hopeful tone: "Do you suppose the man lost his mind, and the ship's constables came to take him away?" Nobody answered her, and Ridge thought her scenario might have some faint grain of hope, but then again he'd never heard of an arrest going down in quite this manner. Wouldn't they leave one guy to knock politely on the door and tell everyone it was okay to come out? Ridge shrugged. "We'll carry guns and watch our backs. We cannot afford to slip schedule. Everyone okay with that?"

He received only pale, scared looks, but nobody refused. He thought grimly, as Tomson handed out the rest of the side arms, they wouldn't dare-they get paid too much. "The show goes on as scheduled," he told them. Nobody made a sound in reply. Armed and uncertain, they all fell back as Tomson rolled open the door. Ridge felt the blast of stale, oily, almost decaying air from outside. He felt goose bumps on his arms, and prickles of fear up and down his spine. There was not a sound to be heard, except for the distant dripping of water, and all the faint little noises that a huge ship naturally made, like wind rushing through tunnels, and metal popping as ambient temperatures changed.

"Door's open," Tomson said as if they needed to be reminded to step outside.

Chapter 4

Ready?" Ridge said. He was the first out, followed by Tomson. Ridge and Tomson stepped gingerly about on the clanging, vibrating, gridded steel platform outside. They kept their guns aimed straight ahead and looked carefully about. Ridge examined the spattering of bloody hand prints on the portal.

Tomson said grimly: "We were not dreaming, Ridge."

"No, we weren't. I wish we were." Ridge's gaze followed the trail of fresh blood away from the portal, over the railing, down into the blackness below.

Tomson stepped up to the steel railing and touched the thick blood there with one fingertip. "No doubt about it. That is blood. What do you suppose that was all about?"

"I cannot imagine," Ridge said.

Brenna stepped up behind Ridge, briefly putting a reassuring hand on his shoulder. Her touch went through him like the warmth of a heat lamp. "Probably some poor soul lost his mind," she said. "The ship's constabulary had to take him away, and the Captain will give us a talk about it later."

"Yes yes yes," came a murmur of assent. The group were digesting and denying, processing and getting on with things, as humans wanted to do. Ridge felt the urge to put it behind him also. He said: "Let's lock down the workpod completely." It was SOP anyway, some esoteric Corporate regulation probably having to do with insurance rules.

"Let's get our jobs done and get the hell back here where it's safe and sane," Lantz said as she buckled up her web gear. "Yes yes yes," came the chorus, and the others secured their gear. Each of the eight technicians wore a light-weight rig similar to hers, olive drab in color, held together with adjustable straps and consisting of cylinders and pouches sitting snugly against the chest and back.

Under Tomson's direction, Yu and Mahaffey used hand-held wireless devices to make the twin doors slide shut. They locked the portal tightly, and Ridge could see nobody smaller than a crazed hippo could force his way through there. At least their home was safe, although now they had no way back in. The only way to re-enter WorkPod01 would be when they returned and telephoned Captain Venable to have him transmit the entry codes.

"We're ready to rock and roll," Tomson said. "Are we going to open the workstation down under?" He meant the lower floor of WorkPod01, which contained practically an entire factory, tool making facility, whatever one could think of. Normally, it was an island brightly lit from inside, with its doors open and a ramp laid down to truck in heavy parts, motors, assemblies, special tools, even portable generators and hoses.

"No, let's hold off," Ridge said. "Let's go out on Ring 61 and assess what we have going on. Then I'll decide whether we come back here for tools, or bring the shop out there with us." Implicit in his thinking was the fact that it took a lot of work, a lot of energy, and a lot of time to move a fifty ton room made of solid steel and containing all that equipment. He'd need a special auth from Venable plus possibly assistance from one or two other workpods. It was tricky running the shop out there, separating it from under WorkPod01 and then trucking it out like a gondola at a ski lift. It wasn't something to do unless one had to.

With that decided, for the first time Ridge was able to focus on the platform and the guts of the huge ship beyond. The steel grid platform, big enough to park a truck on and surrounded by safety railings, seemed jammed among the massive girders making up the ship's inward skeleton. The men and women in their suits and helmets, with miners' lamps atop their visors, stood in puddles of light, while all around them loomed darkness. The sun itself was too far away now to shed anywhere near the bright heat it did on Earth or the Moon. The ship's nuclear reactors were on minimum output, and the ion drives did not ordinarily power internal systems.

Ridge counted heads. "Everyone ready?"

Single-file, looking like old-fashioned miners going down into the bowels of the Earth, the eight technicians with Ridge in the lead started on their journey. Their voices echoed hollowly in the nocturnal void that stretched in all directions, offset only by the faint glow of daylight from that distant little star, that pinprick known as the sun. Huge girders, much lighter than their massive shapes suggested, curved through the darkness. Their crisscross members merged and blended with other gloomy shapes, like large round containers and tanks, work platforms, ring shafts, and other features. That was just the inner cylinder, with zero G at its central axis. The precious cargo was stashed in blisters, pods, and hangars in the inner skin of the ship. Deserted stretches of walkways represented the loading and unloading bays for when she was to dock in orbit of Triton.

As they carefully made their way along catwalks high in the air, Ridge tried to call Venable again, this time on his collar com. No reply. Ridge tried calling the other numbers he knew, including the Provost Marshal, the Chief Engineering Officer, and more, but the communications grid appeared to be dead. Ridge kept getting a prickling feeling up and down his spine that they were being watched.

The others were voicing questions of their own. Mahaffey was never one to be put off. "Hey, this place looks like it took a direct hit from an atomic bomb."

Yu said: "Come on, it's not quite that bad."

"It sure is dark and spooky," Lantz said. Her normally pale, freckled features looked ashen.

Ridge walked ahead, with Tomson bringing up the rear. Ridge told them: "Keep your eyes on the path ahead and your hands on the railings at all times." He took a deep breath. "If you feel the need for oxygen, pull out your mouthpiece. Tomson tested all the bottles and gear, so we should be in good shape."

Tomson, in the rear, said dryly: "If you trust that I'm not ready to be yanked off the window by any guys in white coats."

"Those weren't guys in white coats," Jerez said. When she was nervous, her Universal Anglo slipped deeper into a classic Castilian Spanish complete with lisped letter 's.' Yu thought it was cute and told her so, for which he got a tongue-lashing in Tagalog. Several persons laughed.

"Eyes on the path," Ridge reminded them. He was troubled, though. Nothing was as he remembered it. He did not remember the vastness and cavernous nature of the ship's interior, at least not around Ring 61, which he had always assumed to be a Ring of many small compartments. Looking around in the dim light, he began to think that the devastation here was much worse than anything he had seen in other decks they'd worked. He tried to picture the other decks, but couldn't put a number to any one. It scared him a bit that his memory was so vague in places. He wondered if he were going insane. At first it was just a nagging thought. He kept seeing Brenna's alluring look over her shoulder as she pranced away in her turban and robe a while ago. Did she do that on purpose? Was it just how she was? How could a seductress have slipped through the fine toothed comb of Corporate industrial psychologists? Or was it all in his imagination, and was he having problems with Dorothy without knowing it? Then he got a real scare. He couldn't remember the names of his children. This made him tremble with fear. He had chills going up and down his arms and back.

"Ridge, are you okay?" Jerez asked from nearby.

He nodded, but tears were running down his cheeks. Am I going insane? Or is it fear of heights, something new I didn't know I suffer from? What is going on here?

"Ridge?" Brenna asked from mid-line of slowly moving figures in a phantasmagoric landscape. Nightmare within nightmare. He was in love with her, and it was eating him up. Why did he suddenly now realize this? Why was her tone so warm and concerned, as if she knew what was burning inside of him? Was it in her too, this desire to hold and be held, this longing for one another's warmth and reassurance?

"Speak to me, Ridge," said Tomson in a worried tone.

"I'm all right," Ridge said. "Just thinking."

Jerez imitated in an annoying falsetto: "Eyes on the path. Eyes on the path, or we'll fall in the manure." Several persons laughed, and Ridge laughed too, which sort of broke the tense and scary atmosphere.

A minute later, there was a shriek. The line stopped and people bunched up. "What is it?" Tomson said.

Ridge had one hand on the gun in its web holster on his belt as he looked around. Jerez had shrieked and stood pointing. She was pale. "Look, did you see that?"

"You're hallucinating," Yu sneered.

"What are you smoking?" Mahaffey added.

"No no no," Jerez said, "I saw one of those guys in gray suits or whatever they are wearing. Looks like those sugar candy guys from the Days of the Dead in Mexico, the *Dias de los Muertos.*"

Ridge felt a new shiver on his back: he thought he spotted a pale gray figure, just for a second, across the chasm on the other side. It looked like a man wearing stitched rags and red sunglasses, fleeting from one hole in the wall to another. He heard a scurrying sound, and a noise like air blowing softly through a flute, just for a second before silence reigned again. Amid the silence, water splashed in distant places, as if the place were terminally leaking.

"Get yourself together," Lantz said. "You're trembling, and I hear your teeth rattling." She did what she often did when nervous, which was to loosen her coppery red hair and tied it back in a pony tail with rough, freckled hands.

Ridge raised his hand. "Everyone be still." He listened intently. Why were there holes over there, a thousand yards or more away? Why were there no decks? He thought he could make out twisted, melted girders, but it was too damned dark in this general gloom, and the lights on their helmets did not carry far enough. Just bright enough the lights were so they became targets if someone malevolent were watching them. But who or what would be watching them? What kind of nonsense am I thinking? He listened another second, but heard no more sounds.

"This place is trashed," Tomson said drawing up alongside Ridge. "This place is truly trashed, man. I don't mean just impacted or zipped or zapped by some pebble. This place caught the Huge Bazongo, and I mean long ago."

Ridge had to agree. He nodded and pointed across acres of blackened slag that seemed to hang like a frozen river below.

"You're right. This is ancient damage, Tomson. What is going on?"

Tomson frowned and looked back. Ridge involuntarily turned his head back and looked at WorkPod01. Their home gleamed distantly like a white lantern amid gloomy bronze and brown shadows. Tomson said under his breath: "Don't let on you just shat your pants."

"I feel like I might," Ridge said with dry, terrified humor. "I've never been this scared in my life."

"There is something totally wrong with this picture," Tomson muttered.

"Are we going forward or not?" Jerez said with staring eyes.

"Of course," Ridge said. "Let's keep on schedule and stop being distracted. The sooner we get our day's work done the sooner we get back home and lock the door." He wished he hadn't said that, as soon as the words came out, but it was too late.

"I'd like to go back now," Jerez said.

"Me too," Mahaffey said.

"Guys," Ridge said, "we can't-"

"No, bullshit," Mahaffey said loudly, "we're civilians. We don't get paid to risk our lives or a heart attack from fear."

"Really," Jerez said. "I wouldn't mind if we went back now."

"Yeah," Yu said, "I'd like to get some reassuring words from Venable before I drag my tired butt out here and get scared to death."

"We can't go back now," Ridge said. "There is no reason to." He felt a rebellion rapidly brewing in his hands, and the worst part was he wanted to join it himself.

Tomson stared at him. "Your call, Section Leader."

Ridge knew he must think fast. They could not stay here, suspended a thousand feet or more in thin air above an alien-looking field of charred objects embedded in slag. Were they hallucinating or were there pale men running around who had just dragged a stranger to his death. What had the stranger been trying to tell them? Ridge wished he were a lip reader. No time now for nonsense; he must make a decision. Should they go forward or back? Instinctively, he knew the answer. "We can't go back because we are locked out, folks."

Several persons, including Jerez and Mahaffey, protested. Fear was written on their features.

"I don't know the answers," Ridge said, raising his hands and dropping them. "I don't even know at the moment how or why I got to be in charge of us, because I can't even remember my first name right now. Can any of you remember much of anything?"

"What the hell are you saying?" Tomson said, his face suddenly contorted with emotion. "You're crazy, man."

"Am I?" Ridge looked at him. "We can argue later." He turned to the others. "Folks, we're standing on a noodle high up in mid air. We're asking a lot of dumb questions and we have no answers. Suddenly, our whole world is like a house of cards. All I can suggest at times like this is that we hitch up our pants, put aside all the dumb questions, and get on with the job. I don't know what else to tell you. Those who want to go back, you do what you want. I'm going forward and I hope the rest of you follow me. Frankly, I think it's our only option." So saying, he started marching forward at a brisk pace. At first he was afraid nobody would follow. Then the gangway behind him, and under him, began to vibrate in a kind of familiar unison as they all marched in step, single file, holding on to the railing on both sides as they crossed the abyss, and for a short time the illusion of normalcy once again prevailed.

Chapter 5

When they arrived at Ring 61. Ridge was relieved to see lights and hear music. They emerged from oceans of darkness on all sides into an island of light that seemed suspended in gloomy midair.

"What was that all about back there?" Tomson asked. The self-assured sneer was back on his strong, dark visage.

"Temporary insanity," Jerez said as she strode confidently up the last few yards of steel and onto the main platform under a row of large bluish-white lights. The music was common, universal rock stock, the kind one heard in every city of the world, and which had been playing in WorkPod01 as they got ready for the day's work.

The catwalk broadened and opened onto a wide ledge that curved outward toward them as they drew near. In the curving wall some 25 feet beyond the ledge were caves. Narrow-gauge rail tracks ran out of the largest cave and stopped halfway across the ledge. The ends of the two tracks were twisted upward and deformed, as if they had begun to melt long ago. The heat that had caused that was long gone. Ridge stepped onto the ledge with his gun in one hand and a light in the other. Heart pounding, he licked his dry lips and stared from side to side. The ground here was like rock, as though part of the ship had melted and poured inward, covering the metal grating that was partially visible through the long-cold slag. Dust was everywhere, covering bits of broken machinery, casually thrown rocks, debris too desiccated from age to be recognizable.

"Look," Mahaffey said, pointing to a spot where the uneven wall sloped down to the ledge. With the pounding rock music and its frenzied, indecipherable words, Ridge was startled to see the hollow eyes of a human skull peeking from the dust.

Mughali walked over in her bulky suit and nudged the ground around the skull with her boot. "It's old," she said simply. "No smell of putrefaction. No traces of flesh or skin on it." She knelt down. "Tomson, look at this." She pointed with a delicate finger along the temple region of the skull.

Ridge and Tomson walked up behind her to look. Ridge kept an eye on the cave entrance and had his gun ready. Tomson knelt down beside Mughali. "Wow, look at that," Tomson said wonderingly. His larger finger traced along a curving mark, following her smaller and more delicate finger. "That's a fracture," he said. "Looks like something bit into this person's head."

Ridge looked over their shoulders and noted that the edges of the fracture were about the same grayish hue as the surfaces of the skull. "It's old," he said. "Any more information?"

Tomson ran a probing hand around the skull, pushing dust away. He shook his head, rising. "The rest of the body is elsewhere. Someone or something carried the head here and set it down or threw it down, maybe to..." He stopped and gave Ridge a worried look. "Maybe to gnaw on it."

Ridge scratched his head. "Great." He glanced at the other staff members. Yu, Lantz, Mahaffey, Brenna, and Jerez stood huddled together on the edge, as if ready to bolt back across the catwalk into the darkness from which they had come. "Come on and join the fun," he said, waving his arm. He pointed to the cave. "I'm going to take a look in there."

Yu looked angry and confused. "Where is the work area? What is this place?"

Ridge said: "I'll let you know as soon as I get more information from Captain Venable." He turned to Tomson. "You stay with them. I'll go into the cave. Probably just a misunderstanding. I'm sure our work area is in there someplace."

Tomson said: "You sure we have the right coordinates?"

Ridge nodded. "I've checked and double checked. This was supposed to be a power relay station, and we should be seeing people from WorkPod09 around here, checking circuits while we extract, test, and reset the more complicated wetware and biocybernetics." He shook his head, but that did not clear his thinking. "Keep an eye on them," he said simply, "I'm going in." He told the group: "Just stand down for a few minutes. I'll be right back."

"Be careful," Brenna said with concern, folding her arms around herself as if she were cold, though it was relatively warm and the air had a kind of damp, ripe balminess to it. Ridge could see she was shivering. He wanted to embrace her, hold her, tell her everything was all right, but it didn't seem like something he should do. Jerez and Mahaffey didn't look much happier than Brenna. Yu was a stronger, more reserved and analytical type, and he took his place by Tomson's side. Mughali offered: "I'll go with you," but Ridge waved her back.

The cave, when he started cautiously along the railroad tracks, curved around a bend into darkness. Stumbling over dusty objects, Ridge made his way slowly down the tunnel. The walls were steeped in darkness, but rough edges and ridges shone like black anthracite. Ridge heard Tomson's voice echo: "Are you okay in there?"

Ridge did not stop cautiously moving forward. "Yes, I'm okay so far." The music suddenly stopped.

"What's going on?" Tomson and Mughali both called out.

"The music stopped," Ridge said. He listened in the silence, feeling sweat dribbling down his temples. The gun in his slick right hand felt heavy, and the flashlight in his left wavered.

"Hear anything?" they called out.

"Be quiet so I can hear," Ridge said. Almost immediately he regretted having ordered them to be silent, because he longed to hear their voices. He was around a leftward bend now, out of their sight and out of touch. It was a lonely feeling. The tunnel curved on in a rightward bend, and he heard a faint scratching noise. He called out: "Is anyone there?" He waited. *No answer.* He raised the gun and flashlight and walked slowly forward.

"Talk to me," Tomson yelled from far away. Ridge ignored him. Air blew softly around him, and he smelled something putrid. Each time he caught a whiff of whatever it was, a fresh current of air blew it away.

Suddenly, the music again started playing loudly. It was an ancient rock and roll tune about cars and girls and racing. Ridge flew back against the wall, trembling, and waited. Nothing more happened. The song looped endlessly, playing the same several stanzas over and over again.

Slowly, Ridge walked forward. He was becoming angry now. What could this tomfoolery mean? He was responsible for the safety and well-being of the other seven members of his team. "I'm beginning to take this personally," he called out. "Whoever you are, I'm going to have a few issues with you when I get my hands around your neck." No answer.

Ridge timed his steps carefully on the dusty train tracks. With each step he glanced down among the debris to see where his next footfall might land, and then up again to make sure he missed nothing, should something come flying at him. He kept seeing the bloody hands of the man in the window, and then the frantic expression and the man's wide eyes as he was yanked away backward into oblivion. As the minutes passed, Ridge was beginning to doubt this was a simple matter of taking someone by the neck to straighten things out. His anger was beginning to yield to questioning and fear again. As he walked forward, he sensed that he was entering a large open space. Cooler and drier breezes blew on his face and dried the sweat on his neck.

With a crash of heavy steel breakers, a surrounding circle of blindingly bright light winked on. In the same instant, the music fell silent. Ridge almost dropped his gun and flashlight. With a yelp of pain, he brought his wrists up to his eyes and staggered backward.

"You come to help us?" a voice said. It was an odd, high voice, but firm.

"Get that light out of my face," Ridge ordered.

The light dimmed considerably. Ridge stood with olive-drab curtains of blindness floating before his eyes. Even if he were attacked now, he'd be shooting blindly. A voice said: "You can put your gun away. You're one of us." Ridge hesitated, still holding up the gun, but slipped the flashlight into a holder on his tool belt. The voice continued: "You have nothing to fear. Are there others with you?" Ridge hesitated to give information, and the voice said: "What WorkPod are you from?"

"WorkPod01," Ridge said. "I have a full crew of technicians with me. You have a name?"

"Caulfield. Are you armed?"

The voice, Ridge began to realize, was that of an elderly man. "I'm Ridge. We have several handguns."

The voice laughed. "You'll need a lot more than that, my friend." He sounded bitter. "We're out of time, Ridge. You're too late."

Ridge felt anger welling up again. He felt frustration, confusion, fear. "What the hell is going on here? We came to do a job."

"Oh yes you did," the voice said. It was an old man's voice, with a quaver in it, and a sibilant halt at the end of each phrase as if the speaker's lungs had make an effort to refill. "Come out into the center. Go on, don't be afraid. They won't go near light."

"Who won't go near light? What are you talking about?"

"Mudmen," the voice said. "They are muddled, dirty purpose-bodies built from muddy DNA and broken codons and mismatched body parts. Lots of old body parts."

"What on earth are you talking about?" Ridge slipped his gun into its holster. He rubbed his eyes with both hands. His sight was returning. He was in an irregular clearing under a high, curving roof that looked like a farm of stalactites. The cavern branched off in two side directions, but the central tunnel was blocked off by a mass of debris in which Ridge recognized a battered work cart, broken lights, torn canvas, glass, bent metal pipes, and shreds of cloth. Looking up, Ridge saw at least two dozen round spotlights in black metal canisters had been mounted in the ceiling all around, and those now winked out in batches. Ridge could hear the breakers cutting out as someone opened them. An elderly man in a ragged jumpsuit stepped out from the central tunnel onto the pile of debris. He looked pale and emaciated, dirty, with wind-blown white hair on a partially bald skull.

"Did the captain send you?"

"Yes. Captain Venable."

"Venable, that louse!" Caulfield wiped the back of a soiled hand across his mouth. "He has betrayed us all, more than once."

Ridge pressed: "What is this work we're supposed to do? We came to make repairs, but I don't remember the ship being this badly damaged."

Caulfield's eyes were wide as he stared into some memories Ridge couldn't imagine. "It must have been a terrible blast," Caulfield whispered in his broken voice, with spittle foaming from the corners of his mouth. "Melted the walls, burned out the catwalks, killed the astronics." His eyes were hollows of nightmarish vision within gaunt features. He looked as though he had gone through a cauldron of horror and come out transformed. He wore the remains of web gear: one canteen, one holster and gun, as dirty and dusty as the man himself. Ridge tried to press him for information, but the old man was in a world of his own. "You're too late," Caulfield said, still staring into the distance and hardly noticing Ridge. "They're all dead. I'm the only one left, and I have very little time. There is no time to sit and talk. We have to go."

For a moment they stood confronting each other, the old man ten feet up at the mouth of his refuge, and Ridge in the middle of the clearing. It looked like a defensive position. Ridge said: "I've got seven techs and engineers back there waiting to find out what we are supposed to do here."

"Do?" The old man laughed. "Do? Hah! Survive, if you are lucky. Get them out of here. Go back where you came from."

Ridge felt more puzzled than ever. "What is going on here? Is it the air in the ship?" He felt a bit faint, and shook his head sharply once or twice, tapping a palm against one temple. "I can't seem to remember."

"You'll figure it out soon enough," the man said, bounding down toward Ridge. "My name is Caulfield. WorkPod09." He held out a bony hand, and Ridge shook it. Caulfield's eyes had a tragic yellowish cast, and his face looked like a mask of irony. There was something he wasn't telling. Ridge could feel it. Why? "Get those people out of here," Caulfield said. "I'm coming with you." He grabbed Ridge roughly around the shoulders, turned him back the way he'd come, and pushed.

Ridge resisted, but with the other man pressing roughly on his back, he let himself be propelled along. "What happened to the rest of your work group? Did you send a man to warn us?" Seeing Caulfield's opaque expression, he added: "We watched a man get torn to pieces banging on the window of WorkPod01. Any idea who?"

"No time, no time," Caulfield whispered, looking back over his shoulder. "Go go go," he urged. "See that on the ground?" Ridge looked down and saw what had given off the putrid smell: a corpse lay huddled against the wall. It was nearly hidden in the shadows by the track. It had a putty-gray color with a greenish-pink sheen of bacterial decay on its naked, stitched up skin. Ridge glimpsed something misshapen, off-center, a sightless face that was only vaguely human, with hands curled up on either side of sunken cheeks. The fingers on those hands were abnormally short, but it looked as though the creature had long claw-like fingernails. The claws were yellowish, almost birdlike or reptilian. Ridge froze a second, until Caulfield roughly shoved him on. "Don't worry. You'll see more of them."

"What are they?" Ridge said.

"Ridge?" Tomson called out in a worried voice.

"Coming. I've got someone with me." Even as Ridge responded, he felt Caulfield's hand drop away. Turning, he saw that the old man had pitched face-forward and lay gasping on the wood-like rail ties. Ridge called out: "Tomson! Medic!" he knelt down on the tracks, even as he heard scrambling feet coming close.

"Save yourselves," Caulfield gasped. His eyes were staring, and his body lay hunched and helpless. Suddenly he looked small and frail. Ridge saw dried blood on his back, and a dirtied rip in the fabric of Caulfield's jumpsuit. The feet running close were those of Tomson and Mughali, their booted soles pushing heavy, sandy dust aside with each fleeting stride. "What is this?" Tomson said. Mughali skidded to a halt kneeling beside Ridge. Her face looked worried and confused. Tomson looked more implacable as he started to open the first aid kit slung over his chest.

"Help him," Ridge said frantically. "He has information we need."

Tomson shook his head slowly. Mughali looked from Caulfield to Tomson to Ridge and back with wide eyes.

"We need to know what he was talking about," Ridge said. "Mudmen. Danger."

Tomson shook his head slowly. His big dark hands were frozen on the first aid kit, but he showed no sign of opening it.

Mughali said: "Look at him, Ridge. The man won't need any help from us."

Ridge looked down at Caulfield. Ridge's eyes strained to take in the sight of Caulfield's face, from whose mouth and nose a thick black stream of gore had splashed. Tomson turned the old man on his back and used one hand to check the man's neck for a pulse. Tomson shook his head. Ridge stared at the body, whose eyes were already sinking inward and whose brown-spattered mouth gaped. Something about that face troubled Ridge, but he couldn't think what it might be, and there was no time to leisurely puzzle things through. Ridge heard Jerez's voice from a distance and looked up. Jerez seemed to be arguing with Brenna. "Some of us want to go back," Jerez said. Brenna replied: "We have to stick together, and Ridge is the one in charge." To which Jerez said: "The hell with Ridge. He doesn't know anything more than you or I do." To which Brenna replied with silence, bless her. Ridge held his head in his hands and shook it slowly. What to do? What to do?

Tomson shook Ridge's shoulder gently. "We can't leave our people scattered all over the place. Want to go back or dig in?"

Ridge looked up with sudden determination. He rose. "We came to do a job. That's what we'll do. Get the others assembled in the cave. I'll go in for a look at Caulfield's little hideout." Without stopping to answer questions or objections, he left Tomson to carry out the order, and strode back into the cave.

Ridge clambered over the rampart Caulfield and his compatriots had erected. He noted the strung lights, which appeared to be lined up to drive back whoever these creatures were. Ridge guessed that the mudmen did not like loud noises either. There had to be a way of reaching the Bridge. Congratulating himself on having made the best of possible bad choices, Ridge descended through a short shaft into what looked like a WorkPod, minus the luxurious living quarters, showers, weight training equipment, and so forth. Where had Caulfield's fellow technicians gone? Had Caulfield gone crazy and killed them all? Was the whole song and dance about mudmen the raving of a sick mind? Ridge remembered the body on the tracks. Could it really be the body of some being cobbled together with chemistry and stray body parts? Or was it part of some insanity of Caulfield's? Horrifying as the latter possibility might be, Ridge hoped it was the case, rather than even scarier and far murkier alternatives. Somehow, he had a bad feeling about the whole matter, and his feeling got worse as the minutes wore on. He found a series of concrete-like tunnels housing some of the electronic nerve centers of the ship. Room after room contained similar huge banks of lights, coils of cable, workstations, and generators. There was a bathroom with a toilet, and a single sink with one cold-water faucet. Ridge cautiously tested the sink and was able to draw a liberal supply of clean, fresh water. Satisfied, he stepped back. That was a major plus. He completed a quick tour of the facility. Noting tools strewn everywhere, he surmised that many work crews were working here around the clock, and had been for a long time, to restore functionality to the ship. How long had it been? The question nagged at him, fueled by the disturbing age and destruction of the ship. In the back he walked into a long, narrow greenhouse, the first of a bank of such greenhouses, easily two or three miles' worth of fruits and greens growing in hydroponics tanks. Somehow, Caulfield's and other work teams had kept strings of special lights working, which kept the plants going.

Did this have any relationship to the excellent functioning of WorkPod01 and its like? Filled more with questions than understanding, Ridge returned to the entrance of the work area. There he found that Tomson had assembled the other six staff members, whose expressions ranged from scared and unhappy to sullen. Tomson said: "We're ready to start work. What do you want us to do?"

Chapter 6

The Bridge CP or Command Post did not respond to Ridge and Tomson's urgent attempts to obtain guidance. Time and again, they tried to raise Captain Venable or anyone in the CP, to no avail. There were several antique, scratched wall screens in various parts of the work area, and they powered up easily enough, but all they yielded was either a white blankness or a greenish, grainy static. Sometimes, there would be a black screen with irregular, faint bluish sine waves undulating in apparently random patterns. Never was there a written or spoken, or a talking head; just endless cryptic silence.

"What are we doing here?" Jerez said with a pale face, embracing herself with pudgy arms and shivering. Her eyes looked large and scared, and she spoke for everyone. At times, Mughali seemed very strong as she bantered with Mahaffey or Yu, and at other times she might sit in a corner sobbing.

Tomson had definitely assumed his place as Ridge's second in command, and Ridge was grateful for the support. At times he wished Tomson would just take over, period, but the tall dark-skinned man seemed too smart to pick up that load. "What have we gotten ourselves into here?" Tomson would say at odd moments, examining the dusty and half-ruined work area to which a crisp and chipper Captain Venable had sent them just hours earlier.

Brenna found the clothing of several lost workers tossed in a heap near the rear exit that led into endless yawning night. The uniforms were torn and bloody, and thrown haphazardly among the rail ties leading into other industrial areas of the ship. The discarded web straps were frayed and severed as if something with great force had chewed through them. "There is no sign of any bodies," Brenna said with a gloomy expression on grayish-brown shadowed features. The lovely lines of her face looked moody and shadowed, as if inked along with the onyx of her large, weeping eyes. It was the first time that Ridge ever touched her, standing beside her, putting one arm around her. Her shoulder briefly nudged against his ribs before they both pulled away. Nobody had noticed, since the others stood at an angle before them in the tunnel with its single yellow light in a wire cage above.

"Could be Caulfield's shift," Tomson said as he squatted to touch several pieces of torn and bunched khaki cloth. He lifted a piece and sniffed it. "Still smells of blood and sweat--mostly sweat, sour with fear." He made a distasteful expression and tossed the cloth down. He rose. "Ridge, let's get it over with and go back to WorkPod01."

"Agreed," Ridge said. He looked at his chronometer. "Thirty two hours left in our obligation before the next shift comes here."

"Shouldn't we warn them not to?" Lantz said. She undid her ponytail and tightly rewound it.

"We're trying to raise the CP," Ridge said. He worried about hysteria spreading among his seven charges; or worse yet, that he might succumb to the irrational desire to bolt and start running madly in the direction of WorkPod01. Remembering the fate of the man beating on the window with bloody palm prints, it seemed like the worst thing to do.

Tomson seconded: "We're doing everything we can, and it's up to each of us to act cool and remain professional."

Lantz flared back: "You think we aren't being cool and professional?"

"Speak for yourself," Jerez said, defensively wrapping her arms around herself.

For a moment the entire work group stood staring at Ridge, as if on the verge of breaking ranks and leaving. He couldn't blame them, but he hoped he could hold the group together until help or advice or guidance arrived-anything, to break the increasing air of confusion.

Mahaffey spoke up bravely: "I saw a tangle of cables back there leading into the transformer. Until I'm told otherwise, I think I'll go sort that out." He looked at his fellow metallurgic tech, Lantz. "Care to join me?" Lantz nodded with looked almost of relief at getting some direction. Brenna, as Chemical Engineer 1, nodded. "I'm with you guys. Anything to keep busy until someone sends us a signal." She almost smiled, and several people laughed nervously in response.

"Good! That's it," Ridge said. "We have three handguns, and we'll take turns standing watch so everyone's back is covered. I don't know about you, but I hate to sit around and be idle. Let's find and tackle the work that is all around us, crying out to be done. There's obviously been a disaster here, and we need to fix the mess." He almost added "or we don't get home" but that seemed like a ridiculously pessimistic thing to say in this already dire situation. Tomson nodded in agreement near him, and he was quietly grateful for the man's support.

Yu, as Bio-Engineer 1, turned to Jerez, who was a Cyber-Engineer 2. "If you can find us some wetware neural nodes, I might be able to start tracking what's wrong here."

"Good point," Jerez said. She glanced stoutly toward Ridge for approval, but did not seem to be waiting for his go-ahead. "What do you say, Ridge?" even as she and Yu turned to go back into the bowels of the work area. As a Cyber-Engineer 1, Ridge had to agree. "It's as good a plan as any," he told her.

Within a short time, they had full power restored. "Looks like Caulfield was conserving," Ridge said as he paused. He was covered with sweat. He wiped gloved hands over his forehead. Nearby, Tomson cut off a small brazing torch. His dark skin glistened with droplets of sweat. "Man, this place is spooked," Tomson said in a low voice. "Don't let the others hear, but I think it's going to take an army of technicians to get this place working. Maybe that's how the whole ship is."

Ridge laughed nervously. "Come on, you're giving me goose bumps. You know we were safe and sound in our nice warm WorkPod01 just a few hours ago listening to music and showering and stuff. This is strictly nuts."

Tomson looked at him strangely. "You think we're going to get back to WorkPod01 in one piece?"

Ridge felt a dryness in his mouth that belied his own jaunty reply. "Yes I do. Lighten up, Tomson."

"Something dragged off those workers. They wouldn't just leave their clothes lying around, unless you think they went nuts and ran off singing."

"They were here a long time," Ridge said. "The blood and sweat were still fresh, but Caulfield was an old man. The Corporation wouldn't let an old man ship out on the Neptune run, so figure it out for yourself."

"Yeah?" Tomson leaned chin-forward and said: "Oh yeah? Then figure this out. We were supposed to be on Triton in one year. Caulfield was a man at least seventy years old when he died there a little while ago heaving half his body organs out of his mouth. You figure that out and tell me when you know the answer." Tomson slipped his brazing goggles back on, making his eyeballs look opaque and inscrutable. They glittered and flashed as his small hand-welder flared back up. He resumed repairing severed wires.

Frustrated, Ridge threw down the metallic flowcharts he'd been studying and went out to visit the others. He found Jerez and Yu on station with their guns in the entrance. "Any signs of funny little gray men?" They did not share his sense of humor, but shook their heads darkly in reply. Ridge checked the gun on his own belt. "I'll be back to relieve one of you in a few minutes. Yu, I'll relieve you and you can go help Tomson. He's bitching and moaning back there in the communications center." Ridge wandered on through tight, dark spaces--through the galley, through darkened and uncomfortable chambers stuffed with equipment--until he came to the main transformer and throughput node for wireless transmission. The two women, Jerez and Lantz, hung on the sides of a globular pod. Its round, pewter-dull metallic hood stood open, and they leaned inside to work. Their headlamps were on, and their expressions mirrored confusion while their fingers flicked idly from one tangle of wires and coils to the next. "Ridge," Jerez said, "this is like trying to find a meatball in fifty tons of spaghetti."

"It's hopeless," Lantz chimed in. "These circuits are dead cold. We're trying to find a spark, a glimmer of data potential anywhere, and it's like she says. Where's the meatball?"

"Wish I knew," Ridge said. "I'm starting to feel just a bit hungry now that you mention food. If nothing else, we can get together and cook a hot meal."

He wandered further back into the guts of the station, to the experimental greenhouse. Corporations were forever experimenting with growing things in space, trying to combine the characteristics of crystals and charge particles and chlorophyll-driven Earth biology to come up with better ways of sustaining travelers in space. There, under a whitish light that made the outlying walls look all the blacker, he found Brenna. "What are you doing?"

She looked up with a faint smile of bravado. "Checking the plants for abnormalities."

"Why? You're a chemical engineer. Do something chemical."

"Ha ha, like what?"

"I don't know. Chemical." He gestured helplessly as he stood very close to her. He could almost smell the heat of her body emanating up from the shadowy recesses of her dark suit. Never had he longed so much to crawl into a dark space and curl up, to hide from reality. There was no place he wanted to be so much as beside her right now. He studied the minute peach fuzz on her fine cheekbones, the tiny scar on her right eyebrow (from a childhood accident with a swing, she'd told him). He leaned close to the pale, fragile column of her neck and inhaled the warmth rising from her body. He could smell the faintly lavender fragrance of her shower soap, and closed his eyes.

"What are you doing, Ridge?" she asked in a low, teasing voice.

He snapped back, straightened out. "Just wishing we were back home."

"Home home, or pod home?"

"Right now, honestly, I'd take pod home."

"Me too," she said, examining a tangled mass of roots attached to a dense ball of green sprouts.

"I'd curl up in my bunk," he said.

She grinned, and her white perfect teeth gleamed like ivory in the soft light. "So would I. Look at this plant." She held it up in the growth luminescence.

"I'd pull the covers over my head," he said, "and dream of you."

She froze and stared at him. Her eyes were very large. He'd said something he should not have said, and they both knew it. In that moment, as her smile changed into something arrested and uncertain, they both knew she felt the same way. It was a betrayal of the people they loved. "What about Dorothy?" she whispered in a voice so faint he could barely hear.

He did not know the answer. "What's with the plant?"

She looked at the plant in her hands as if rediscovering it. "Oh. This. It's been growing wild. See how the stems loop around each other? I was trying to figure out the pattern." She pointed with a soil-crusted fingertip. "See how the whorls go around in ellipses? It probably means these plants were exposed to some sort of diurnal solar cycle."

"In here?"

She shrugged. "We have a lot of research to do, and few answers as yet."

Tomson walked in. "How are you two doing?"

Ridge was startled. "Fine, fine." Brenna looked up, blushing, as if she'd been caught in a moment of intimacy. Tomson looked bewildered, but there was no chance for him to stare questioningly at them.

A scream resounded through the corridors, followed by cries, and then a man's voice wailing.

"That came from up front," Tomson said. Guns drawn, he and Ridge left Brenna where she stood and raced down the narrow corridors. "Don't leave me here!" Brenna wailed and started after them. Ridge glanced back at her, extending a hand to her. She was a trifle too slow, and he forged on as another scream resounded.

"Sounds like Yu or Mughali," Tomson said breathlessly as he and Ridge clawed and bounced their way through passages choked with equipment, some of which came pouring down out of rotting boxes and rat-gnawed bags as they struck shaky shelving with their shoulders. Music began loudly booming from all sides. "Over here!" Mahaffey's voice came. He sounded hoarse with fright. Ridge and Tomson burst into the entrance area behind the piled debris. Someone had turned on the banks of bright lights. Ridge found a bloody sight. Yu held the gun in trembling hands while sobbing uncontrollably.

Yu and Mahaffey stood at the base of the rocks. Yu had a gun in his hand, while Mahaffey held a flashlight. On the ground between them lay Mughali's weapon. Halfway up the pile lay the bloodied and ripped remains of the brilliant, diminutive Indian engineer. "Oh my God," Ridge said, feeling a ball of vomit welling up under his diaphragm. The woman's face was oddly mangled, so that her eyeballs stared in different directions, and the rest of her features were ground up so that the still wetly gleaming skull was partially visible under reddish gore. Her body had been torn and twisted by multiple powerful forces acting from different directions. Her uniform was twisted around and around, and her small boots pointed in odd directions, while her arms were pulled up and twisted and broken behind her oddly angled back. The sight of this vibrant, warm human being now nothing more than a tangle of shredded meat and bone made Ridge turn and toss the contents of his stomach violently against the wall. Mahaffey had apparently already done the same, judging from the ropes of yellow goo hanging from his lips as he stared in silent horror at Mughali's remains. Yu ran hysterically to the top of the pile and yelled: "Here, you sons of bitches, come and get this!" He fired two or three times into the dark, silent corridor. Zigzags and wireframes of bluish light flashed blindingly. The reports crackled in the air and faded. A stink of scorched dust drifted back as Yu readied to fire once more.

"Stop that!" Tomson and Ridge both hollered. Ridge said: "Don't run down your charge. Whatever killed her may be back for the rest of us any minute."

"Come on!" Yu hollered, waving his gun. "I'm ready for you." Mahaffey clambered and pulled him by the wrist, trying to calm him.

Brenna came running into the area, saw the body, and blanched. She kept her composure, raising both hands to her mouth, but observing: "There was another scream. Whom are we missing?"

Ridge and Tomson looked at each other. Tomson said: "Lantz and Jerez." They turned and ran. Ridge tossed his gun to

Brenna, who caught it deftly. "Watch that doorway and shoot anything that comes through." Brenna nodded, and Ridge ran after Tomson.

They encountered the two women running toward them in the corridors. Both had spatters of blood and grayish gore on them. The two men nearly collided with them, and the women clawed past them with panic-stricken eyes. They carried bloodied tools-Jerez a wrench, Lantz a hammer-and their mouths were open but they were too breathless to scream. Looking past them, Ridge spotted a pair of moving red eyes glowing in the darkness. He made out clay-like gray figures with clawed hands drawn up ready to strike. "Mudmen," Tomson whispered, raising his gun. Ridge fired first. The first strike was on target, and a pair of red eyes winked out. It was dark, but Ridge thought he saw spattering body fluids. He and Tomson fired repeatedly until the air smelled like a mix of burned plastic and ozone.

"They've stopped coming," Tomson said, lowering his depleted gun.

"For now," Ridge said.

"We're in trouble," Tomson said.

"You got that right," Ridge said. "Come on, let's get the others together. We're leaving right now." His eyes were still flashing from the after-effects of the gunfire in close quarters, and he knew his own gun had weakened considerably. Unless they found a specially designed power source and adapter, they would not be able to recharge the weapons. Ridge burst into the small hall with Tomson behind him. Lantz and Jerez stood in the middle, breathlessly still waving their crude weapons about, while Mahaffey, Yu, and Brenna surrounded them.

"Nobody is watching the entrance," Ridge shouted as he ran toward the mound with his gun up. He half expected mudmen to come pouring over the top any minute. All he saw was darkness in the tunnels. He heard a regular, calm plashing as water dripped someplace.

"They came out of nowhere," Lantz said breathlessly. Her face was spattered ruby-red in the slightly off-light, as were her muscular bare arms.

"Out of the walls," Jerez said. Her face had streaks on it, as did her bare neck and shoulders. Sweat and streaks of blackish oil added a surreal sheen to the women's skin.

"Be real," Mahaffey said.

"Okay, it was like out of the walls," Jerez amended.

"She means they just popped up out of the shadows," Lantz said.

"Silently," Jerez said, gulping for air. "Stealthy."

Lantz nodded and gasped also. "We didn't know what hit us at first. They aren't real fast, but they just keep plodding along. They're stupid, like moths. You can kill them if you're fast enough."

Jerez said: "They know those tunnels backwards and forwards. We don't have a chance hiding in here. It's a wonder Caulfield survived as long as he did."

Ridge nodded. "That does it. We're heading back to WorkPod01. Everybody make sure you have some kind of weapon. Stick close together and watch each other's backs."

"Listen," Mahaffey said. His normally dark skin seemed pale, and his eyes were wide. Everyone grew still, and they listened. Ridge's skin crawled as he heard the mudmen singing their hunt-song for the first time: flute-like, at various low timbres, so soft you had to strain to hear them, as these enigmatic dwellers of the darkness sang to one another of their next meal.

Chapter 7

The seven surviving techs and engineers of WorkPod01 formed up on the ledge outside the work area where Mughali lay dead, stored with minimal dignity, posthaste, in a food locker. "Keep an eye on each other's backs," Ridge repeated. "Those of us with guns, don't fire unless you have to because we're running low and we won't be able to recharge until we're in WorkPod01 with the door locked."

They started for home. Single-file, they walked on the high catwalk above seemingly bottomless darkness. The light around them was darkly brassy, muted but hard, a sheen of copper like at the bottom of a deadly well. Ridge took the lead, with Tomson trailing. In the middle, Yu carried a gun, while Brenna, Lantz, Mahaffey, and Jerez carried improvised tools like hammers and crowbars.

The swaying, rocking metal grid was in many places a ribbon so narrow one had to put one foot carefully before the other while holding to the railing on one side, and not look down into the abyss on the other. Tomson joked: "At least they can't fly, so far anyway, so we're safe as long as we have the bottomless pit beside us." A few chuckles rose up in the flat air.

At first the going was slow and quiet. Ridge could hear everyone's breathing. Then there was a sudden creak, a screech of metal, a clatter of dropping steel, and Brenna screamed loudly enough to waken the dead. Or the mudmen. Ridge whirled, full of concern at losing her. "Grab her!" But someone already had grabbed her, even as the section of catwalk under her feet broke off and fell twirling down into the darkness in a long curve. A minute later, they heard a faint crash. "That's a long way down," Mahaffey whispered.

"You got that right," Jerez said softly behind Ridge. "At least this artificial gravity still works."

Yu walked behind Jerez, and he helped Brenna onto safe territory. Brenna reached behind her to tow Lantz along.

"Keep going," Tomson urged as he clambered after Lantz. "Must have been old. Or else it was a trap set up by the mudmen."

"They aren't bright enough," Jerez said.

"Don't be too sure," Tomson said. "Never underestimate the enemy."

"Probably just old and rusty," Mahaffey said. "How can that be?"

"Let's talk about ourselves," Ridge said. "Everyone has at least one good story to tell about home. Let's think about home, okay? I'll go first. Back in San Diego, I like to get up early in the morning and take my coffee and stand on the back patio. It's still foggy because the marine layer hasn't burned off, but it's not really cold. I can see dew drops on the oranges that are clustered on several little trees on the back lawn. A neighbor's big fat orange cat slinks by, stalking a mouse. It's the only time of day I really have any peace because my wife and kids are asleep and the family dog is in the kitchen eating the kibble I just poured for him."

"What kind of story is that?" Jerez said behind him. "What's the punch line?"

"There isn't a punch line," Ridge said. "That's the beauty of it. Unlike this paradise in which we find ourselves walking, it's safe and quiet and uneventful at home. About all that ever happens is that a check bounces and I have to call the bank to straighten things out."

"There are no checks anymore," Mahaffey said. "Nobody uses checks anymore."

"Just keep talking and we'll be home soon," Ridge said with a wary grin, glancing over his shoulder. His strategy seemed to be working. Keep them talking, and it would take their minds off their fears. He had to remember to keep his hand on his gun and keep an eye out for mudmen, since he was walking point.

Jerez said: "I spent my childhood in Singapore but married a Norwegian man whom I met in Belgium while I was studying engineering at Louvain. I have cute little blond children and a husband who looks like one of those college students who does puppet shows at kindergartens for spending money." Several people laughed-a nervous, low laugh that told they were relieved to dump some of their anxiety, even for a few seconds. "We have a low spot in the backyard of our home in Ostende. We call it the Low Country. When it rains, which is often, the low spot fills with water and becomes a little pond. It has slimy black salamanders in it, some of them with orange zigzags on their backs. They are harmless, and the children like to put them in a glass aquarium to watch them eat insects. We always make the kids put them back because we tell them the salamander mommies are looking for their kids."

"What are your kids' names?" Mahaffey asked, and Jerez looked at him uncomprehendingly.

Yu told his little story. "I grew up in a small apartment where the older men all smoked and played board games. They didn't like a little boy around, so I spent a lot of time on the fire escape. My mother was afraid I would fall off, but I was agile as a mountain goat. As I got older, I started climbing on the rooftops and pretty soon I could see the city around for miles."

"What city?" Mahaffey asked.

"Shanghai. Pudong," Yu said. He was silent a few moments. "It was gray and smoggy a lot because the city is so huge. There are parks, but they sit under gray rain clouds. Sometimes the sun breaks through. I saw a really lovely rainbow once, a perfect semicircle with red and blue and green like neon lighting in it. I met a girl on the rooftop too, when I was 18."

"Did you screw her?" Mahaffey asked.

"Mahaffey," Brenna said in a warning tone.

"Must you be so crude?" Jerez said.

"I never did," Yu said. "However, there was an older woman. Well, she must have been about 25 and she was a little bit stocky. Her family owned a skin theater over in Fengjiang, and she sold tickets there. She used to come home for lunch every day and sit in the sun on the roof, with her top off. She had these heavy breasts, and one day she caught me staring at them. So she looked left and right and smiled at me. I was 18 and what did I know? I went over and for one dollar she let me feel them both."

"That's a crock of crap," Mahaffey said.

Ridge turned and said to Mahaffey: "Are you trying to make trouble?"

Mahaffey's dark skin looked darker, and his eyes were wild and angry. "You know what I'm getting at, Ridge. Quit dicking around with us."

"I'm not dicking around," Ridge said softly. "I'm as confused as you are, but I'm keeping my mouth shut. In a second or two, I'm going to slap your mouth shut for you if you don't zip a lip."

"I'm ready for you," Mahaffey said. He rose in a threatening pose and pursed his lips as he walked. His eyes blazed. Ridge noticed a tear in each outer corner of Mahaffey's eyes.

Tomson growled from the rear: "I want to hear some more stories, man. Keep your tongue in your head and your eyes on the road before we all drop down the drain."

"Did you squeeze her tits?" Jerez asked.

Lantz giggled. "He probably gave her another dollar and sucked one."

"Maybe," Ridge said, "we can come back to this story later. Mahaffey, since you are such a pain in the ass, has anything ever happened to you?"

"Yeah. I'm here. Isn't that enough?"

Yu turned and smashed Mahaffey across the mouth. Yu's face was contorted with rage, and his head trembled so that his black hair shook. "You bastard. You needle me again and I'll throw you down into that shit below. I'll throw you so hard you go splat. I hope those little gray men eat you alive."

Mahaffey stopped and felt his chin, then his jaw. "Ouch." Blood ran between his fingers. Ridge was afraid the two men were going to go at it, but Mahaffey grinned sheepishly. "Okay, I had that coming. Try it again, Yu, and next time my foot is going through your head. Understand, geeko?"

Yu's eyes still blazed, and his lips quivered with revulsion. "You damned lowlife. Let's make a deal, worm. You don't talk to me and I won't talk to you. Better yet, let's not even look at each other."

"Whoa," Ridge said. "Guys, we all have to live together."

Brenna started singing in a high, thin voice. It wasn't words but a sweet keening sound. Everyone was so shocked that all further conversation fell silent. The group stopped in mid-air, in just that sphere of dim light from their collective head lamps, with no view backward or forward. "Keep moving," Ridge said, and Tomson in the back said "Go! Go!" The group obediently started moving again, but Brenna did not falter in her song.

Somewhere in the darkness, a fluting noise sounded. Chills ran up and down Ridge's spine again. What on earth (or not on Earth) was going on here? More fluting voices joined in. Ridge found he had to listen very carefully or he would miss the low sound of air hitting air as those deadly mouths in the darkness communicated with one another. It was scary in one way, and yet nothing new in another way, since they knew they were being shadowed by these deadly terrors that had torn Mughali to pieces. Ridge found that if he shut out the childlike singing of Brenna, he could triangulate somewhat. His hearing told him, as he turned his head in various directions like a radar dish, that there were mudmen all around on the inner cylindrical surfaces of the ship. Mudmen padded silently along shadowy girders in midair. Mudmen moved in groups along ledges. There were a lot of them, for he could see the occasional flash of a pair of ruby eyes-the backs of their eyeballs, to be more specific, where light gathered and reflected in the tapetum, a reflective structure coating the rear surfaces of a typical nocturnal animal's eyeballs to gather, reflect, and amplify meager light sources. Most earth animals tended to reflect in the greenish wavelengths of light; whatever the mudmen were, they went lower yet, into the red at the edge of visible light. There was an explanation for everything, Ridge thought, and there would be an explanation for all this too. He told the group so, adding, "Soon we'll all have a good laugh about this."

"How about Mughali," Mahaffey said. "She isn't laughing."

"Neither are any of us," Ridge said. "Now shut up."

Brenna stopped singing. "That was a lullaby. I sang it to my babies when they were real small so they would be quiet. I will sing it to you some more if it will make you quiet."

"Thank you," Lantz said sincerely. "Well, you know I grew up near Tacoma. It rains all the time there, but it's very lovely.

When I was small, my dad used to pack us in a minivan and drive us around the Olympic Peninsula. That is one of the largest non-tropical rainforests in the world."

"Is that where you learned to lift weights?" Mahaffey asked.

"Yeah. Shut the fuck up, okay? I'm sick of your crap. Now listen. So we used to pull over in these dark, beautiful tunnels and get out of the van. We'd walk on tiptoes right into the edges of the forest. There was moss so rich and dark and green that it muffled your footfalls. The moss hung down in ropes and beards and sheets from all the trees. You had to climb carefully, but it took you down into these little valleys where fresh water flowed. There were these little waterfalls, and sometimes you could see a tiny little rainbow right in the waterfall, glistening over these slippery looking slimy rocks. These rocks were cold and slimy and wet. They had this green coating on them in little ropes like seaweed and you could see butterflies flapping up around where the sunlight penetrated way down into the deep parts in the forest."

"That's a beautiful story," Brenna said. "I just want to tell you that I loved walking my stroller up and down the boulevard."

"What boulevard?" Mahaffey asked.

She said with sweet patience: "All of them. Ricardo would be off flying to Rome or Cairo, and I'd be alone with the little ones. We had a sort of beat up little green hatchback, and I would take the double stroller. I'd drive down to the beach along the Rio de la Plata. I would find a nice spot to park where the airplane noise wasn't too loud from the Aeroparque Jorge Newbery, and then we would walk along the little concrete sidewalks. The sun would shine, and the bees and butterflies were out in force, the wind was balmy and the flowers were in bloom, and I would sing my lullaby to the little babies in the stroller." She raised her voice sweetly in a humming sound that Ridge found incredibly sweet. As soon as she started, echoes came from the mudmen, chilling imitations, haunting inversions of evil where Brenna shed goodness. Then again, perhaps even mudmen had some sort of soul and life. Maybe they believed in something. Certainly they yearned to eat and drink, and they had a taste for human blood and meat, so maybe they were capable of higher yearnings. Or baser yearnings, Ridge corrected himself. Brenna's lullaby from Buenos Aires trickled away. For a few minutes the mudmen continued their faint puffing and lowing, and then that stopped. Only the sound of water trickling randomly from high places to low places was audible now.

"We are getting closer," Ridge said. "Faith, y'all. We're almost home." A cheer arose. "Yeah!" Tomson cried. "Plug me in to my music and hand me a stick of stimulay. I'm good for it." Laughter followed his declaration.

They came into an area of increasing light, though still faint. The catwalk on which they trod became more visible, showing its worn metal surfaces and floor gratings.

"Eyes open wide," Ridge said. "We're coming to the end of the catwalk and up the ledge on the home side now. We've made it so far. Anybody got the key to our home?"

Tomson said: "I think we'll find it when we get there. Anybody tried reaching the CP recently?"

"I'll give it another shot," Ridge said. He cranked up his collar mike and spoke into it: "Hello, Bridge. Captain Venable? CP, this is WorkPod01. Do you read? Over." He waited. "This is Ridge speaking. Bridge, this is WorkPod01 calling. Do you read me? Over." No reply came, just a faint crackle of static.

"You all think I'm just a poor kid from Sandtown," Tomson said, "but listen. My dad was an Air Force colonel. He used to fly the most advanced jets and saucers in our arsenal. He'd bring back photographs, when it was allowed, of clouds way up on the edge of space. They were these wonderful photographs in which you'd see a green mass below, and then a sort of a haze, kind of blue streaked with white, or white streaked with blue, and above that the black edge of eternity. That always got me, particularly when my old man managed to get some stars in the shot. That always worked magic for me. We lived in a great big old house on a quiet shady street. There were these huge weeping willows all around on the lawn. Elms lined the streets as far as you could see. I had a real happy childhood there."

Mahaffey cut in: "And then you discovered drugs and whores and became a juvenile delinquent."

Tomson took the needling in stride. "I did develop a case of clap early on, because I discovered those young ladies before I could afford protection. I learn quickly though, and I caught on a lot faster than you are catching on, you son of a bitch." There was no humor in Tomson's voice by the time he reached the last sentence of that short, threatening speech.

"Quiet," Ridge said. "Here we are." They stepped onto the gridded platform that would take them to their front door. Breathing a collective sigh of relief, they closed the railings around the moving platform, which was about the size of a living room. Ridge manipulated the simple lever controls with their black rubber ball grips, and the platform quietly started moving on well-greased chains and sprockets. It made a soft, fatty sort of rattling bicycle chain sound as it traversed the last few yards of the void. The platform swung gently around a turn, around a corner in the high walls, and moved slightly upward into a spill of light. The seven staffers waited as it glided over a ledge richly splashed with homey yellow light that spilled from the overhanging windows of WorkPod01. The platform rose up, elevator fashion, and attached itself like a front porch to the metal hull of WorkPod01. The metal walls were solid steel, well riveted and tough, and painted a dull chariot red. The sealed doors of the small work factory glowered below, visible through the floor grating. Ridge felt a deep sense of relief. "Okay," he said, "now all we have to do is get in."

"That's just the trick," Mahaffey said with a hysterical little rising laugh. "We can't get in. We're locked out, and there is a reason."

"Shut up, you fool," Jerez said, banging on the sealed steel portal with the flat of her hand.

Lantz followed suit. She banged on the steel with her fist, raising and lowering a muscular arm. *Nothing.* Ridge shuddered, realizing instinctively that Mahaffey was most likely right. They were locked out. Like a man in a bad dream, Ridge watched the members of the team look at each other in consternation, wailing and banging on the steel. *Mahaffey is right,* Ridge thought. We are truly hosed. We are never going to be let in there again. All I want to know is why? No, all I want is to lie down with Brenna and pull the covers over our heads and listen to that lullaby. But first we'd have to get in, and it doesn't look like we are ever meant to get in again.

"Okay, now what?" Tomson said as he pushed his way gently through the panicked crowd. He did not bang on the locked, sealed steel doors. Instead he laid one palm on the steel and then closed his eyes as if slipping into some kind of psychoactive dream. Sweat rimmed his face, which turned a sickly shade of yellow. He opened his eyes and shook his head. "Those vibes are bad, my friends. We can never go in again. We're finished."

"That's insane," Ridge found himself saying. Several others yelled out in agreement.

Tomson shook his head again. "Sorry, folks. I'm not being psychic. I was just thinking about all that's happened. There was no key. We locked the place up and threw the key away, so to speak."

Ridge looked carefully along the grating and down the ledge below, but saw no sign of the dazed, bloodied man who had pounded on the window. Mudmen must have taken care of him, Ridge thought. He could imagine the lunch feast they must have had in the dark below. Shivering, he walked close to the riveted wall, beside Tomson, and gripped the railing. "If you and another person will brace me, I'll climb up and take a look inside." With Tomson and Yu supporting him, Ridge climbed up onto the railing. The forward sloping windows were still several feet above his head. The two men supported his legs as he stood on tiptoe. He leaned palms-forward against the wall and pressed his right cheek against the cold steel. It was to no avail. He must get higher. "Grab me if I fall," he said. Carefully, he flexed his knees. He rose up and down several times, aiming carefully how to place his fingertips. Then he jumped. His fingertips caught on the steel rim under the window. Before his grip could weaken, he pulled himself up. As he did so, he slipped his fingers into a flat area just under the thick plate windows. He figured he had enough strength to chin-up for about a minute. Dismissing his fears of plummeting down past the platform, he pulled himself up. His entire torso trembled at the effort, but he managed to raise himself high enough to get his eyes above sill level. What he saw puzzled him. The interior of WorkPod01 was well lit and clean-but there was nothing there. There were a number of oblong, slightly glowing bluish-white objects that seemed to form the tops of a number of boxes. There were intricate designs all around on the walls, which glowed with light from the boxes on the floor. In the ceiling were fixtures that looked like fluorescent tubes, but they looked cold and gray, emitting no light. There was no sign of life in WorkPod01. There was no hint of left over dinners, of chairs, of tables, of moon doors, of showers, of exercise sets, of ancient Homeric poems stashed on shelves. All the clutter he remembered was missing. It did seem that the overall floor plan vaguely resembled that which he remembered from the galley. The only other thing he glimpsed that made sense, before his strength gave out and he dropped down to the grating among his team members, were one or two places on the wall with rounded rectangles that might have been the viewing screens where the crew had seen and heard Captain Venable speak to them.

"Well?" Tomson asked. "What did you see?"

Ridge shook his head as they all crowded around. He knew his face must be pale, and their faces reflected his shock. "Nothing," he said. "I saw nothing that I recognized."

"Did someone clean it all up?" Jerez asked. The others babbled simultaneously with similar questions and anxieties. Ridge shook his head and staggered to the railing, trying to assimilate what he'd seen, or not seen. "It's crazy," he said, feeling a sickness in his gut. He banged his fist on the cold steel and yelled: "There's nothing there. No galley, no showers, no books, no moon doors, no cubicles. It's like we never existed."

"We are ghosts," Mahaffey said. His eyes looked crazy, and he started walking in circles on the platform. "We are dead people."

Brenna smiled. "We bleed when we are hurt, and you see that Mughali died. That hardly makes us ghosts."

"Bullshit," Tomson told Mahaffey. "I pinch myself, I feel it. That means I am real. You're talking nuts."

Ridge tried to grasp Mahaffey by the belt. The young man was tall, and strong, and wild. He was filled with emotions as he windmilled his arms. "Don't you see? It's all a bunch of bullshit." He looked at Jerez. "Can you tell me the names of your children?" She stared mutely back at him. He looked at Yu. "You say the woman with the tits came home every day for lunch. It's a long commute between Pudong and Fengjiang to the south. It would take her hours each way in heavy traffic. It's not real, Yu." He turned from the stricken Yu and said to Brenna: "Your children. What are their names?" She slowly shook her head, her eyes filled with denial. "You see?" he continued. "None of you remember critical things because it's all bullshit." With that, he leapt onto the railing.

He balanced precariously, squatting on the railing. Both feet were on the thick metal bar, and he leaned left with one hand touching the railing while the other hand windmilled in space for balance. Several people shouted, and several reached for him. Ridge wanted to reach out and grab Mahaffey, but felt paralyzed, partly because it all happened so quickly and partly because he had been wondering all morning what were the names of his own children. He couldn't even really picture them in his mind's eye, much as he loved them, much as he thought about nothing but his family. Mahaffey rose fully to his feet on the slender railing. He balanced there for a minute, rotating his arms while several people screamed and reached for him. Tomson dropped his gun to the grating with a loud clang and started to wrap his arms around Mahaffey's legs, but wasn't quick enough. With a wild look in his eyes, and a long trailing scream, Mahaffey jumped. Ridge watched him sailing downward. Mahaffey's shirt rippled in a breeze, and his arms and legs stuck out as if he were jumping onto a horse. He fell out of sight and everyone on the grating fell silent until they heard a single sodden splash far below. It was a splattering sound, like a palm striking down on a countertop, or a melon falling from a window to a sidewalk, and the sound left no doubt as to Mahaffey's outcome, which was the end of all struggle and some sort of eternal peace amid the debris of the universe here in this mysterious place, this dead or half-dead ship of ghosts drifting far from the sun. The remaining six team members held each other and sobbed. Several stood at the railing, clenching their fists around the steel where Mahaffey had last stood, and looked down.

"Ideas?" Tomson said, retrieving his weapon and slipping it into his belt. His eyes had a haunted look as he stared out at the distant surfaces inside the ship. Even then, Ridge thought he glimpsed tiny blurs of reddish light moving stealthily and strategically into position in the void. Were it not for the sobbing of Brenna and Yu, he thought he would clearly hear the flute drones of a dozen rounded mouths amid the slag and dross.

"I'm fresh out," Ridge said. He could almost feel the impact of his words striking his team members like a blow, sending them reeling. He shook his head to clear it. "Look, while there is life there is hope. We have no idea what's going on here. Mahaffey lost his mind and bailed out. That's not the solution I recommend."

"What do you recommend?" Tomson said.

"Yeah, what bright idea do you have now?" Jerez added.

Ridge sighed and looked up and down the steel wall, which was tighter than a safe. "We might try to make our way to the CP. We might try to find Venable in person and have a serious discussion about just what the hell is going on inside his ship, if he knows."

"And where is the CP?" Tomson asked softly.

"Where is Venable?" Yu asked.

"That's the next thing we should try to find out," Ridge said.

Chapter 8

We're going to make our way forward to the CP," Ridge said. What else could he do?

"Where exactly is that?" Tomson asked.

"I know it's toward the bow in front," Ridge said. Seeing the skeptical looks around him, he added: "I am not going to lie to you. I do not know where the Command Post is, where Captain Venable is, where the Bridge is. All I know is we can't stay here because those creatures out on the walls are just waiting to have us for lunch. Look down." There was a collective gasp as his five surviving team mates stepped to the railing and looked down. Way below, they saw a wriggling gray blur. Nobody needed to tell them it as all one could see of the mudmen devouring Mahaffey's remains in the faint twilight below.

"I'm with you," Tomson said. Several others made affirmative sounds and nodded. Ridge noted that he, Tomson, and Yu still had guns. Ridge told them: "I seem to remember that when we headed to the work area, we were going backwards. That is, we were moving toward the stern. That means we need to go that way." He pointed past WorkPod01 into the darkness. He stepped to the railing and looked down along the ledge below. "Looks to me like this platform will travel some distance."

Lantz said: "Anything but stay here. Let's go." Suddenly, Ridge thought, it was three women and three men. The three women (Brenna, Lantz, Jerez) stood in a line and echoed Lantz's sentiment. Ridge, Yu, and Tomson nodded their own agreement. All six heaved a collective sigh and shrugged. Ridge spoke quietly for all: "Let's get going." He moved the well-greased levers of the platform. Ridge felt a slight lurch, and those bicycle noises again of chains dragging through grease-packed sprockets, and the platform began to move. The platform moved laterally along the wall. In minutes WorkPod01 looked bare as the platform moved away from the island of light, and the group were enveloped again in that mix of dim but brassy hard light and equally dim, soft chocolaty shadow inked hard-black around the edges.

At one point, they passed through a particularly grayish-dark, charcoal pool of night. Arrayed on a high wall ledge were about six mudmen sitting in a silent array. They stared directly and enigmatically at the humans from about 50 feet away with dim red eyes. The humans on the platform shuddered and drew closely together. Ridge felt bodies against his. He felt the trembling of his team mates, and he felt his own body trembling against theirs. He felt his teeth chattering, and felt his hands grow cold as he looked at the silently staring, immutable kachina-like mudmen masks with their rounded mouths. They blew noises like a faint wind, a soft susurrus, a tootling that echoed from other spots. The island of red eyes and round mouths passed, but Ridge knew he had not seen the last of the mudmen.

The platform moved slowly through the darkness, an island of light. The monorail on which the platform moved curved gradually along the inner surface of the ship. The surface was curved, suggesting a long zeppelin-like cylinder. The surface was pitted and uneven, and glowed with dim lighting from inside the ship itself. The platform bathed in a patch of hard industrial light as it moved. The moving light rippled over fire-glazed pores, glassy waves, coal-like flows of glittering carbon debris. Here and there like rats on a dockyard, mudmen skittered from one vantage point to another. Always they stared hungrily at the human cargo passing so temptingly by them. Their whispering and moaning and fluting got on everyone's nerves. Jerez sat down on the grating and held her hands over her ears. Tears streamed from her eyes as she sobbed, and mucus spiderwebbed between her open mouth, her chin, her elbows, and her knees. Ridge worried that Jerez might be the next to lose her mind and go over the side. Lantz knelt beside her and stroked Jerez's hair. Brenna squatted on the other side and murmured encouragement. Jerez kept shaking her head and protesting. Her sobs grew louder, and the men exchanged looks of growing frustration. Ridge felt the fear in his bones, and the other two men had that glazed, hunted look in their eyes. Tomson told Yu: "Don't even think about it." Yu's hands hesitated near the butt of his gun. "Save your charge," Tomson told him.

Ridge told Lantz: "Keep trying to reach the CP on your com. We'll take turns trying. We have to keep trying to reach Captain Venable."

"What if he's dead too?" Yu said.

Ridge shrugged. "I can't answer impossible questions. You've heard of living from day to day? We're living from minute to minute here, pal. Bear with us and try not to make it any harder."

Jerez yelled through her tears, without opening her eyes: "He's right. We are all doomed. Mahaffey knew the score. You saw what they did to Mughali."

"Easy," Brenna said. She looked up at Ridge. "We need to find help."

Ridge nodded. "That's what we're trying to do. Everyone, keep an eye out for signs of civilization."

Tomson stepped close. "We've got to be asking some hard questions here, Ridge. I'm all for being civilized and calm. I'm all for singing hymns and keeping a stiff upper lip in the face of adversity. It would help though if we knew what the adversity is."

Ridge felt like slapping him. He wanted to ask why people were asking him these questions. Why me? Then he remembered that he'd accepted the leadership position and now he must perform. This was what he got paid for. Or was it?

"Ridge?" Tomson said, leaning close with a quizzical look. "You okay?

Ridge swallowed hard and couldn't answer. He was paralyzed with fear of the unknown, terrified at what he might learn if his memory really did open up. His brain felt cloudy, and maybe that was good. Maybe it was bad, but it was a kind of balm to ease the echo of questions Mahaffey had left hanging in the air.

Tomson shook him gently. "Man, snap out of it. You look the way I feel." The others were looking at him too, Ridge saw, even Jerez with the spittle hanging dumbly from her chin and her eyes open in animal fascination so that she could momentarily forget her own dreadful thoughts. Ridge could not remember precisely the moment he'd signed the papers or the moment he'd sworn in for Federal Earth Service. Like so much of what he recalled, it was a welter of minute details wrapped around fuzzy generalities. He felt suffocated, as if the air were strangling him. Was there a virus or a chemical in the air that made them forget? "I don't know," Ridge said softly. "I don't know. All I do know is that we need to keep on. We must not lose hope. We must not let fear and terror win."

Tomson laughed. "Those are the moons of Mars. Phobos and Deimos. Fear and Terror. You think the moons of Mars are screwing with us?" He laughed harshly, then stopped. "Sorry, folks. Poor joke. I'm trying to bring a little levity into the proceedings. Ridge is right. We need to sing those hymns and canoe gracefully through that dark jungle. These are the times that try men's and women's souls." He did a little jig.

"You're losing your mind," Yu said. His face looked stark and sweaty.

Brenna laughed gently. She rose, keeping one hand on Jerez's head to offer comfort. "Tomson is the sanest person among us. He's trying to keep our minds off our troubles. Aren't you?" She looked at Tomson.

Tomson grinned widely, and Ridge loved him for it. Tomson said: "That's the idea, lady. I want us all to get back home in one piece. How far are we from Triton? Another day? Another week? A year?"

Ridge said: "We'll find out soon. We'll find the CP and do visual checks if nothing else. Look at the bright side. The ship has power. We were talking with the Bridge just a few hours ago. There has to be hope."

"That's right," Tomson said, "we have to keep going."

Silently, the platform continued its slow sweep along the inside of the ship. As the turn became sharper, it was evident they were coming to the bow section, where the ship's cross-section was smaller and the hull more sharply turned toward an eventual point. As Ridge remembered it, the ship was huge, with rounded points at bow and stern. The ship rotated to create artificial gravity on its inner surfaces. On ships like this that plied the solar system for years at a time, one typically found weightless facilities-cargo storage, certain types of factories like those creating high-precision crystals, and even sporting events-concentrated along the mid-axis. Normal living quarters and work areas were along the inner surface of the central hull, where the diameter was slightly larger, and the pseudograv somewhat stronger. As the platform approached the bow section, they saw more lighting ahead, which meant the mudmen were probably scarcer. The bow section contained a smaller rotating cylinder some 400 feet long and 200 feet in diameter, with about as much floor space as a good-size ten story office building on Earth for comparison. A wall separated the bow from midsection. The wall was covered with lights, viewing bubbles, external elevators, dangling hoses, a thousand features that seemed brownish and ominous, in this half-light, to Ridge's eyes. He saw no mudmen in the area, but that didn't mean they weren't around-or had crewmembers in the bow managed to exclude them?

"Is it me," Ridge said, "or are the lights really turning on as we get close?"

Lantz shook her head. "I think it's all just the way we see it. Why would the lights turn on-you mean, like someone is turning them on?"

Ridge shook his head. "No, more like it's automatic. Like there was no reason for them to be on until we came."

"Because there was nobody here until we came," Tomson added with a sardonic tone. "I'm becoming a pessimist. Someone please help me." One or two persons laughed, and Lantz punched him lightly on the arm.

The platform followed its track along the curving, increasingly bright, but still barren walls, into a dark tunnel that led into the bow area. The platform slowed as it entered a long, dark area that resembled an outdoor trolley stop complete with benches, overhead lights (now dim), and billboard schedules and announcements. The platform made several lurching motions and stopped. "We're here," Tomson said simply, and Ridge echoed: "That's as far as we go." He turned to the others and said: "Stay close together. The bow section is smaller, but it's full of small quarters and narrow passages. If we keep making our way forward, we are bound to reach the CP. If our luck holds, we could be safely in the CP with Captain Venable in just an hour or two."

"Yes!" several persons exclaimed. A few high-fived. The group stepped onto the more solid steel platform. They had mixed looks of relief and apprehension. Ridge understood their feelings. It was a relief to be out of the cargo holds and to have gotten this far. It was a feeling of apprehension to think of what new and unpleasant surprises might await them here, because it was quiet and there was no sign of life. They waited a minute or two on the platform, listening to the hum of air circulators, the soft crackle of fluorescent lights, the muted banging of metal as the platform they'd arrived on cooled and settled in its berth. Each time a relay slammed shut, a metallic clang traveled through the shimmering corridors with their highly polished floors. Each time a thermocouple closed or a sensor triggered some change of state, like time to turn on or off an air vent or a climate control duct, Ridge and his companions jumped. When *Neptune Express* docked, she brought with her an entire industrial capability including factories, hangars, offices, and an internal trolley system that seamlessly linked with the local one. On a busy day in port, thousands of workers might stream through here. The ship would dock in the external secondary moons of Luna or L-5, and an army of workers and officials would get her ready for her next journey-hence the trolley station. A smaller but no less excited flurry of motion and bustling humanity would erupt when *Neptune Express* docked at Triton, which hopefully would be soon.

"This way," Ridge said, pointing to the widest corridor leading forward. The group gladly followed him. "Look!" Jerez exclaimed, pointing to a huge image in a wall between two pillars. The image glowed with a lovely blue light against the black backdrop of space. The image looked much like any of the live action shots they'd become accustomed to seeing during their earlier days of passage. Neptune had a light, almost happy blue glow. As the legend inscribed digitally on the glowing signboards related, Neptune was slightly over 30 times as far from the sun as Earth, averaging nearly five billion kilometers or nearly 2.8 billion miles from the sun. Neptune measured roughly 156,000 km around its equator, or almost 97,000 miles. As a gas giant, it had a mass roughly one third that of Earth. It had about 58 times the volume of Earth, and just under 15 times the surface area if one could call the outer edge of its gaseous, wispy atmosphere a surface. An astronaut floating there would appear to weigh about one and one sixth as much as he or she would on Earth. If that sounded hospitable, the next fact quickly shot down any hope of comfort: the hydrogen, helium, and methane based atmosphere stayed at a chilly minus 214 degrees Centigrade or minus 353 degrees Fahrenheit.

"Those pictures are so beautiful," Jerez said with a tear in one eye.

"Aren't they though," Tomson said shaking his head.

"Almost feels like we're halfway back to normal," Ridge said with a grin. He recalled the warmth and comfort of WorkPod01 as he remembered it. He remembered how good it had felt to crawl into his warm bunk and snuggle up in the privacy of his dreams in his down sleeping bag. It occurred to him that he wasn't tired at all yet, though they'd been on the go for hours now, and stressed to their utmost with several horrid deaths. He should be mentally, physically, and spiritually exhausted, but he wasn't.

"Look, there is Triton," Brenna said, pointing. Ridge noticed that she had the faintest lisp, for there was a tiny gap between her upper front teeth. The more he saw of her, the more he longed to be with her. The feeling was so strong that he wasn't fighting it anymore. His wife Dorothy was a distant condition right now, a possibility rather than a factor. If they ever got back home alive, he might tell her about Brenna, or he might not. Maybe when the world got back to normal, he'd wonder what he had ever seen in his soft-faced young woman with her wine-dark hair and eyes a darker blue than the dangerous atmosphere of Neptune. Ridge shook these thoughts away. His gaze followed her pale, pointing finger toward an image of Triton rising over the cusp of the eighth planet. Both worlds glowed with distant sunlight, and the faint rings of Neptune curved like a veil uniting them. Triton's diameter was 2,705 kilometers (1,623 miles), compared with Luna's approximately 3,476 kilometers or 2,086 miles. Triton's thin nitrogen atmosphere glowed grayish-white above the Sea God's blue atmosphere. Neptune looked deceptively Earth-like in these images, but Triton's surface temperature at minutes 391 Fahrenheit made it the coldest spot in the solar system.

"I don't like it in there," Yu said. Ridge looked in the direction Yu was looking. "The corridors are too empty, too quiet," Yu said.

"Yeah, it's scary," Jerez said. Her teeth audibly chattered. Her eyes were large and scared.

"We'll wait here," Yu said. "I have the gun."

"We shouldn't split up," Tomson said.

"Let's all go together," Ridge said. He felt sorry for Jerez, but Yu was beginning to really irritate him and he almost welcomed the idea of parking the bio-engineer someplace until he could sort out what was going on.

"We'll stay here and guard our retreat," Jerez said with false cheer.

"What retreat?" Tomson said. "There is no way back out there that I can see."

"Back to WorkPod01," Yu said seriously. "That's the only place we know."

"That's home," Jerez said vehemently. "We're staying here."

Ridge and Tomson exchanged looks. Tomson shrugged, seeming to say 'let's get on with it.' Ridge rolled it around in his head. He had no real authority, just a thankless position as Senior Engineer. "Okay," Ridge said. "You call your own shots. We'll keep in touch on the collar mikes."

Jerez touched the large black button clipped to the edge of her collar by her throat. "We'll hold the fort over here. If you find the Captain, give us a holler and we'll come running."

Reluctantly, Ridge gathered his diminished team together. Tomson, Brenna, and Lantz. "Anyone else want to stay?" he asked halfheartedly. They shook their heads. "We're sticking with you," Lantz said. Together, they marched off down the wide central corridor. The corridor itself curved, so that they had limited visibility under its constantly low ceiling, but they could see through strategically placed windows. In the distance, they made out a trolley station on the opposite hull. Part of a white tubular object protruded-the nose end of a high-speed rail car. This must be the internal, working rail line, Ridge thought, and that the commercial, fancy one for docking purposes. Once they were away from their station of egress, there were no more ceiling panels to look through, and Ridge became nervous about the limited visibility.

The four walked slowly and carefully down the corridors. It looked as though humans had just stepped outside for a few minutes. In glass-windowed cubicles on either side, desks and chairs stood empty. Dozens of persons must work here, Ridge thought as he looked at coffee mugs on desks, digital pads open to receive dictation, family holocubes knickknack shelves. It looked so congruent with his memories of life on Earth that he almost forgot they were closer to Neptune than to Earth or Luna. The others appeared to be thinking the same thing. Brenna tried a door in passing, and it swung open. Silently, the door crept open a few inches and stopped. The four persons stopped to listen. They heard air in vents, wind in airshafts, small machinery clicking in the walls as a million Microsystems fine-tuned the climate. "Wonder where they all are?" Brenna said.

"If you see any calendars," Ridge said, "let me know. That might give us a clue."

Tomson gave a humorless, nervous laugh and ran a hand quickly over his short, kinky hair. "Man, this is almost as creepy as that wasteland outside."

Lantz pointed to a glass case that stood partially open. "Look, emergency equipment. I see guns." They stepped into the office. Carefully, Tomson and Ridge sidled in holding their guns ready. Lantz and Brenna crowded behind them. Ridge sniffed. "Smell that?"

Tomson wrinkled his nose, shook his head, looked at Ridge. "What?"

"Dust," Ridge said. "Stale air."

"Cold," Brenna said, wrapping her arms around herself. Lantz followed suit, and goose bumps appeared in pinkish-white fields on her triceps.

Ridge said carefully: "If I had to guess, I'd say this was all shut down for a long time and just turned on when we came. You know, sort of like those lights that snap on when someone gets near your house back on Earth." It did smell stale in here, he thought.

Brenna put her finger on it: "There are no people smells. No perfume, no sweat, no mothball sweaters, no shaggy coats, no leather gloves or purses. Not that we'd see them in space, but civilians on Luna or Triton might have them. There's nothing like that here, nor are there any people sounds, like someone flushing a toilet, laughing, pouring coffee, sneezing. Nothing."

"It's a black hole of people," Tomson said softly. "Why?"

Ridge pointed to the open locker, where a half dozen long-arms stood in perfect soldierly alignment with their buzzmuzzles pointing up and their trigger guards pointing outward. Along the inside walls of the cabinet, left and right, were several small-arms plus all the expected equipment, from cleaning kits and synchronizers to spare charge packs. "Take a look at this." He walked over to the locker and knelt. With one fingertip he traced back and forth on the steel floor of the gun case. A fine layer of dark dust coated everything. From there, rising, he tracked the black dust to desks, chairs, ledges. "It's on everything," he said.

"Soot," Tomson said, sniffing his fingers after rubbing them on a ledge. "There was a fire in the ship."

Lantz pointed to several chairs standing around as if the owners had just risen a minute ago for their lunch break. "Nobody has sat here since it got dusty," Lantz said.

Tomson gestured with both arms. "Look, all the chairs are turned as if they suddenly rose and headed for the door we just came in."

Brenna pointed to a cup lying on its side on the floor farther in the office bay. "Looks like a few people did drop things. A cup, a handkerchief, a slipper."

Ridge added: "In and orderly fashion, I'd say. Like it was a drill. Or an emergency, but they had trained for it. But losing a slipper and not going back for it is a sure sign there was something extraordinary happening."

Brenna examined the closet and pulled out a rifle. "It's charged, but it's been on Sleep." She pulled the Wake pin, and the indicators glowed green along the stock under the barrel. "God knows for how long."

"Arm yourselves," Ridge said. "Let's take all the rifles. We can use them." He handed each of them one of the stun-rifles and pulled down two extras with Yu and Jerez in mind. "If you see lights, we can use those also."

A minute later they strode quietly down the corridor. Ridge felt a trifle more at ease now that they were better armed. "Keep an eye out for spare charge packs," he told them.

The corridor led to a central rotunda. The floors were coated with that faint black soot, but otherwise everything gleamed as though cleaning crews had been working nonstop.

"Ridge," a voice said. *Yu.*

Ridge whipped his hand to his throatcom. "What is it?"

"Not sure. Something is happening."

"We're coming back." Ridge turned and started to run. "I knew we should not have split up."

"What is it?" Brenna said with a worried face as all three fell in behind Ridge at a goodly trot.

"Not sure," Ridge said, "but why take chances. I want us all together from here on in."

They heard Jerez scream, and that was when they knew something was really wrong. They started running back to the trolley stop as fast as they could. Their footfalls echoed around the gleaming windows and walls. Dust kicked up lightly around their feet as they pattered along the rubbery floors. They heard shouting-*Yu,* Ridge thought-and then another scream—*Jerez,* Ridge thought—and then muffled shouting from both.

As they emerged into the trolley station, they saw swarms of frantic movement. A number of mudmen bodies lay spattered on the tiled floor surfaces, smearing the fine blue and white decorator tiles with greenish-brown blood. Yu and Jerez had left the moving platform and had their backs against a dead-end wall. The platform rocked as mudmen clambered up from underneath. Jerez looked dazed and bloodied as she fought two of the creatures off, wielding a wooden staff she'd found, with which she swiped at them. Her face was contorted in a silent scream, and her eyes were half-closed in terror. Yu's face looked calm, and his eyes had a mechanical, methodical appearance as if he'd shut down all emotions and was acting with his last shreds of rational calm. One by one, he shot deadly sizzling charges into his attackers. He aimed his gun again and again until it ran out, and then both he and Jerez disappeared under a pile of attackers.

"Careful!" was all Ridge could shout as he and his three companions appeared in the midst of this roiling chaos. It must be clear—they were armed to the teeth with fresh weapons, but a single stray shot could sever a limb or a head, and those must not belong to Jerez or Yu.

In another ten seconds, the appalling truth became clear. Ridge and his companions fired away at the edges of the mudmen crowd. There must be three dozen of the creatures, Ridge thought, shooting those that turned and ran toward him with their talons open to grasp and kill. The mudmen had a kind of fungus-like, mushroom smell, of forest floor and rotting wood and moisture in pulpy crevices. When scorched with the charge guns, they gave off a stench like burned rubber. They were leathery, and when they came apart under the darting energy rays, amid the smoke and carbonization, Ridge could smell the odor of their half-digested food, their feces, their rotting-leather blood. Several mudmen heads exploded as Ridge and his companions fired. It was all over in a minute or so, but by then the disaster was complete. The few surviving mudmen scampered away, throwing themselves over the sides into the dark to escape. They left the platform littered with the bodies of their fellows—and the bodies of their two human victims.

"Damn you!" Lantz sobbed as she walked through the roiling smoke, kicking mudmen body parts aside. Brenna, Ridge, and Tomson stepped over mudmen bodies. Ridge found himself slithering over their slime and offal. He slipped at one point, and nearly sprained his free hand bracing himself against the wall while holding up his rifle with the other hand. The fall brought him face to face with the mudmen's handiwork. Brenna screamed hysterically.

Ridge felt tears of anger, sorrow, and pity rolling from his eyes as he regarded the torn bodies that lay propped up against the wall. The remains were largely skeletal. The mudmen were like the fierce flesh-eating *piranhas* of the Amazon rivers. With their blank faces, slitty buttonhole eyes, and those little round mouths full of rows of tiny teeth, the mudmen had swarmed over their victims. They had sucked and torn and ground and whirled the flesh away right down to the bone. If they'd had another few minutes there would be nothing left but bone. As it was, most of the flesh was gone, and what remained in the torn and twisted jumpsuits were grinning caricatures of death.

"There is nothing we can do for them," Ridge said quietly. "We've got to get to safety." Seeing the hesitation on the others' faces, he added: "We can burn or bury them later. We'll talk about them, maybe have a service. For now, we need to get out of here. Stay with me!" So saying, he started back toward the rotunda at a jogging pace. The others fell in behind him. They ran with their rifles at ready.

Nobody spoke, nobody cried—the situation had gone from desperate to grim, and Ridge could not fathom how it might get worse, but it surely could. Each knew they had to be prepared for some final stand, much as Yu and Jerez had just been forced to make. Hopefully, the end would be less ugly if it had to come now.

Chapter 9

Ridge was now more aware than ever of the claustrophobic effect as they ran toward the rotunda. They were four sooty, sweaty persons in dirty jumpsuits open at the collar where helmets should have fit, had they any helmets to wear or a vacuum to wear them in. They bristled with guns and fear. The corridor ran along the curvature of the ship, so that they seemed forever to be headed down under the ceiling. They seemed to be forever descending, and the ceiling ahead and behind robbed them of visibility.

In the rotunda, under a dome about 50 feet high, they stopped at a directory plaque. Ridge looked quickly around and noted closed doors all around, and a mezzanine of unknown function above. With Brenna, Tomson, and Lantz crowding around him in a sea of gun barrels, Ridge touched the view screen on the directory plaque. Simple interactive controls responded to the tip of his index finger. He moved his fingertip about and brought up a succession of images. They stood at the entrance to a warren of tunnels leading into the sensitive command structures of the nose. "There is the CP," he said, tapping on an image of a small area near the tip. He moved his fingertip, and the images rotated. A succession images and blueprints scrolled by. "There appears to be some kind of huge warehouse."

"It's a dormitory," Tomson ventured. "Kind of like a giant WorkPod01 without the galleys and other amenities."

"How odd," Brenna said. "You think they all went there to sleep?"

"Where else could they have gone?" Lantz said. "Push here."

Ridge did as she told him, pressing the first of a row of orange squares. He zoomed in on a stylized image that showed rows upon rows of sleeping tanks. "They must have gone under the gas," Tomson said. That was the lingo that meant they'd gone to sleep, and that immediately cued the four that there must have been a catastrophic emergency. "Why else would they have gone under?" Brenna said.

"Comet? Meteor? Something hit the ship and caused all that burn damage we saw out there," Tomson said.

Ridge bit his lip and swallowed hard. "If that's the case, then we need to think this all through from the start. Remember how old Caulfield was? All the signs point to this having happened a long time ago."

"We must have been asleep a long time," Brenna said. Her face contorted in horror. "My children! My husband!" Tears ran down her cheeks, and she dropped her weapon. Her hands flew to her face. The others stood stunned, soaking in the realization that Ridge knew they had been suppressing. He said quietly: "I was afraid of this. That's what Mahaffey was thinking when he pulled the plug."

"I'm going to kill myself!" Brenna cried. "I don't want to live without my babies!" She wailed loudly, and nobody had the fortitude to stop her. For a moment, Ridge wished he had joined Mahaffey. It would have been an easy way out. "No," he told Brenna. "No, you don't understand, do you?"

She wiped her eyes and stared at him through a grimace of glittering tears. "What?"

"Your babies aren't dead," Ridge said. "You're thinking that a long time passed and they grew big and died of old age. Or maybe they are grownups now and they think you were lost in space."

She nodded, running wet fingers over her sorrow-swollen features. Lantz and Tomson weren't faring much better.

"It isn't so," Ridge said. "Trust me. It's almost more sad than all that."

"What do you mean?" Lantz cried feebly, her voice distorted with grief. She, too, had loved ones who might have long ago died if the ship and its passengers had really gone into long-term hibernation as a way of escaping death, until someone could come to rescue them.

"I'd rather not speculate," Ridge told them. "It's just—I hate to see you so torn up over how this has all turned out." His three companions stared at him in varying degrees of realization and a newly dawning horror. "You see, there were no babies."

"No!" Brenna mouthed. She held her fingers to her mouth and appeared beyond speech. No words came out of her pale, distorted features. Her eyes glittered with bereavement, as did those of Lantz and Tomson, each in their own way. Tomson was still more stoic, while Lantz appeared to be a denier to the last. Feeling terribly sorry for himself, but more so for Tomson and Lantz, and especially for Brenna, Ridge said: "You remember the questions Mahaffey was asking? Can you name your children? Of course we couldn't. None of us has children."

"You think we're not human?" Tomson asked somberly.

Ridge sighed deeply, holding Brenna as she collapsed against him. "I want to think we are."

Lantz was still defiant, at least partially. "You'd better explain this crazy shazzle, man. I think I'm going to puke right here, right now." She looked green around the cheeks, and her tongue worked feverishly in her mouth as if saliva were gathering for a violent projectile heave. Ridge couldn't blame her. "I'm just piecing it together logically," he said.

"Go on," Tomson urged. "You're on the right track, man. We need to know the truth so we can understand what we are really up against."

Ridge said: "Maybe the ship took a hit. Maybe we are beyond help. A long time has gone by, and nobody has come to rescue us. Who knows where these mudmen have come from. Who knows what any of this is about. Fact is, I looked over the edge and there was nothing in WorkPod01. Nothing. No galley, no books, no showers, nothing. Just a bunch of hibernation beds for..." (he paused to swallow, and almost could not speak) "...for the next crew just like us."

Lantz hurled just then, a stream of yellowish breakfast or whatever that twirled in the air and spattered loudly on the gleaming floor in the rotunda. Her red hair hung around a feverish, flushed face in sweaty strands. Her face looked emaciated like her body.

Ridge continued: "We were grown somehow with our memories forced into us the way you add piggyback medications to an intravenous drip. Memory codons. Everything we know, everything we remember, is fake."

"Not everything," Tomson said quietly. "We are human. We know what that is. If we didn't, we wouldn't be human, and none of the rest would work." He looked at Brenna. "Our grief," he said. He looked at Lantz. "Our desperation." He pointed to himself. "Our disappointment."

"Is that what you feel?" Ridge said, tears springing to his eyes. He sobbed with his own grief. He had thought he was married. He had thought he had children. "Disappointment?" He wanted to hit Tomson. "Is that what it is in the end? You are disappointed?"

Tomson was stoic. "Maybe it's the wrong word, Ridge. Each of us has to take this in his or her own way. I didn't have children or a wife. I had a girlfriend I was going to go back and marry, but I knew she was cheating on me. That made me feel sad, but I felt I could go back and turn it around. Somehow I was going to get her to love me. Now I know it was just an illusion. Makes sense what you said. It was all a big fraud." He looked up and hollered. "Damn you, Corporation. Why did you do this to us?"

They waited in silence, and nobody answered.

Brenna wiped tears away with the stiff fingers of one hand. "Something went wrong, didn't it? I mean, this ship doesn't seem to have any plan."

"It's Science," Lantz said bitterly. "Progress. Human advancement. We can do anything. We are masters of the universe." She looked up. "Fuck you!" Her voice echoed grimly among the shadows in the mezzanine.

Ridge said: "Bottom line, do we want to live?" He looked from one to the other. "Do you want to live? Do you? And you?" They all nodded hesitantly. "No," he said, "it's not good enough. You can't hesitate, or you are lost. You have to make up your mind. Do you want to live? If you do, you have to do the impossible and shove aside all your grief and anger and disappointment, because the mudmen will be back any time soon and they are looking for a meal."

"We weren't made for that," Tomson rumbled in his big, implacable voice. "It's too complicated."

Lantz laughed coldly. "Maybe it's the other way around. Maybe we are on some long trip and the mudmen were created to be food for us, but the tables got turned somehow."

Tomson shook his head again. "Too complicated still."

Brenna stood back and looked in Ridge's eyes. "Are you sure?"

"What do you mean am I sure?"

"That we aren't real."

"We're real," Ridge said. "Parts of our memories aren't."

Brenna shook her head in continuing shock, but her tears had dried up. Lantz stepped up beside her and put a strong freckled hand on Brenna's shoulder, seeking warmth and companionship. "What a nightmare," Lantz said. "You know what? Already, I'm forgetting more stuff."

Tomson nodded. "That's because it's not necessary. Your brain is compensating. Once the veil of illusion is torn, the illusions blow away."

"What does that leave?" Ridge said bitterly. He felt terribly empty. He wondered if he'd ever been to San Diego, or if there was a woman named Dorothy there, or even if San Diego existed at all.

Tomson said: "It all seems so clear and logical to me. It's like a storm has passed and it's one of those clear, moonlit nights. Anyone know what I mean?"

Ridge could picture it exactly. "I've seen a clear, moonlit night." He had, somewhere.

Brenna ran a grimy sleeve across her face. "You didn't. Someone else did, and that person lent you their memories."

Lantz put her hands defiantly in her pockets. "I'm a human being, a woman, from Tacoma. I love that place. I can almost smell the moss in the rainforest."

"Me too," Tomson said. For the first time, a smile flickered on his features. "You know, if we can remember things in common, it probably means they are real. Like, is there a

Philadelphia, or is it just some parlor trick of gene splicing done by the Corporation?"

"I was never in Philadelphia," Ridge said, "but I know they have these meat things, these sandwiches..."

"...With cheese on them," Brenna said laughing.

"Bad for your heart," Tomson said, laughing. "Cholesterol factory." They all laughed.

Ridge said: "What else can go wrong today?"

"We want to live," Tomson said. He looked angry. "Whoever made us, and why, we do have the will to live. Mahaffey may have lost it, but I'll go down fighting."

The others all agreed. "Okay," Ridge said. "It's settled. The best we can do is continue as before. We have no other choice. We can deal with the emotional stuff once we're safe again."

Brenna grew serious again. Their sunny moment had been fleeting, like on a meadow swept with rain clouds on a day that wasn't winter any more but wasn't spring yet. "We could go back to WorkPod01, get back in our dream machines, and go back to sleep."

"And never wake up," Lantz added. "Good way to go if we have to."

"I think I want to do better than that," Ridge said. He stared into the turbulent dusk in Brenna's eyes, and she looked away to avoid his gaze. Don't go the way Mahaffey did, Ridge thought silently. I want to be alone with you.

A flute-like sound rolled across the air. It was delicate, probing, and menacing. Other low round-mouth sounds floated in the air as the mudmen spoke among themselves.

"Let's get out of here," Tomson said.

"Up the stairs over there!" Ridge said, pointing across the floor to a curving staircase that looked like *faux* marble. "Maybe we can save ourselves, save the ship, end up back on Earth after all!"

Lantz helped stricken Brenna along. Brenna kept stumbling on the stairs. Tomson carried an armload of rifles, including Brenna's.

"Hurry!" Ridge said. Already, he saw mudmen spilling into the rotunda. "Up here!" Ridge led his companions around into the mezzanine. The mudmen milled below, until several looked up. They had not faces, but the suggestions of faces. Their features looked as though someone had sewn them onto a dirty gray sock. Some were darker gray than others, some putty-colored, a few almost off-blue like the color of wet concrete. As a dozen mudmen swarmed up the stairs, Ridge and Tomson unloaded a withering fire into their midst, and they fell back in a tangle of piled, motionless bodies. "So far so good," Ridge said. "Let's keep moving before our luck runs out."

They followed a maze of corridors on this upper level until Tomson found a small lobby with several elevators. The lobby had that gleaming marbled look, resembling office buildings back on Earth—anything to foster the illusion of normalcy for humans trapped vast distances from home in a tin can amid hostile outer space. The material was lightweight but sturdy, and had the smooth, cool feel of marble. It came in a variety of colors and styles, all of them smooth and polished like the real thing. There were reddish marbles with yellow inlay, white in black, black in white, all the possible combinations. They were patterns like in real marble—some resembling ink dissolving in water, others smoke drifting on mountains, others the sedimentation that took place to really create marble. The floors themselves in the cone were doctored further with illusions of glass, gleaming brass, thick carpeting, and echoing high ceilings to further the illusion, to prevent humans from losing their minds on long journeys through the cosmos. *Somehow,* Ridge thought without having much time to dwell on the idea, we ourselves are part of the illusion. But how? Why? He was desperate and angry to find out. A part of him wanted to think: Where are our creators so that we can embrace them and crush their lives out of them just as they have crushed our hopes and our very identities? We want to punish them for playing this cruel joke on us, for toying with our lives like this. Another part of him thought: We are humans too, and we should treat them with mutual respect when we meet them, if we meet them, if we can find them, if any of them are still left. He also thought: Maybe the ultimate joke is that they have gone away and we are left to take their place. Or was that the purpose? He realized how much more he needed to learn, and he would not rest. Survival alone wasn't enough.

He must learn the truth. That alone, the truth and nothing but the truth, would console the grief he'd seen in the eyes of Brenna whom he loved. Finally, he had this good thought that now they were free to love each other. He wondered if she knew that yet. He glanced over as they ran to the elevators, and saw Lantz and Tomson supporting her. She still looked ravaged with grief. Her grief alone lent her dignity greater than the cynicism of those who had created this tragedy; her grief alone made her more than human, he thought, suddenly proud of her and of himself and his companions.

Chapter 10

Watch out!" Lantz cried suddenly as mudmen burst into the elevator lobby. Lantz whirled about, holding her rifle ready in pale, muscular arms. Her rangy body bucked several times as she fired, and damp curls of orange hair jigged about her narrow, intent face. More mudmen spilled into the area waving their claws, and the humans dispatched them in a welter of crackling blue light and flying chips of *faux* marble.

"In here!" Brenna said, punching open the elevator doors. The four remaining humans sidled into the grayish light inside the elevator as shiny brass doors rumbled shut. For a second, mudmen tried to pry the doors apart. Ridge got a lingering glimpse of scaly skin and peeling, horny claws. The claws were at least two inches long, and ribbed with black lateral stripes within, while the outside was coated with a thick layer of horn. "Don't shoot!" Tomson cried. Lantz and Brenna used their rifle butts to slam the clawed hands into bloody pulp, which the owners then pulled away. A puddle of greenish blood dripped onto the floor, and bits of gore dribbled down the crack between the doors. Ridge looked away as he felt his gorge rising.

The elevator rose. Lights flashed by above, indicating changes of floors. Ridge counted twelve floors. The lights were round and bore small black numbers. The last circle was red rather than yellow, and had the letters CP in it. "That's where we want to go," Ridge said. "That's where we'll find Captain Venable and get an explanation of all this."

For a minute or two the elevator slowly rose. The four humans stood tensely with their eyes upcast. Ridge felt the tension in himself, and noticed how his companions' cheekbones were hollowed, their eyes framed in dark orbits, their faces dribbling sweat as they stood with their rifles ready. Then the elevator began to falter. "No!" Lantz cried, punching the buttons. "Go go go!" Tomson muttered under his breath. "Come on!" Brenna said. Ridge felt like smashing his rifle against the buttons. The elevator slowed down, shuddered, and stopped. "Oh no!" they all said. "Damn!" Tomson kicked the splashboard along the wall with his boot. Ridge said: "Let's think it through, guys. Let's be calm. What is happening? The elevator died on us. Looks like we made it about half-way up there. We may need to climb the remaining six floors on foot. We can do it."

The elevator did not start up again. The lights were lit and the lighted buttons promised power, but somehow this was not translating through to the guts of the machine. "Open the door," Ridge told Lantz. All four stood with their rifles pointing, as Lantz gingerly reached over and pressed the button. She sprang back in a ready pose. The doors made a shuddering noise and then rumbled gently open. Ridge expected a mudmen charge, but all was quiet. They stepped out into a wide space, and for a moment Ridge thought it was just another clean, well-lit laboratory or office space. A moment later he began to realize how wrong he was. The first clues were what looked like ancient shreds of cloth lying along the carpeted floors.

"Weapons," Tomson said softly in a warning tone of voice. They moved slowly forward while holding their weapons ready. The air was still but when the climate control fans hidden in air ducts cut in, Brenna let out a little yell, and Ridge nearly jumped a yard backwards. "Damn!" Tomson said. Lantz's eyeballs were rolling left and right and up, while her hands flexed around her rifle. Lantz's cheeks looked sucked-in, and her mouth had a quizzical tilt to it, as if she were about to cry. Ridge felt the same way.

The lobby area was about forty feet long and twenty feet wide, with large open portals leading into darkness on either side. Opposite the elevator doors were high glass walls whose dark hues varied from dark brown through various off-shades of gray to a dirty charcoal. They looked old, Ridge thought with added foreboding. Maybe he was ready now to face the truth, whatever that was. Nothing was as he'd thought it to be just that morning, and he swallowed hard at the thought that he'd have a lot of other unhappy surprises before the tally was done. "Careful," he said. Keeping the others in line kept him from going crazy. Keeping his friends alive meant more than the luxury of slumping inward and preoccupying himself with the gloom he felt slowly spreading through his soul. "Easy does it."

Lantz was the first to reach the high, arched portal on the right. The area around the portal was steeped in shadows from large, stacked boxes, but beyond the boxes Ridge saw light. As Lantz stepped through into the grayer, brighter light, she made a face and cried out. Her face did not lose its mask of dismay as the others crowded around her. Ridge almost did not want to look, but he knew he must.

They stood at one end of a long room like a dormitory. It had a low ceiling of large, square tiles. The walls were covered with monitoring equipment. In some areas were rows of two dozen black chemical suits with staring round eye holes in charcoal hoods; purpose unknowable, but obviously for some type of rescue. Doors on all sides led into more rooms like this one. Instead of beds, the incubators lined up by the hundreds reminded Ridge of the sleeping boxes he'd seen in WorkPod01 while hanging by his fingernails. He did not want to call these containers coffins, though they had some resemblance to containers for dead persons. Their rounded glass lids had a smoky look, but many of the lids had been torn off or hung at odd angles. Many other lids had been smashed, and the shards lay on the skeletal remains they contained. The incubators made an even procession of twenty to a row, and Ridge counted about 40 rows. As they walked in, Ridge saw other rooms like it, and guessed there must be several thousand incubators.

"All dead," Tomson said as he walked from one incubator to the next. Brenna, Lantz, and Ridge did the same in other aisles running among the receptacles.

"These remains are mummified with age," Ridge said. "This happened a long time ago." It was a bone house, a charnel place, Ridge thought. What had happened here? What was going on?

"Look," Brenna said pointing along the floors. Many of the bodies had been lifted roughly from their resting places and left of the thinly carpeted floor. Few of those bodies were intact.

"They've been gnawed," Tomson said in a disgusted voice. Lantz stifled a choking sound, and Ridge felt overwhelmed by the cruelty and insanity of this overwhelming sight. "Mudmen," he said. "It had to be mudmen."

"They had quite a feast here," Brenna said. "What a terrible place."

Ridge walked numbly with his rifle hanging. "For some reason, the ship's crew left their offices and other work stations. They came here, expecting to sleep through their emergency, whatever that was. They never woke up again, because they never expected to be attacked while they were asleep."

"Why asleep?" Lantz said. "On the Luna-Neptune run?"

"Expecting help," Tomson said. "It would save oxygen to go into suspended animation like this. Maybe the hull was punctured."

Ridge frowned. "Thousands of people. How can that be? Unless it was a colony ship, there wouldn't be this many people on board. And I've never heard of a ship where each person had a deep sleep incubator."

Brenna said: "You think the plan was to go to sleep? That would imply a much longer journey." She stared at Ridge, Tomson, back at Ridge. "There is no place in the solar system that would require a fast-moving ship to have deep sleep capabilities. Besides, those are experimental, and I can't think of a single ship that had them." She bit her lip, realizing she had said something that might not make sense.

"Poor kid," Lantz said. "What memories of ours are real?"

Tomson said: "If the hull was punctured, which is my bet since we saw all that slag and charcoal and all those missing decks that simply burned away, then the ship has done a great deal to repair itself. Or it's been repaired a lot. By whom?"

"People like us," Ridge said. "WorkPods. You saw how old Caulfield was. He must have been the last one out of WorkPod09 in many years."

"You saw incubators in WorkPod01?" Tomson asked.

"Yes." Ridge pictured once more the calm, secure, shadowy interior he'd glimpsed. He pictured again the orderly array of incubators. "I think the ship grows generations of us. For generations we've been repairing the ship. Generations of us."

He trailed off. Lantz cried again. Brenna sniffled. Ridge continued: "Venable, that son of a bitch, if he's real. He and a few people, working behind the scenes, out of reach of these damned baseball-heads, have been growing generations of us to slowly get the ship back into shape. For some reason, nobody has come to rescue us, so it all just keeps going like this." He walked among the scattered bones and dried-up scraps of skin of the ship's humans. As he stepped over it all, laughing madly, he saw their clothing disintegrate into puffs of dust. "There is no question now," he said, "we can't deny it. This is a generational ship of some kind, purpose unknown. Colonization? Maybe. It's anyone's guess. I want to know the answer!" He shouted at the rows and rows of dead people. "I want an answer, you bastards!" He shook their incubators, and kicked one. It was heavy and barely moved. "Serves you right, you heartless bastards!"

"Look down here," Tomson said. He pointed down a long central aisle wider than the rest. His three companions followed him into a wide central area crammed with dead machines. Stillness, shadows, emptiness hung eerily over the machines that were choked with dust and had not run in many years. "If I can fire some of these up," Tomson said, "we might be able to figure out what year it is and where we are. We might be able to figure a lot of information out."

Lantz held up her hand. They all fell silent and listened to a distant medley of flute sounds. It was like the noise made by wind pushing gently through drainpipes on a rainy night, Ridge thought. He had no idea where the image came from, but it felt eerie and creepy. Chills traveled up and down his back. Lantz ran a wrist over her forehead and leaned against the metal skins of the computer cabinets. "I don't know how much longer I can take this." She slumped down in one of a dozen or more chairs that stood randomly about. She rested her arms on the armrests and lay back tiredly for a few moments. Tomson did the same in another chair, and looked longingly at Ridge. Tomson said: "Ridge, don't you ever get tired?" He looked at Brenna: "You okay?"

Brenna hugged herself and nodded uncertainly. Her lips trembled, and her eyes flicked sideways as if she were glancing back into her wonderful memories. "I'll be okay once I get over it," she said faintly.

Lantz spoke for her. "I wish I knew if any of it was true. Do I really remember smelling the moss on foggy morning? Or is that just bullshit, like the memory of a butterfly wing beating in stillness so profound you could almost hear the wing flutter as the little guy moves from one big purple flower to the next. Or are the purple flowers bullshit too?"

"None of it is bullshit," Brenna declared in a small, firm voice. "All of it is real and sacred because those are our memories. We are people, and that is our soul. Our memories are our souls, and it doesn't matter how the memories got there." She suddenly burst into tears. "I had two beautiful babies and they were not bullshit." She threw herself against a tall computer cabinet and hugged it, crying. She hauled back and planted a resounding punch on the cabinet surface, which echoed like a flat cracked gong down the corridors. The flute music paused a second, then grew louder.

"They are getting closer," Tomson said. He moved weary eyeballs right and left as if wondering—should he run again? Was it worth it? Ridge had the same feeling, but wouldn't let it get the best of him...not yet, anyway. "Come on," Ridge said, "we need to find our way into the CP. We need to interview Captain Venable."

"I'd like to strangle him," Lantz said, jumping to her feet. "Come on," she said, offering Tomson a hand. "Let's go."

"Yeah," Tomson said with a sigh as he pushed himself erect. "Ridge, lead the way. Where's that man with the answers? Where is that handsome captain of ours? I'd like to have a few words with him before I wring his neck."

Ridge grinned. He listened carefully and heard the flute sound getting closer from several directions. He could have sworn he heard running feet. If the mudmen could run that fast, then there was little hope of escaping them. Sooner rather than later, they would catch up with the four remaining team members. Until then, Ridge thought, we'll give them a run for their money. "I think I see more elevators down there." Ridge pointed down a main artery to its end against the curving hull. "We're close to the nose area. Maybe we can get into the CP and barricade ourselves in. It's a small area and we can defend ourselves."

"If there is food and water," Lantz said.

Brenna shouldered her rifle and stepped forward. "I'd rather die of thirst than have those *things* tear me apart."

Once again, Ridge found himself a step closer to falling in love with Brenna—or was it awe? Her demand for dignity made Ridge feel quiet and content inside, even if they were about to be killed.

Brenna said: "Everyone, stop looking so glum. We have each other, we are still alive, and we have a CP to find. Let's go!" She started briskly off in the direction of the elevators by the hull, and Lantz was the first to scramble to try and keep up with Brenna. Ridge and Tomson followed, Ridge feeling glad for once he did not have to lead.

Behind him, the dull brush of mudmen vocal chords on rounded mouthfuls of air grew louder.

Chapter 11

Slowly, cautiously, they stepped out, one foot at a time, into a carpeted receptionist area on the top and final floor. This was no lobby, but some kind of executive suite. The curvature of the nose area was evident on all sides. The two elevators opened on a small round area that was comfortably claustrophobic. It was a tight little space with inward curving walls narrower on top than bottom by a good two feet. The ceiling looked like a plate that could be removed, probably revealing miles of tangled cabling. Under the tan, stylish modesty of the ceiling were two banks of tiny silvery light globes on tracks. These lit up as the four stepped into the room. Several single-panel doors led away into unknown rooms, presumably the Bridge or Command Post or command module of the entire operation. Around the walls were thick greenish glass windows inset in small, massively built sills. Breaking the circle of doors and windows was a cramped reception counter built directly into the wall on their right as they stepped from the elevator. The four eased in and Ridge nearly expected to hear music softly playing. Instead, a screen in the wall behind the receptionist's abandoned desk flickered suddenly.

"Watch it!" Lantz said jumpily. She turned and nearly emptied a charge into the empty air where the receptionist had long ago risen and walked away to the elevator, never to return.

"It's a view screen," Ridge said. "Hold your fire."

For a few moments the screen—a square about two feet per side—flickered with grainy bluish light. Then an image of Captain Venable resolved itself against a bright background. Under white lighting, Ridge clearly made out chairs, cabinets, even a young woman sitting in the distance at a console chewing gum and sipping coffee. The background was blurry in the extremely bright light bathing Venable's background. "Greetings," the Captain said.

"Can you hear me?" Ridge said, leaning across the dark-blue counter of the receptionist desk. "This is Ridge. I'm the Lead Engineer from WorkPod01."

"I can hear you and see you just fine," the Captain said. His eyes looked merry, and his fresh youthful cheeks were stipple pink. His teeth were bright, his lips shiny, his enthusiasm infectious.

"We're dying out here," Ridge said, slamming a heavy palm down. He felt too overcome to say anything more.

"It's rough out there," Venable agreed.

"Get us out of here," Ridge said. "Get us to safety."

"Sure. Can you get in here?"

"Can we get in?" Ridge said, phrasing the question in a different tone that suggested 'may' instead of 'can.' As he spoke, Tomson and the others tried door handles. "All locked," Tomson muttered. "Same here," whispered Brenna and Lantz. All were angry, yet all were suddenly overcome with a memory of respect. This was their captain, and he should save them, after all. Ridge burned with concern as he leaned into the view screen. "Captain, I've lost four people in the last few hours."

"Really?" Venable said vaguely. "Who were they?"

"Mughali, Mahaffey, Yu, and Jerez."

"That's very sad," Venable said sincerely. "You should be safe where you are."

"Then you know about the mudmen?" Tomson barked.

"Yes."

"And you let us go out there without even a warning?" Tomson's face was contorted with rage. He looked old and betrayed. His mouth hung open, and his teeth were parted in a gesture of utter contempt. He showed a pink tongue rumpled in utter distaste.

"I had no choice," Venable said. "I have no choice about these things. We are locked in a crisis, and we have no choice. I'm terribly sorry."

"We?" Brenna said. She pushed Ridge aside. "Do you know I thought I had two children? Or did I? What happened to my babies?"

Venable blanched. His features retained their smooth, handsome babyness, but his eyes grew more sympathetic. "You understand, Brenna..."

"You know my name?" She placed her fists on the counter top. Her shoulder dug into Ridge's ribs, though it was a rounded shoulder and did not hurt. Ridge did feel the tenseness in her body, and wished she did not have to suffer so.

"I know all of your names," Venable said. "I know you all."

"What about my children?" Brenna said. Tears ran down her cheeks.

Venable shook his head. "It seemed better to let you be happy than to have you know the truth."

Lantz shouted over Brenna's shoulder: "It was more efficient to have us think we had lives, is what you mean."

Venable looked sad now. "Don't think that way. I am a prisoner here, and I have no illusions. I have only the thought that we are serving mankind. We are on our way to a better world."

"Isn't this the *Neptune Express*?" Ridge asked, feeling foolish. He felt as if he were a passenger who had taken the wrong train after a night of drinking, and now must ask strangers the embarrassing questions to get home. "Isn't this a cargo ship traveling back and forth between Luna and Neptune?"

Venable shook his head with a sweet, sad smile. "What a fine story."

Ridge waved a fist. "So what is the story here?"

Behind Venable the scene changed to one of deep space. Ridge glanced at the stars in their various diamond hues, but did not recognize any constellations. The sun was not visible. Gone was the lovely, glowing blue orb of Neptune, with the crescent Triton rising like a gray bubble of nitrogen over the Sea God's shoulder. Venable said: "The engineers and thinkers who made you dreamed up a nice name. The real name of our expedition is *Nebula Express*." He turned his head slightly and flicked his eyes like pointers to the crabbed tangles and spidered webs of stars that looked almost like explosions of wetness in a meadow. "That is deep interstellar space, and we are many light-years from Earth."

The little lobby was silent as they digested this. Ridge felt a hardness in the pit of his gut. "Things can't get any worse now, I'm sure." As if to give his hope the lie, he heard distant thumping noises in the bottom of the elevator shaft. With a sudden inspiration, he said: "You won't let us in there, will you?"

Venable blinked sadly. "I can't."

Brenna said suddenly: "We're not the first ones in here, are we?"

Venable blinked again, this time with a slight shake *no* of the head.

"Then this has been going on for a long time," Lantz said.

Tomson said: "You had no right to do this to us."

"It was either this or let mankind die out. Earth perished in a swarm of comets that circle around every hundred million years or so. There is no home left to go back to. The *Nebula Express* is moving faster and faster through deep space seeking a new home."

"Do you know the mudmen ate all the colonists?" Tomson said.

"Not all of us," Venable said. "Not any of us, in fact. Those were the original colonists who set out. We all donated our memory information, our DNA, our hopes and ambitions and the good and the bad of us, into the ship's laboratories. It's all automated and a hundred times redundant. The cleaners started turning sour and eating the freight, but we have plenty of growth stock and the electrochemical soup to cook it with. That's how we made you."

"You cooked us from stray memories and left-over love affairs," Brenna said in a tone that made Ridge cringe, and he hoped Venable felt her disdain. "You made soup from human lives and created us for what purpose? To fix things that cannot be fixed?"

Venable gave his clean-cut, cheerful smile. "You fix things that will require generations to fix, but they can be fixed. They must be fixed, even if eons are required. The ship was badly smashed by a stray comet."

"That would explain the charred and glazed wasteland out there," Tomson said.

Venable said: "Your kind have been laboring for ages to set things right. You are winning the battle."

"Yes, but we live our lives in those cold black tunnels," Lantz said, "while you sit in your nice cozy little CP. Is it warm in there?" She ran around the desk and banged her fists on the view screen. "Is it cozy in there?" Tears flowed down her strong features. "Is it like our workpod in there? Do you lift weights? Take showers? Listen to music?"

"No," Venable said, "I am all alone." He said it so plaintively that the four humans fell silent. Ridge felt all anger and rage leave him. It was clear that Venable was somehow as much a victim as they were. "Are you real?" Ridge asked Venable. "Are you a person?"

"Yes."

"You are the captain of the ship?"

"Yes."

"You are the captain but you are trapped in there and cannot help us?"

"I am safe from the cleaners," Venable said simply.

Tomson grew animated in the remnants of his own anger. He waved his arms and made faces to imitate the mudmen. "Those are the baseball-heads with the stitches and the slits for eyes? Round mouths?" Tomson made fishlike mouth gestures at Venable, thrusting his chin aggressively forward. Sweat glistened on his dark skin, and his eyes looked ravaged from the continuous succession of frightening revelations.

"They are the cleaners," Venable said. "They were made to take away your bodies when you die."

"Damn!" Lantz welled up with anger, then punched the desk with a loud bang. "Just like that, eh?"

"I'm sorry. It is the truth. It had to be. Things got out of control. We are hoping you can make it right. Then we can all be free again."

"What do you mean?" Ridge asked.

"When the ship is fixed, then we can go away."

"Like my children and my husband," Brenna said.

There was a moment of silence in which Venable appeared to be thinking, while the gossamer cobwebbing of stars sprawled behind his head. "Think of it this way, Brenna. You are a composite of many people, but you are the impression of some primary woman who lived a life much like the one you remember. Your babies lived in Buenos Aires and probably grew up to be fine men. They would have listened to *tango* and drunk and played *futbol* in *La Bombonerita*..."

"But you don't know for sure?" Brenna said. Her eyes were wide and hopeful, her teeth like little chicles of desire.

"I have no idea, nor would the most loving mother have control over their lives."

"But they lived?"

"Yes, they lived."

"Oh, thank you," Brenna said and started to cry again, this time for joy. She turned away, dabbing her eyes with her fingertips.

Ridge wondered if it was a lie, but he was happy for her. "What about Dorothy?" he asked. As Venable smiled again, before Venable could reply, he blurted: "What were their names? I loved my children but I can't picture them and I don't know their names." Truth was, he'd nearly forgotten them, and that made him sad.

"Here they are," Venable said. "Patrick Jr. after you, and Robert after Dorothy's dad."

"Then my name is Patrick?" Ridge almost laughed. Tomson did laugh. Brenna and Lantz joined in.

Tomson yelled "This is all more bullshit!" and punched the screen. He couldn't harm the wall, and Venable was unfazed. "No," Venable said, "these are all real people. They lived long ago. Brenna's two boys Ricardo Jr. and Matteo would have lived their lives back on Earth, two or three thousand years ago."

"They are dust," Brenna said, losing some of her joy. Then she brightened again: "But they lived. They had their lives." She bit her lip before continuing: "I hope they loved me as much as I

loved them. Or as much as the woman who I was..." She was
unable to say more.

"You see," Venable said, "it's not so bad. The engineers and
thinkers meant well. They were kind people who tried to think
of everything. They tried to think about how we would feel."
The screen flickered, and he looked up. "Power is fading. Will
need a few hours to recharge." He laughed. "I haven't talked this
much in ages. I am all alone here."

And half nuts, Ridge thought.

"...Many secrets," Venable said, his voice breaking up.
"...Largo, the city of the future."

"What is he saying?" Tomson asked.

"When we orbit New Earth, we'll drink to that," Venable
said. He grinned. His image pulsed weakly as the batteries fed
their remaining juice into the com nodes. "Great view from
Largo. You and I won't be around, but our descendants will
remember us."

"Tacoma!" Lantz shouted, desperate to get her share of the
information. "What street did I live on?"

"Off Pearl Street near Point Defiance Park."

"Yes!" Lantz said. "Pembroke Court."

"Pembroke Court No. 34, the house with the basketball hoop
on the sidewalk. That's where Dr. Werner Lantz lived, the
geneticist at SeaTac University."

"So that's it," Tomson said. "You dumb shit. You gave it
away. Some guy named Lantz was mixing test tubes at the lab,
and he cooked a few people up."

"Shut up!" Lantz said.

"Easy," Ridge said, putting a hand on Tomson's powerful
arm. "Let her have her memories. We don't know how much of
this is real and how much is phony, but that's all we're going to
get."

The screen flickered again. "Please come talk to me again,"
Venable said. He smiled as before, but against a dimmer
background. The stars were gone, and the background with the
coffee-drinking woman had been replaced by a kind of neutral
cottony fog.

"Let us in there," Ridge said."

"I cannot, but there is a key."

"Where is the key?" Ridge pressed, leaning close.

In a fading voice, Venable said: "WorkPod01."

"How do we get in there?"

"Hurry," Venable said faintly. "Tell them the code."

"What code?" Ridge said through gritted teeth. "What is this code?"

Venable's voice was a mere whisper: "Function Check Largo." His image was now only a faint outline on a dull gray square. It was like seeing a ghost. His eyes flicked upward, to the right, as if to help his ears hear. "I hear the cleaners. They are coming up in the elevator. They can't reach me, but they can harm you."

As Venable's image faded, they could hear the turning of the elevator gears. They heard a sound like thick cables smeared with grease, stealthily clicking while coiled around their turning pulleys as the elevator car rose.

"Here," Lantz said, "there is a stairway or something. She was on her knees, pulling up a round steel trapdoor in the carpet. Ridge glimpsed yellowish light, steel ladder rungs, a steel tube leading down. "In here!" she said, lowering her wiry frame down into the vertical shaft without waiting for approval; fear for her life, Ridge supposed. He heard the fluting now, the push of air, the plaintive and deadly notes that hung in the air like drifting leaves, like phrases looking for one another to complete a thought. The elevator was audibly rumbling and shuddering now as the car drew near. Ridge thought he heard the chitter of claws on marble, the ripping sound of paw-callus on carpeting. He could well picture their round mouths. He could imagine the slit eyes opening into pairs of round goggle-shaped eyes to find the next human meal. Cleaners, Venable had called them. All part of a plan.

"Down the hatch!" Tomson said, following Lantz. Brenna followed. Even as Brenna's auburn ball of hair sank slowly down the shaft, and Ridge swung himself around to follow, the car rocked to a halt in the elevator shaft. Ridge heard the chorus of excited, hard mudman breaths now. It sounded like a complex note from a calliope, a steam-driven chord of anticipation, a regular up-note from diaphragms meant to sing in hell. Ridge banged his knee on a hard steel rung, and a knock against the ribs took his breath away, but he was too intent to notice. He was intent pulling the trap door down on his head and twirling the lock wheel which dropped steel tumblers into place to seal the floor even as the car doors rumbled open and a half dozen baseball-heads tromped out with their claws and mouths open, their sewn-up skulls and slitty sock eyes expressionless, their nostrils just pairs of yellowish holes poked in borrowed and decaying skin the color of bread-crusts.

Holding a finger over his mouth for silence, Ridge gestured to the faces looking up at him from below. "Down, down, go," he whispered.

The shaft led down interminably. It was lit at intervals by hard little industrial lights the size of one's palm, set back behind steel gratings that resembled shower drains.

"Where are we going?" Lantz whispered. She was still at the bottom, going first. Ridge could see the goose bumps on her shoulders past the quickly moving jumpsuited elbows and knees of Tomson and Brenna.

"Just keep going," Ridge said. "We have to get to WorkPod01 and blow our way in if we have to. Venable says there is a code in there."

"I just want to curl up in there and rest," Tomson said. He slowed for a moment, hung on the ladder, and took a deep breath. Brenna collided with him and apologized. Sweat ran down Tomson's dark face. His eyes were large, white, and desperate. "You want to rest?" Ridge asked full of concern.

"You're not tired?" Tomson looked up, huffing.

"Not yet," Ridge said, "but if you talk about it I might just want to curl up and sleep for a day or two."

"We've got to get to safety," Lantz whispered. Her freckles glowed in the amber light. Her eyes looked blue amid yellowish sclera.

"WorkPod01," Brenna said as if it were a promise.

"Once we get in we can rest," Ridge said. "We were safe there before. We'll be safe again."

"Oh God yes," Lantz said, climbing faster. Her bare arms made a freckled blur. Ridge wondered if she didn't get cold. He hoped the shaft would take them totally out of the nose section and maybe back onto that wall they'd seen when approaching on the moving platform. No telling how long their charges would last, and he did not relish the thought of fighting their way inch by inch out of the nose section. Now that the mudmen were triangulating in on them, it was a guess how narrow their escape might be if they succeeded in returning to WorkPod01. He didn't want to share his pessimism and fear out loud. If nothing else, WorkPod01 was their birthplace and might be the best place for them to die.

Ridge and his people were busy clambering as fast as they could and ignoring banged shins and elbows and knees. Ridge's mind kept focusing on visions of the underside of the nose area. He remembered it as a large round surface filled with protruding cubes and domes and other geometric shapes; hoses, lines, lights, elevators frozen on their cables, long thin ladders like the one they were climbing on.

Suddenly, the dark shaft seemed to brighten up to a faint, hard coppery light. The sides came away and mudmen claws reached in. Lantz screamed. Tomson bellowed and fired his rifle. Brenna shrieked as claws tore her hair. She made fists and battered at the foul-smelling faces that reached toward her with dripping, protruding teeth in little red round mouths. Mudmen were taking the sides off the shaft, and the metal parts came away with banging and clanging noises.

"We're coming into a car of some kind!" Lantz said. Her voice choked into a gurgle as something wrapped around her neck.

Tomson swore and lashed out, but a brace of mottled mudmen arms reached for him. Their skin hung in shedding shrouds, Ridge saw. Up close they smelled like a mix of dry earth and mushrooms and motor oil, plus rust and fish. It was an indescribable smell, faint like their flute words, but nauseating. Ridge struck out left and right with the butt of his rifle, hurting them, bashing their faces in and smashing their clawed fingers on the hard rungs. Brenna shrieked madly and tore at her hair as if it were infested with bugs-or maybe she was losing her mind finally.

A moment later, Ridge saw what Lantz had meant. The shaft ended at the mouth of a tank of some kind. It was a round airlock sort of thing whose lid was open.

In an explosion of action, the mudmen crowded around with reaching arms, all four humans hollered or screamed, the shaft seemed to collapse, and a chrysanthemum of light erupted from somewhere. Or was it the wind being knocked out of him by those callused fists beating them into submission? Ridge fell, and with him Tomson. Brenna and Lantz seemed to be swallowed up by a collapsing wall to one side, and they disappeared into a vast falling mountain of black anthracite and rust liberally splashed with gouts of muddy ruddy water the color of apple cider. The mudmen stared in perplexity. Brenna and Lantz were gone under a collapsed mountain of rotting hull material, and Ridge and Tomson crashed feet first into this thing that resembled a large milk canister waiting to be delivered to some Victorian household millennia ago on a leafy London street, or in Boston or someplace else where horses clattered by on early morning delivery rounds and nothing so weird as a mudman would ever show its face. Or was that another shred of memory cooked up by the engineers and thinkers Venable had mentioned? Ridge landed on top of Tomson, who collapsed with the wind knocked out of him. One or two mudmen spatted against the outside of the riveted steel container, not that Ridge could see them so much as he could hear and almost feel the soggy breaking of their bones and the sickly twisting apart of their arteries so that their sour green blood mixed with the bile inside them. Inside the container it smelled of cheesy mold and dirty socks and rotting milk, but there were no mudmen. There were no features in the container but two tightly riveted, thick plate windows the size of man's face, just enough to look out through, in a ring of shiny brass rivets. The inside was so tight and cramped that the two men were wrapped around each other with the breath knocked out, and could not help but look out the window plates. The canister shot out of the bottom of the nose and whizzed like a child's bottle rocket into the vast black interior of the ruined and burned out hulk of *Nebula Express*.

Chapter 12

The canister sailed through dark space inside the void hold, with its lid hanging open. It sailed through the air on some trajectory Ridge could not understand anymore than he could figure out the canister's purpose. "You okay?" he said, trying to separate his heavy male bulk from the longer but also heavy bulk of Tomson.

"Yeah," Tomson said. "I think I have a sprained ankle, that's all." His face looked ashen, but his eyes were alert and bright. "This thing wasn't meant to hold a couple of big bucks like us."

"More like a pair of little tiny elves or something," Ridge said. They both laughed. "Oh no," Ridge said, "here we go." The canister was sailing on its merry path, which had a slight curvature implanted by the ship's spin. The ship's inner hull curved inward at the rear half, and right about there the canister sailed through that faintly glowing coppery light and impacted near the base of a rocky looking mass of slag and rust and burned out carboniferous material. The canister hit, rolling, made a sound like that Victorian milk canister being tossed empty out the kitchen's back door, and it then rolled a bit and ended up stuck in a crack between two humps of shattered coal. Ridge and Tomson were bashed around inside, but gravity was light until the moment before impact, and the hit was a glancing one whose spin left them more dizzy than its shock made them stunned. After a moment, as he heaved himself out by pushing against the "Must be some old cargo transport tube," Ridge said. He reached in to help the other man out. "Can you make it?"

"I'm fine," Tomson said as he heaved himself out and lay on his side favoring his sprained leg. "This does hurt a bit. If we see any mudmen, just shoot me because I can't run."

Ridge looked worriedly about. "I'd shoot us both because I don't want to be alone with these freaks." He didn't want to say the other thing out loud, which was that, with Brenna gone, he really had little desire to live.

Tomson seemed to sense his feelings. "Don't give up on that woman yet, Ridge. If the mudmen ate them, then they are at peace. Otherwise if they are alive it's our duty to find them."

"Spoken like a great general," Ridge said.

Tomson grinned. "With all that crap Venable was talking, who knows what sort of stock we sprang from."

"Good stock," Ridge said. "They wouldn't have used weak stock." He helped Tomson up and together they clambered and crawled and inched their way up the wet surface. There was a lot of water in the ship's ecosphere, Ridge thought. The seals separating the ship from space must be really tight. Water hung in the atmosphere like a haze. Water made the rusty, slaggy, crushed-coal and onyx-glowing waves and ripples of the hull surface slick. Puddles like rusty milk lay in low spots. In the humid air, the decaying metal sweated moist rust. The air smelled of it. It was a smell much like wet human blood in an open wound. Like good fresh blood in a lung, it sucked oxygen molecules to itself until it was saturated like a full sponge.

"It's drier up here," Tomson said as Ridge pushed him on ahead, up the slope, toward the fine steel band of that their platform had traveled on. That seemed like a long time ago. By now, their jumpsuits were partially in shreds, though the stiff hoops around the necks were still in place. Those were for attaching helmets, if one had any. Luckily, Ridge thought, they had not needed helmets. The ship was still that much together. Venable might be right. Maybe there was hope, not for Ridge or Tomson but for some far-future thing made of flesh and coded memories. It was almost laughable, Ridge thought as he and Tomson crawled up the slope. The humans who would be born then, who were all that remained of mankind, would be constructs much like the denizens of WorkPod01. How were they any more or less human?

Ridge helped Tomson up the last few feet. They clambered onto the steel ribbon, which was about six feet wide, with railings on both sides. That was a lot better than they'd had coming out of the work area earlier, when they'd had to go one foot at a time.

"Where are we?" Tomson said as he hobbled painfully on one leg.

"I figure halfway between WorkPod01 and the work area. Which way do you want to go?"

Tomson turned and stared at him with a strange, haunted look. After a pause, Tomson said: "The work area. That's a lot easier, man."

"I hear you," Ridge said. "Okay, let's go." He hauled one of Tomson's long, hard arms over his shoulder and helped the other man hobble along. "Goes faster this way. Gets us away from any mudmen who may be chasing us."

"Maybe they all went to the nose," Tomson said. "Maybe we get to have a respite from them for a while."

"We can rest in the tunnels," Ridge said. Then he remembered that the mudmen had forced their way in there too, and Lantz and Jerez had fought them off with tools. "We need a miracle," he added *non-sequitur*.

"You're telling me," Tomson said bravely.

"Desperate times call for desperate measures," Ridge said. "We'll have to split up. You rest in the tunnels, and I'll work my way back to WorkPod01 and see if I can break in."

"Good plan," Tomson said with a tone of hollow courage. Ridge had the feeling there was something Tomson wasn't telling him, and it probably wasn't good. "I'll be just fine in the tunnels," Tomson said.

"Sure you will."

Slowly, they made their way to the work area. This was where their world had first started falling apart that morning (if the start of their long day could be called morning, Ridge thought).

One step at a time, they cautiously made their way along the narrow footpath that spanned the last little distance between where they'd caught the moving platform and where they'd left the ledge on which Ridge had first met Caulfield. Coming ashore on the ledge was an oddly dispassionate matter for Ridge. He was surprised he was not more taken by the ghosts of Jerez and the others, of Mughali who had died here, and especially of Brenna. He could still see her holding up that plant with the twisted roots, her face aglow as she related her theory about why the plants in the greenhouse area grew this way.

"No sign of any bodies," Tomson observed as Ridge helped him negotiate the last few hundred feet into the tunnel and then the living area where Caulfield and his WorkPod09 crew had grown old and died one by one.

"I'm not surprised," Ridge said. "The cleaners would have had a nice lunch here." They clambered up the pile of rubble, down into the clearing, and then toward the living quarters and greenhouse area in back. Mughali was gone, as was the mudman in the corridor, and Caulfield's cadaver was long gone.

"All gone to make more mudmen," Tomson surmised. "I'll sit here." He removed his arm from Ridge's shoulder and seated himself on the floor in the narrow little galley. There, he could easily get to the sink and the pantry, which still contained a few bottles of unknown content from the Caulfield era.

"All right," Ridge said. He found a cup that Tomson could use to drink from. He opened a few of the jars sitting around and found they contained nothing but dust. "Are you hungry at all?" he asked Tomson.

The man shook his head. "Not really. A little, but not seriously. Why?"

"Don't you think it's unusual we don't feel hunger or thirst or tiredness?"

"I feel tired."

"We should all feel tired." Ridge did not feel fatigued, which surprised him. He closed the jar and put it back, though its contents were worthless. "Well, I'll get ready now. Check your rifle and make sure you can defend yourself while I'm gone."

"Don't worry about me," Tomson said. He winced a bit as he shifted his leg about. "I'm going to putter with this rifle here a bit, and then I'm going to wander back into the greenhouse and look for a little cabbage or something."

"If you figure out how to cook any, let me know."

"I'll do that," Tomson said.

Ridge explored around the tunnels. He found that at least two of the back channels, by which the mudmen must have come in and surprised Jerez and Lantz, could be closed. The steel gates rolled on wheels and worked fine, once Ridge had figured out the lever mechanism for starting the heavy gates rolling. No mudmen would be coming through the back way, as far as he could see. He returned and found his friend sitting at a chair in the kitchen with the rifle. He led Tomson to the clearing just this side of the rubble area and told him: "If you could sit with your back to the wall, you could probably pick off any mudmen who make their way into the work area."

"I'll do that," Tomson said. "Come back here with me and I'll show you something." It was Ridge's turn to be surprised, and he let Tomson lead him to the greenhouse. They stepped down into the low, narrow stone paths amid the sagging plastic tables. The air smelled of sage and other herbs as they negotiated their way among hanging balls of various flowers and herbs. "Look what I found," Tomson said. He pointed to a table and chairs. The table was round, and the chairs were missing most of their upholstery, but the springs were intact. "Sit."

"Okay," Ridge said, sitting on one of the chairs while Tomson eased into the other. The springs were rusty but still had some life in them. "They maintained this stuff for a long time," Tomson said. "Nobody has sat here for a long time."

"Nice," Ridge said.

"Yeah, but that's not all. Look over there."

Ridge followed Tomson's pointing finger, which made a long oval sweep from left to right and back, pointing at the wall. Tomson said: "There is a window there. It must open at regular intervals and let in the light from somewhere. Maybe from outer space, maybe from some artificial sun, whatever they have that powers all this and keeps the ship alive."

Ridge gaped. "My God. That's what Brenna was trying to tell me. The roots get regular exposure to some form of external light."

Tomson laughed bitterly. "Don't get your hopes up. It's not all a bad dream. The sun isn't really shining on the other side. I'm thinking maybe there is enough starlight to make the plants think there is a full moon, if that. The plants have become so light-sensitive that they shoot out at the slightest sign of more light than this dim glow in here."

"And the dim glow?" Ridge said, sitting back and spreading his arms over the back of the chair. He felt a little tired now also. It was good to rest a bit.

"Bacterial lighting," Tomson guessed. He sat back like Ridge and put his arms over the back of the chair and folded his legs as if he were at some nightclub watching a fine dancer and enjoying himself. "Fluoros. Some combination of weird glowing sources that the engineers and thinkers built. Must have been a little time before they had to run, before the comets devastated the earth. Must have been like when the dinosaurs perished, hundreds of millions of years ago, only our kind got away and old T. Rex didn't."

"You daydream on," Ridge said. "I'm going to look for the gadget that calls the platform back. Must be hidden around here somewhere." He left Tomson to enjoy his view, should the window ever open.

Ridge carried his rifle loosely in one hand as he made his way through the narrow, glowing corridors of the work area. He sidled around stacked boxes, some of which crumbled at his touch. Dust flowed from their unknowable contents and dissolved in midair, making Ridge cough. He poured himself a cup of water in the kitchen and washed down the dust in his throat. He refilled the cup and took it to Tomson, who stood in the greenhouse pruning a few of the plants there. "Sure is a nice garden," Tomson said with a happy glow on his face. "Could use a gardener. Say, maybe I'll just move in here and settle down. Lock myself in like Venable over in his CP and get so I'd be talking to these little green fellas." He flicked his finger lovingly over some lush green leaves.

"Whatever turns your crank," Ridge said. "If you stick around and the shade slides open on that window, you might get the same treat those plants do."

"There can be nothing like the sunlight we enjoyed on Earth," Tomson said. "At least we are lucky enough that we inherited other people's memories of it."

Ridge found a tool shed lower down with lots of valuable equipment in it. The metal tools in particular had not aged significantly. Many objects with moving parts still had their packing grease intact, though it had changed colors and looked a rancid, bacterial white.

Ridge also found the small control room for the work platform. There was a little window overlooking the bleak light in the damaged areas. He had a clear view of that thread of the monorail as it ran parallel to the curving slag-surface of the hull and disappeared beyond the glimmering light globe formed by the ship's stray lighting. The controls were not much-some levers, a wheel, one or two gauges. He figured out how to send the signal that would make the platform roll back from the nose area to the ledge nearby. A green winking light in a steel plate suggested that the transfer was probably taking place.

Ridge stopped in to see Tomson. His friend sat at the table and chairs, pointing excitedly to the oblong in the wall. "It's a kind of steel curtain, and I heard all sorts of whirring and humming. It's going to open any time now and give the plants their little bit of daylight or starlight or whatever it is. Sit down and watch the show."

"I can't," Ridge said. "I have the platform rolling back here. Don't forget, we need to watch for mudmen or they'll come crawling up our backs when they figure out we aren't in the bow area anymore." He waited a little while with Tomson, and when nothing seemed to be happening, he went out to the ledge. On his way out he noticed how tired Tomson looked. Tomson's face was ashen, as if the mixture of pain and exhaustion were racking him.

Ridge walked out to the ledge and watched the platform rolling slowly back from the trolley stop in the bow. As he watched, he noticed an anomaly. For the first time ever, he had a clear view of the underside of the platform. In the dim light, with its high yellowish tones and mid-browns, and then the quick recession all around into black shadow, the underside of the platform was a tangle of girders and shadows. Ridge was able to see that the underside had a secondary platform, probably originally intended for carrying tools, tow motors, and other equipment. As he stared at the slowly and smoothly approaching work platform, he began to realize that the underside was filled with mudmen. Like some collection of worms, they filled the space under the floor. Ridge was sickened to think that he and his now-lost companions must have ridden that way, quite innocently, on their first trip to the ship's bow, without ever knowing that death was riding under their feet. With their dirty-white heads glimmering in the faint light, they hovered in the shadows like the predators they were. All the faces were turned expectantly his way, and that decided his next move.

The platform rolled more slowly as it approached the ledge. Any moment now, the mudmen would come silently pouring from underneath the platform and make their way to the work area in search of Tomson and Ridge. As the platform drew near, Ridge came out from a side service tunnel. He stepped onto a small steel bridge holding a funnel in one hand and towing an ancient red cart behind with his other hand. As the platform rolled by overhead, Ridge lit the nozzle on the welder and ran the mouthpiece from the hydrogen and oxygen tanks together over the flame. The entire platform was engulfed in a blaze of brilliant yellow-white flame. There was one continuous, pulsating globe of blinding light. The mudmen caught fire. Some melted together, holding each other, while others jumped. They did not do any fluting now, but formed their mouths into small trumpet shapes and brayed loudly like elephants. Several brayed all the way down until their body sacs splattered on the slag and rocks far below. In all, by the time Ridge turned off the gas and lowered the funnel, he estimated he had wiped out two dozen of the creatures. He left his new fire-cannon where it sat, shouldered his rifle, and separated the tanks. He pushed the tanks back into the shed where he'd found them, and hooked them up to the master bleeders to refill them. While he waited, he made his way back upstairs to tell Tomson. He was a bit thirsty now, and a little bit weary, and got himself a cup of metallic-tasting but cool water from the kitchen. Holding it in a dirty white plastic mug with child's cartoon figures on the side, he walked back into the greenhouse.

"Tomson! Guess what I did."

No answer.

He walked among the narrow passages, inhaling the fragrance of oats and parsley and just plain earth grass. He sipped his water as he went, and when he was done sipping, he threw the last into the flats of mint and oregano growing near that window where Tomson had been awaiting dawn with his plants. He found that the shade had risen, exposing a window filled with stars. The window was about eight feet across and four feet high. Already, the rolling steel curtain was slowly closing again, to await its next day cycle. The plants of course loved it and would be curling their little white feeler sprouts as frantically as possible for maximum growth. In the chair sat Tomson with his head back and his mouth open. He sat slumped a little bit to the left, resting on the back and arm rests. His right arm lay curled comfortably over the neck rest. His eyes were half-open and glazed. "Tomson! Don't go!" Ridge said and stepped close. He felt Tomson's neck and found no pulse. Already, Tomson's skin was growing cold since no more heat came from the heart of him, from the inside, to burn away the chill. All that had been inside Tomson, the nutrients with which he had been born into his short life-the very sun inside him, his soul-had burned itself out. "Ah geez," Ridge said out loud as he gently pressed his friend's eyelids shut. "You got away. You're past it. Wherever you are, I hope you are looking at New Earth. I hope it's pretty. I'd like to see it too." He sat opposite his friend until the steel shutters had closed and the plants were in their night again. He emptied the dented metal cup of water Tomson had been sipping.

He carried Tomson's body out on the bridge where the scorched platform still hung, some twenty feet above. He laid Tomson out on the slag beside the bridge and turned the funnel on him. He smelled burning cloth, hair, and flesh, and did not look until the smell was mostly of scorched paint and hot steel. When he looked, all that was left was a blackened skeleton that had twisted sideways a bit, corkscrewed while there were still muscles to contract, and its arms had risen to point toward WorkPod01. The skeleton's face, however, had sunken downward in the opposite direction as if signaling WorkPod01 was sadly beyond reach.

"I'll show you it's within reach," Ridge said. "I'll show you it can be done. I'll come back for you when it's all over." With that, he pulled his flame throwing device up on the platform. It took time and effort, and he was out of breath by the time he was done, but then he turned the platform on and while it rolled slowly to its destination, he sat with his rifle in his lap, resting his back against his flame thrower, and dozed a little bit.

While he dozed, he dreamt of walking in San Diego. He was on the sand, walking along the beach. The sea curled in. The breakers came in hard and white, foamy, but their heart was luminescent green like a bottle held to the sun. The sky was blue and wrapped all around. There were no children on the beach, just a woman. Brenna. She wore a white shawl over a yellow bikini that showed off her tall, lithe figure. Her hair was a dark ball with red highlights, like the blood boiling for her in the chambers of his heart. She smiled at him and waved, and the wind blew her hair while he ran toward her. He smelled the fog, the sea, the kelp drying on the sand.

Chapter 13

Ridge realized he must have dozed a little. What startled him awake were the bright lights pouring down from the windows above. That would be WorkPod01. He rose, rubbing his eyes and yawning. His knees felt a little stiff from all his exertions and from the abuse he'd taken during his long day so far. He walked over to the control levers and moved them. The platform stopped making bicycle-chain noises and shuddered to a stop. Now the platform sat exactly as it had early in the day when the door had opened and Ridge and his crew had walked out. Now he was the only one left.

Rather than damage WorkPod01 by burning its doors, as he had planned, he decided to wait patiently. He was able to clamber up onto the hydroxide tank and look inside without having to tear his fingernails. The scene was exactly as before, but one difference. The empty hall had an array of sleep incubators. Now the incubators were not lying flat anymore but had propped themselves up. Since he saw nobody moving around, he had to assume it was all automated. He did see a number of flashing red and blue lights, so that was also different. Maybe something was about to happen.

The event he had hoped for occurred shortly thereafter. The sleep incubators opened up. Each incubator emitted its sigh of steam as its vapor lock unclenched and the gases inside mingled with the air outside to form a new and vital combination-78% nitrogen, 21% oxygen, and one percent trace gases. Each had a translucent glassy looking door, and those doors slid open. Inside each incubator was a fully formed human being wearing a clean new jumpsuit with collar markings of rank and function.

There were four men and four women, none of whom looked like Ridge and his crew. So, Ridge thought, each shift consists of different personalities. They had name tags, and Ridge could make out a few of the names. The man with the single black bar, who was their leader as Ridge had been of his crew, was a strong-looking young man with dark hair, whose nametag read Ludovico. That meant Ludwig, Louis, what have you. Lucky Louie. He was about to be born and lead his crew on a charge against impossible odds. Right now, if Ridge read it right, the smile on Ludovico's face meant that he was joking with some of his team mates. They all half-stood, half-leaned in their newly propped up incubators. Each had his or her arms at their sides and their eyes closed, but their faces mirrored the laughter and pleasure of life in their artificial environment. Maybe Ludovico was carrying on a little subtle mating dance with some new version of Brenna. Maybe there was a red-haired body building gal in there pumping iron so sweat ran down over her freckles. Maybe there was a sour, cynical, but loyal Tomson there grumbling about the lack of proper music or proper toothpaste or who knew what. Maybe this, maybe that. Ridge stood on the tank outside and braced himself with his fingers against the window. As he had suspected, there was a significant difference between real time and dream time. Already, the team members stepped dreamily from their incubators. To them, it was still WorkPOd01 as Ridge had known it-a messy, cozy, steamy sort of warm place. There would be sweat on the exercise equipment. There would be cereal in the bowl, *The Odyssey* under the table, a Captain Venable speaking to them on a view screen as they waited in a loose formation. When all that was over, the doors slid open and they walked out onto the platform. Had they seen a wild-eyed man banging bloodied palms on the windows? Probably not. That would have been real-time and not in their dreams.

Before the door could open, Ridge spotted one or two baseball-heads stealthily moving up the slope below. They would be tracking the team members-probably riding under the platform the whole way. They would wait for the team to spend a little time in the work area, under the pretense that the old mission still worked as plotted by the engineers and thinkers.

Maybe it was against the mudmen's ingrained instincts to attack and eat at the doors of WorkPod01. No matter. Ridge took his time. He aimed his rifle and picked them off, one by one, a good half dozen of them. Then he lifted the nozzle of his flame thrower and crept to the edge of the platform. He looked underneath and saw two stitch-heads standing close together there. Ghosts. He flamed them, and watched their blazing carcasses plummet through the air amid roiling black greasy smoke while their stitches came undone and sausage offal popped out from under their skin.

Smoke drifted across the platform as the doors whispered open. Ridge figured the ship's systems must have priorities that would include keeping WorkPod01 oiled and functioning in prime shape. With grim satisfaction, he determined figure out all of the ship's secrets in time. The ship had many powerful secrets, and he would figure them out if he had time. He stared anxiously at the faces of the team who emerged, coughing and waving their hands at the smoke that was just beginning to drift away. There was no Brenna among them. Of course not, he thought. Each of us is unique. There can never be another me or another you, even if we are slapped together from old dreams and bootleg lives and bits of this and chips of that. Of all the things he had learned here in this life, the one he treasured most was the dignity and truthfulness he'd seen in Brenna. From her, he had learned to be proud of his uniqueness and humanity.

The team members laughed and joked loudly. For a second, Ridge was mentally transported back to the world as he'd seen it a day ago, when the ship had been *Neptune Express* as far as he'd known, and as far as these poor candles understood it to be.

Ludovico stepped forth. "You from another workpod?"

"Yes," Ridge said.

Ludovico noted the black bar. "You're a team leader, eh? Where are your people?"

"They are where they are supposed to be."

Ludovico nodded as the others jostled light-heartedly around him. The men were strong and handsome, the women healthy and attractive. They were all young and filled with love for their families back on Earth, and that world made complete sense to them.

"Is everything all right with you?" Ludovico said. He looked genuinely concerned, if a bit puzzled and almost defensive about his own naiveté. His crisp black eyes crackled with intelligence and thoughtfulness.

"Everything is as it should be," Ridge said. He had meant to grab them, shake them, tell them the truth, enlist their aid. Now that he saw their innocence and faith, he couldn't bring himself to shatter their illusions. He couldn't bring himself to fight against the strength of their innocent convictions.

"You look as though you've had a hard day," Ludovico said.

"It has been a long day," Ridge said. "Excuse me. I have to get my things."

"You can't go in there," Ludovico said, raising a hand in alarm. "Hey," someone else said, "we're sealing this door. Keep out." A third said: "Go to your own workpod, pops."

"I'm exactly where I should be," Ridge said, and nobody dared stop him because he wore the black bar; not even Ludovico, who saw that Ridge looked worn and experienced. Therefore, as a young man and woman drew the doors shut, and as Ludovico stood staring with a look of alarm on his face-he had his collar com going and was trying to raise the CP, and Ridge grinned *good luck* at him-the doors closed and Ridge was inside WorkPod01.

Ridge looked out the window and watched the platform drift away along its monorail track. When the darkness beyond the streaks of light had swallowed them up, Ridge turned to examine the inside of the workpod. He was startled at the contrast between this and what he remembered. There were no cubes, no moon doors, no showers. All of that had been a biomnemonically induced dream.

As he explored the sealed environment of WorkPod01, Ridge almost sobbed with relief. For the first time that day, he felt safe from the mudmen. For the first time, he felt secure enough to relax, except there was this great emptiness in his heart at having lost all of his companions and now even their home had proven to be an illusion. WorkPod01 was a clean, barren environment. The light was even and quiet, the floors polished, the air clean and smelling faintly of solvents without any unpleasant harshness nor undue sweetness.

The ship's systems made sure that each crew was birthed in surroundings free of contamination, or else the illusions would not work so seamlessly. There was little here, except a blank room with eight incubators in the middle. Ridge ran his hands over the walls, looking here and there. The walls were gray and blank, unless one looked more closely and saw the myriad patterns of darker gray that indicated embedded circuits. At regular intervals were fine lines that looked as if they had bacteriolumes built in. But what turned it all on? How could he communicate with the room, the ship, the CP here?

With a soft whirring sound, the incubators shuddered, startling Ridge as he examined the instrument-rich walls. The thick glassy lids of all incubators simultaneously swung closed. With a soft clatter of steel on glass, the lids locked shut with tight frosted-glass in frosted-glass seals. Yellowish oil soaked the seals, instantly creating an impermeable barrier between the inside of each incubator and the air around it. The noise of all this made Ridge jump. He flattened himself against the wall, then relaxed as he watched the incubators slowly lower from standing to horizontal positions flat on the polished floor. The large, coffin-like containers upon closer examination appeared to be shells of stainless steel and thick glass. The glass was inlaid with myriad electronic and bionic circuits, busses, chips, pipes, and the like. The base of each incubator was of the same marble-like material Ridge had noted in the lobby in the bow. The marble settled on the softer plastic floor with a sigh of air escaping, almost making a vacuum seal. Then hidden plumbing in the walls make banging sounds, and Ridge heard a rushing sound. The lids winked softly with tiny green and amber lights, in running sequences. A moment later, water rushed in to each incubator. Ridge was reminded of how one filled a small pool or hot tub. Under an aquamarine light, purified water gushed out from hidden nozzles. The water whirlpooled until its surface bubbles settled. Ridge watched in fascination as one incubator started going through a new birthing cycle. A tiny shadow appeared inside the incubator on the floor near the middle. The shadow was no larger than a dark-gray pinprick on the white ceramic floor. In minutes, the shadow darkened and grew larger. Ridge understood what it was: a zygote rapidly multiplying in its nutrient broth. Every ten minutes or so, the number of cells doubled. Pretty soon, it was a bluish ball of cells like a volley ball with many seams. The ball grew at a good clip until it was the size of a peanut, much faster than *in utero*. Ridge guessed that the nine-month gestation was probably telescoped into a fraction of its natural time in here. The next dramatic phase occurred as the cluster of cells appeared to elongate slightly. Ridge knew that if he stayed long enough, he would see another eight team members go through their embryonic and then fetal stages until the time for birth came. He did not have that kind of time, so he sought a clue about what Venable might have meant in saying there was a key here. What could he have meant? What was a key to the Command Post or CP? Anxious and frustrated, Ridge turned his attention from the miracle of growing embryos to the mystery of getting into the CP.

Try as he might, Ridge could not raise an image of Venable on the two or three surfaces that looked like view screens. He couldn't get anything-not even static. Those areas began to seem like simply light shadows on the wall, and Ridge thought he must have been mistaken in thinking they were viewing surfaces.

"If I were a clue," he said, "where would I hide?" He explored on. He ran his fingertips along the grooves and joins of the walls and ceiling. The metallic or plastic surfaces did not yield. Puzzled and frustrated, he sat down, crossed his legs, and tried to meditate about his quest. He said to the mythical clue that Venable had promised, which persisted in hiding its face from him: "Come out, come out, wherever you are." No clue appeared, and he broke off in frustration.

The place was a cipher. Ridge squatted in a cross-leg Yoga-like pose for what seemed like hours. The incubators were filled with water and the jets had shut off. The room reposed in a peaceful semidarkness. Machinery whispered softly in the walls, in he ceiling, in the floor, in the incubators themselves.

As he squatted, listening intently to the faintest nuances of the place, he began to detect a certain rhythm. He closed his eyes and sat with his hands palms-up on his knees. He tried to make himself part of the room itself so that he could understand its spirit. This was a place of birth. It was a place that gave life, while the rest of the ship appeared to take life. Pipes in the walls dropped ovum and sperm somewhere in a incubator, where the two conjoined and became a zygote. Twenty-three chromosomes joined with 23 more chromosomes to create a single-celled organism of 46 chromosomes. This then dropped into a incubator that acted like a womb to nurture the new human being into life. Ridge imagined there must be hormones and enzymes to speed up the process. In all of that, with its many nuances and complications, Ridge began to detect a faint interplay of rhythms. He counted, not using numbers but his own heartbeats, not by touching fingertips to his pulse, but by feeling the pulses as blood coursed through his brain in much the same way that fluids pumped through this room. He began to decipher the on-off of cooling pumps, the whirr of fans, the gurgle of tiny bubbles in relief valves. He even thought he could almost feel the slick motion of oil molecules around one another in hydraulic systems smaller than his thumb. As he did all this, he detected one simple set of rhythms that made him rise to his feet. His legs were stiff, and he bent to massage them, but he hobbled over to the nearest incubator and then the next and so on. What they all had in common was that, in the thick glass of their lids, amid the intricate miniaturized wiring, amid the cities of chips and buses there, were the softest imaginable little white lights. They were barely visible, and they pulsed in quick patterns, racing around corners, up one side, down the other. As he stepped back, he saw that the same pattern occurred on each lid. Already the person growing in each was the size of a walnut. Each sat on the floor of its tank, and when he looked closely he could see masses of tiny air bubbles around each, and microfine tendrils looping around each other. The only motion in the room was the coursing of those fine lights in each lid. As he looked from one incubator to another, Ridge noticed a commonality about the patterns. They started out the same-a quick motion in the upper left area, branching out into multitudes of unique configurations left to right and top to bottom before winking out to let the whole thing start over.

Ridge looked up and saw the same patterns racing along the ceiling. He guessed the ceiling had receptors in its surface to track the pattern. Somehow, perhaps this sent messages to the room, to the ship itself. Perhaps this was how the birth codes came down. Perhaps the ceiling sent the messages to the glass lids, and not the other way around. That didn't matter. That was beyond his understanding. What he did understand was the repetition. He began to figure out that maybe at one time inspectors had come around to check the growth of the fetuses. Judging by the condition of *Nebula Express*, the inspectors were long gone, dust amid interstellar dust. The automata functioned on, however, and functioned smoothly. He leaned his palms on the glass of one incubator and stared closely at the code of lights, so that he saw the glowing reflection of his own face in the glass. There was a lot of information in the code of lights, and most of it was binary or some other machine-readable code that he could not decipher. What he did decipher, however, were the letters *W and P* and then a number, *92*. Could that mean WorkPod92? If so, it meant that all the workpods were coming out of one factory-this place. If there had been more, perhaps they had all succumbed to age and deterioration, and the ship now routed all the birth activity to this pod. It was a guess, anyway; and he had seen no evidence that other pods still existed. What pod had Caulfield said he was from? Ridge could still picture the old man mouthing the words: "WorkPod19."

Second in the code came what looked like the function and rank ciphers each person wore on their collar. The code appeared in a faint color scheme. Ridge compared the various patterns for members of WorkPod92 and found one that suggested a black bar. He rubbed his hands lightly along the polished glass and thought: Here is my equivalent. Maybe I was born in this incubator.

From there, the code diverged into myriad streams, loops, circles, rising and falling lines, that he could not decipher, but he had seen enough. He went back to his squatting position on the floor. After a while, he was attuned to the faint rocking of pumps and lights and could actually tell each time the pattern of lights repeated itself. Was there a clue in that?

It came to him after a while: Venable must have been born here. Maybe that was the clue. All the birthing in the ship went on here. Now what? Ridge racked his brain. Yes! Venable was older than some number of workpods. Maybe the ship assigned numbers randomly to the workpods, judging by the sequence. Whatever the intricacies of the process, this must be the clue at which Venable had hinted. Did that mean the CP was open somehow when a new captain replaced the old?

Ridge shook his head. Did he even know that Venable was not some ancient machine? Chances were that even in that case, the wetware, the bionics in the Captain, must be regularly replaced as they aged and died. If that were the case, then knowledge could be passed from one instance of a person to the next. He frowned and rubbed his aching brow with eyes pressed tightly shut as he tried to sort out the implications of that idea. It seemed intuitive that knowledge could be passed along through birth-else, how could he have memories of San Diego, Brenna memories of Buenos Aires, and better yet, any two team members memories in common, say of Tokyo or Perth? Even if these were random fragments from the lives of long-dead persons, it didn't matter for purposes of present analysis, Ridge thought. The key was that memory could be transmitted through some biochemical broth, some culinary tricks with RNA and DNA. The question then was, why did he have no memories of previous iterations of himself, since it appeared there were no more than 99 workpods, and so the groups had to repeat. Was each iteration slightly unique? Was each iteration therefore a totally unique human being whose thoughts and experiences were lost forever as it died? That wasn't the pressing issue so much, as the question-could he somehow reinvent himself as Venable and thus enter the CP? Was that the clue?

Still frustrated, Ridge walked back to the incubators and leaned over the nearest one. He stared at his own reflection again and shook his head, as if he were communicating with some other person. That was his moment of inspiration. Glancing up at the darting tiny lights in the ceiling, he waved his hand over the lid. His shadow briefly passed through the beam and nothing happened. Now he did something he had not yet done, and which probably had not occurred since the last inspector passed through here a generation or a century or several thousand years ago with a barcode reading wand of some type on a routing inspection: he placed both hands over the lights. He covered vital parts of the person's code with his hands. After a few seconds, the incubator began pulsing an amber warning light. Ridge leaned his whole body over the lid to cast darkness over the growing life inside.

Lights came on in the room. The walls flashed alight in panels of white fluorescent light. One by one, work panels lit up. The room spoke to him in a mechanical voice that was neither male nor female, but pleasantly and smoothly articulated: "Is there something wrong? We detect a malfunction."

"Yes," Ridge said. "This entire ship is a wreck."

"We do not grasp what inspector says. Can you identify your badge and pod number?"

"Ridge. WorkPod01. Lead Engineer."

"That is not an authorized inspector I.D." Buzzers began to sound-faintly, nothing raucous, nothing to disturb the clinical peace in this reverse tomb where life sprang out of coffins.

"I want to enter the CP and talk with the Captain."

"What is the code?"

"The code is..." Ridge tried to remember. What had Venable said?"

"What is the code?" the voice repeated.

"Function Check Largo."

"Wait."

Ridge waited, while the panels winked out one by one. The incubators resumed their quiet patterns of moving lights. A hundred tiny pumps and circuits went back to normal whisper-function. The walls became blank again as the built-in circuits shut down. The fluoros shut down, leaving gray shadows. Ridge started to think he'd failed.

Then a panel in the wall slid aside. Instantly, Ridge grasped the meaning: the CP wasn't in the nose of the ship, but in here. Where he'd seen a solid wall was now a raised opening like an airlock. He had to raise his feet to step over the threshold, and the panel slid shut behind him. He was in an environment of shapes rather than furnishings; whispers rather than noises; ripples rather than liquids. The very walls seemed to move about as if they were impermanent. Sheets upon sheets of semitransparent circuit sets floated in the air. A constant process of sorting went on. Cool air whispered around Ridge's neck, sliding down his body to his feet. "We must keep you isolated from the cryovironment," said a voice he recognized as Venable's. "Come closer."

"Where are you?" Ridge said. He raised his arms and waved them as if fending off cobwebs. Some of the diaphanous sheets rippled in the wind caused by his arms, but returned into focus. Other sheets swirled as though they were made of liquid.

"Here," said the faint voice that came out of the walls somehow, not from any specific place but from the room as a whole.

Ridge stepped carefully, one foot before the other. He was afraid to hurt the delicate environment around him. He was equally afraid that he might be poisoned. He pictured atmospheres of nitrogen, ammonia, and other poison primordial gases. The floor shimmered as if drenched in excited phosphorants. "We are here," said the voice.

Ridge waved his arms as if brushing a curtain aside. This brought him through the hanging ciphers into a brighter area. It was a cluttered lab about the size of a typical living room at home. A number of sights assaulted Ridge's senses all at once. He cried out involuntarily and took a step back, holding one arm before his face, but he lowered the arm and looked at the secrets of the command post.

A bank of overhead biolume tubes cast a fog of harsh bluish light downward. Dust motes drifted like stars in the empty air. Motes of dust drifted like tiny organisms in some underwater world. The room was cluttered, dusty, and dirty. Old-fashioned wire racks full of dead gray circuit boxes were stacked ceiling-high on all sides. Masses of multi-colored cable snaked among them. The cables all had a uniform snow of gray dust on them, as did the primitive signal lights in the boxes. On the tables were bottles, test tubes, open digital manuals with now-blank pages, discarded ASCII styluses, and more. Rags, watches, socks, toy cars, dolls, pictures of New England houses, sheets of *tango* music written in ink on paper, towels, dirty glasses, the bric-a-brac was endless. It resembled a surreal sculpture.

The tile floor was white, the grout greasy looking, and swaths of cobwebs fluttered around his ankles as Ridge walked. He half expected cockroaches or rats to scurry by his shoes, but there was no life on that floor. There wasn't much room to walk, but he took a few steps.

"You see where the memories were made," the voice said.

"Where are you?" Ridge looked about. He expected to see a view screen on a wall, but there was almost no wall space devoid of clutter.

"Here," said the voice, and Ridge looked on the small lab bench before him. A bank of grayish steel camera lenses pointed down at a white enameled tray sitting askew on the black tile surface of a lab bench. Tubes and wires by the thousand snaked into the water there, and in the water lay a human face. *Venable.*

Ridge gasped.

Venable had that bright, hopeful look. "In all the melancholy and sadness of my existence here, I look forward to the resurrection of all our bodies and life everlasting on the New Earth."

Ridge understood what he had intuited earlier: the Captain had gone mad, as had the entire damaged ship carrying humanity on its last desperate journey. "Where is New Earth?" he said.

"We have not found it yet."

"We?"

"I am the last of the captains." Amid the ripples in his constantly refreshed water-and Ridge spied lobes of gray brain matter under the face, as well as misshapen bits of bone and gristle, maybe part of a nose that had not formed right, maybe a twin or a predecessor or a random growth-Venable smiled and moved his eyes rightward.

Ridge stepped a few feet closer to the hanging red and white checkered curtain and pushed it aside. He looked into a circular command room with high-backed chairs and banks of instruments. He thought it was like looking at a massive church organ with banks upon banks of keyboards and ranks upon ranks of pipes, only the music it made was not sound but sight. The plate view screens were black and spattered with light. It took Ridge a second or two to focus and understand that he was looking at the Milky Way galaxy from a high altitude, meaning light years, meaning they had been traveling for thousands of years to get here.

"Where are we heading?" Ridge asked.

"Counter the flow of stars and nebulas," Venable said. "We are moving against the rotation of the galaxy, which increases our velocity manifold. It makes our search for the New Earth more efficient."

"Then we do not know where we are headed," Ridge said.

"Life is most likely to exist in the mid-disk, where it had time to evolve rather than in the younger, more active center, so that is where we are looking. The ship searches constantly. All its energies are dedicated to that task, except the small effort to just stay alive and keep our cargo viable." Venable smiled very logically. "Without human life to reproduce on New Earth, there would be no reason to continue on. So you understand the purpose of our suffering. You and I are broken mirrors. We shine with borrowed light. We are living borrowed lives."

"You are wrong," Ridge said. "I am a man, and I have loved a woman."

The water rippled as Venable shook his face. "You still do not quite understand, Ridge."

"I understand only one thing," Ridge said heatedly. "I want to live. I want the woman back, Brenna. Where is she?"

"Largo. You might find her there."

"What is Largo?"

Venable smiled enigmatically, and Ridge angrily raised a fist as if to smash the thing in the water before him, which was little more than a photograph forever developing in a tray of chemicals, or biochemicals, given that its brain lay in there under its face. Invisible forces in the air grasped Ridge's arm. He felt himself being immobilized, and a cold numbness shot through him. He gasped for air.

"You cannot hurt me," Venable said calmly. "I almost wish you could. I might enjoy passing on into the limitless relief of eternal peace. Then again, like you, I dream of living. I dream of the old Earth. I know what it is to *tango* with a woman, or to ride a horse, or to sail a boat, or to sleep late and drink coffee on the patio before driving off to log in and check my e-mail. Do you get a lot of e-mail, Ridge? Nobody has contacted me in centuries, except now you are here and I am entertained. Please don't go."

"I am a leader," Ridge said. "I will not desert you."

"For that I thank you. Then we can be friends."

"Yes, Captain. We are friends."

Venable laughed. "We have little choice, do we?"

Ridge walked into the control room. He brushed aside cobwebs and coughed in the dusty atmosphere. There were at least ten or twelve high-backed chairs before the banked instrument panels, and in each chair reposed a mummified officer. Their uniforms were intact after centuries. Their collars were encrusted with rows of gold and black bars. Each had donned a jumpsuit open at the collar, with a wide ring where a helmet might fit. Perhaps they had suited up during the ship's great emergency and never made it. The ship had somehow put a mission together, using the cells and tissues of the last surviving officer-a man named Venable. "I understand the scenario," Ridge said quietly and tapped his hand on the back of a chair, as if saying goodbye to its occupant. Then he left the star-blazed control tomb, pulling the checkered curtain shut behind him. He addressed the face in the water: "We might be able to save the ship. What other choice do we have but to try?"

"None," the Captain said. "I might be able to help."

"I can't do it without you. If we can't do it, let's just blow the whole thing up and end this charade."

Venable looked dazed. "We could do that?"

"We could and we should." Ridge leaned close, and the ship did not stop him. "Think, man. How long should this living hell continue?"

"We must find New Earth," Venable said stubbornly. "Nothing else matters."

"Do we have any candidates?"

In the water beside Venable's chin appeared a blotch of shimmering black, a vision of space, and in it a faint shining object. "This is a star about five light-years of travel from here. We will make a pass by its heliosphere in another hundred years. If there is a habitable planet there, we will insert the ship into orbit around that planet, which will be called New Earth. Then the bones will come out dancing, and the music will start playing on the decks of Largo."

"This Largo," Ridge said.

"Two women are in there," Venable said. "You can go there if you wish."

"Are there Cleaners in there?"

Venable's eyes grew blank as he looked into distant data galaxies. "Cleaners inhabit every corner of the ship, keeping it sanitary and orderly."

"The cleaners have gone mad," Ridge said. "They have eaten all the colonists."

Venable shrugged, a mere ripple in the water. "No matter. The genetic material is safely stored and available."

"Where?"

"Largo."

"Then..." Ridge suddenly wrapped his head in his arms and felt like weeping with frustration. Talking with this poor demented creature was like consulting an oracle. For every second of truth one had to endure a minutes of smoke and tricks. "What should we do, Venable? Keep breeding temporary purpose-people, temps, throwaways, like you and me? Is that fair? Does that make sense?"

"We must reach New Earth. Go, Ridge. You have served your purpose. My purpose is not yet over but you deserve your rest now. Go to Largo. Find your woman. Sleep."

Invisible forces grasped Ridge so tightly he almost could not breathe, and moved him bodily out of the CP. It was all he could do to move his feet in small jerky motions and keep his face up to keep his windpipe free. He heard Venable say: "We will do as you say. We have tried a dozen worlds and failed, but the next one will be our last try. After that we'll do a swan dive into the sun. We'll *tango* off into the sunspots. We'll let the sun tear our atoms apart and make us into hydrogen. We'll return to the beginning of time and start over with a great big bang." Venable laughed. "Thank you, Ridge, and goodbye."

Ridge found himself thrown backwards, landing on his heels and butt and elbows, on the smooth floor in the workpod. The wall winked shut, and with it the CP closed him out.

"You can never come back in here," Venable said in a distant whisper that trailed among the quietly bubbling incubators. "Pity, because I so enjoyed talking with you."

Ridge rose to his feet and staggered to the nearest incubator. Inside was a human fetus, curled on its side and sucking its thumb. In its lap beat a huge bloody heart with trailing arteries and blood vessels. Its eyes were closed and it smiled in some distant dream of sunny castle ruins along the Moselle River in Luxembourg, or hordes of yellow taxis racing along Manhattan streets under a gray winter sky, or bare-chested Jivaros Indians hunting with blowguns in the Amazon basin while the white snow caps of the Andes loomed god-like in the distance.

"Hurry," Venable's voice whispered from the walls. "There is so little time."

Chapter 14

Brenna ran down the shaft, rung over rung, as fast as she could. Above her were the comforting footfalls of Ridge. Below her was Tomson, and below him Lantz. At the moment, she had one thought foremost in mind, and that was to escape the mudmen. She could hear their fluting sounds in the air, both inside the long shaft that trailed off into darkness below, and in the air outside. She could hear the chitter of their claws on the metal. "Hurry!" Ridge said above, and Brenna heard Lantz cry out below. An instant later, the world exploded in light as the panels of the shaft came apart. Light flooded in, and with it came the clawed grasping hands of the mudmen and their nightmare faces. She screamed as she smelled their mushroom smell, saw their round mouths with cobweb teeth, their slitted eyes with dull red retinas. She felt the cold wind of air from open rooms and shafts in the ship's nose area. She felt the rush of wind as mudmen crowded in for a meal on the four helplessly exposed humans.

In that same instant, the combined weight of humans and mudmen made the shaft collapse. Brenna clung to a steel rung as she felt Ridge's heavy body plummet past her. She slipped down several rungs. She ignored the bright red and yellow flashes of pain in her mind as she slammed into more rungs and as her ribs brushed against a body. She had no idea whose body. She tried to scream, but had no breath for it, as the ladder with her and Lantz on it tilted crazily and then fell into open space.

She glimpsed the two men falling below her. They seemed to be falling into the mouth of some brass machine that swallowed them up. It was the last she saw of them because she and Lantz were falling backwards into a heap of slag. She looked up helplessly in slow motion as a dozen mudmen grasped hungrily after her with their claws. She saw their mouths grinding as if already chewing on her flesh. Then everything went black as the dusty coal and wet slag sucked her into it like a mass of quicksand.

Moments later, she lay on her stomach coughing. The world was a dark place flashing with mauve and olive drab lights. Her head throbbed and her lungs wanted to puke forth the dust in them. She raised herself up a few inches by pushing on the wet, foul-smelling slag with her palms. She was alive. But where?

She stirred, pulling herself into a half-seated, half-reclining position still leaning on her palms. She looked about and expected to be killed by the mudmen any second, but she could not smell them nor could she hear their fluting noises nor could she see any eyes glowing in the dark.

A large baseball thing lay in the slag nearby, and she shrieked. It was the head of a dead mudman. They came apart easily, and this one had not survived the tumble through a cubic acre of falling slag. The dust was still settling on its canvas-like skin and sleeping face. To be certain it was dead, she lifted a chunk of anthracite and slammed it down on the head. The head split like a bag of liquid and splashed green bile into the grainy black slag. She regretted having made the added mess, and pulled back.

She heard a feeble moan. "Is someone there?"

The moan again. "Lantz, is that you?"

"Brenna, help me out. I'm stuck here."

Brenna crawled on her hands and knees until she saw a glimmer of gray light. She felt a breath of air on her face, and smelled distant rain. She saw Lantz's pale neck and reddish hair protruding from a pool of dust and oily sand. "Hurry," Lantz said. "I'm sinking. This stuff is like quicksand."

Brenna flattened herself and crawled across the surface of the stuff until she grasped Lantz's hands in both of hers. She felt the gooey sand pulling at her torso as she flattened herself and pulled, and it seemed the sand was winning. The sand seemed to be sucking them both down. Nearby, she noticed a grill with several vertical metal bars. Desperately, she swung herself around until she could lock her ankles around the bars. She prayed no mudmen were on the other side to pull at her feet. "Hang on," she said gasping.

Lantz choked and sputtered. "I'm going down."

"I've got you."

"God..." Lantz was starting to suffocate as the weight pressed down all around her. Her hands were under the slag, pulling Brenna down. Brenna's hands disappeared under the wet heavy quickslag. Only Lantz's face was visible now. Lantz's eyes were wide with desperation and were starting to cloud over with fatigue and anoxia.

Brenna hooked her boots around the metal bars and flexed. Pressing her forearms down flat to distribute her weight better, she pulled her own body toward the bars using her feet. For a moment, nothing happened. Then she felt the sand yield a bit. Inch by inch, she pulled Lantz out, until both women were able to pull themselves up using their hands on the bars. "That was awful," Lantz said, brushing her red hair back with muddy looking hands.

"We're in some kind of shaft," Brenna said. She saw that the shaft had been filled in by a collapse of the slag, so there was no way to go back out the way they'd come. "I think we're buried under an acre of this stuff, and we're lucky that we slid into this drainage tunnel or whatever it is."

Lantz rattled the bars. Metal chattered and sounded as if it might yield. "No way but forward then."

Brenna sniffed. The air had a vinegary tang. She pointed to the dimly glowing red and white flowers of decay and fungus in the separating metal walls. "Watch out for that stuff--it will burn you."

"Too bad it doesn't burn the mudmen."

Brenna shook her head. "I think they're made from it, and other ugly stuff. Come on, stick with me. Let's get out of here." Together, they grasped the bars and shook them until the round grating of which the bars were part gave way. The grating fell forward onto slag, and the two women crawled forward in the gloom. "You hear that?" Lantz said, lying on her side.

Brenna stopped also and listened. "Water." She sniffed. "Smells fresh, like rain."

Lantz's face looked luminous in the dark. Her freckles almost seemed to glow. "Oh God. Sounds like mudmen paradise. Water, darkness, probably rats too."

They crawled forward, because there was nothing else they could do, except stay here and die. Brenna said: "I imagine they'd love eating rats. It would be like eating their own kind."

"I think I see light," Lantz said. She stopped again, resting on her elbows, and looked puzzled. She looked at her hands, which shone grayish-white. "Light. It's artificial daylight, made from bioluminescent bacteria."

The two women dug their way out through a last heap of slag and emerged in a part of the ship they had not imagined. They crawled out from a wide pipe in a trail of falling slag, and emerged one after the other on what looked like a concrete subway platform. A dangling sign read in large blue letters on white enamel: *Largo*.

Water dripped rain-like all around on the dark tracks, while bright biolume shown down from under the ancient green glass canopy overhanging the length of the platform. There wasn't a living soul in sight, but lights glowed with comforting strength and regularity. Several placards revealed pictures of attractive, smiling young men and women looking out with happy eyes. If it was advertising, it was enigmatic. Only the word *Largo* appeared again and again.

The platform amid the tracks was of piled stone, with moss growing around the edges of the individual stones. In a passenger shelter of rippled greenish glass stood two wooden benches whose slats had grown black and brittle with age, but otherwise the place looked as though a crowd of commuters might come running up the stairs any moment to greet a train, should one come rushing out of the tunnels at either end. Instead of a train, and instead of a buzzer or a whistle, they heard mudmen fluting in the tunnels. Brenna thought she glimpsed red dots of light in the tunnels.

Brenna and Lantz ran as fast as they could, across the wet slippery tracks. They clambered up the stone face onto the platform, ran across its chilly wet concrete squares, and down into a well-lit white tile tunnel. "Wish we still had our rifles," Brenna said.

"We'll make new weapons," Lantz said. "No way are we going back for the rifles."

They ran along the clean, well-lit underground. The tunnel was oval. Placards of advertisement for *Largo* lined the walls. Faces smiled on them as they hurried to escape the mudmen. In a motif of cobalt letters on white background, a tile sign read *Exit*. A blue arrow pointed in the direction they were running. They redoubled their pace, ran up a wide flight of stairs just like in a subway, emerged in a small but ornate station.

"Wow, look at this place," Lantz said as she walked into the center of the hall with her hands in her pockets. Brenna followed her across the lavishly marbled floor with its inlaid images of earth globes. There were six such circles: one looking down on the Arctic, one looking up at the Antarctic, one each looking at the Americas, Europe and Africa, Asia, and the Pacific region. A glance told Brenna the maps reflected Earth around the end of the 21st Century.

Over Lantz's head, about 40 feet up, was an expanse of glass panels, and beyond that lay the blackness of outer space. A luminous band of stars must be the Milky Way galaxy, Brenna thought. The glass panels were held in fine wooden frames that warmly covered the ceiling. A band of finely work oak several feet high ringed the transition from ceiling to walls. The oak was richly carved with gargoyles, gilded leaves, and jungle animals with glowing green glass eyes. The basilica structure had brownish-reddish marble walls dripping with creamy white inclusions, like clouds on taffy. Ornately beveled archways supported on Corinthian pillars led off in various directions, all of them devoid of humans. Still, everything looked clean and functional, if thoroughly dusty. They spotted a ticket counter with brass rails and frosted window, closed. They spotted men's and women's bathrooms behind black wrought-iron doors, locked. They saw windows all around containing advertisements that said *Largo*. Brenna frowned, savoring the name curiously.

"Look here," Lantz said striding through a long hallway with a curving ceiling of metal struts and fancy Art Nouveau stained glass. As she walked, lights turned on around her and turned off just as soon as she passed. "It knows I'm here."

"What knows?"

"Largo," Lantz said spreading her arms as if introducing Brenna to a friend. Lantz looked up and laughed. "Largo is the name of this place."

"How do you know that?" Brenna walked after her, amused.

Lantz tapped her forehead with one index finger. "It's all in my head. I was in a place like this once. It wasn't called Largo, and I don't remember the name."

Brenna shook her head. "The ship is messing with our minds. Maybe none of this is real."

Lantz stood with her arms akimbo. "Try falling down on your head. If it hurts, it means it's real."

"I'll take your word for it."

They walked through the train station, expecting hordes of passengers to come pouring through the gates on all sides any moment. Not a soul obliged. "Maybe it's a trap," Brenna said.

"Doesn't feel like a trap."

"Feel that?" Brenna felt a breeze on her forehead as they pushed through the swinging walnut doors, which had shiny brass fixtures on the inside and black iron hinges on the outside. "Smells like a rainy evening in Paris," Brenna said, pinching her collar up.

"Someplace smaller," Lantz said. "Brussels or Cleveland or Sapporo." She wrapped her arms around herself and shivered. Brenna could hear the other's teeth chatter and said: "Are you finally getting cold? Want a coat?" Lantz nodded, and Brenna pointed to a clothing store across the street. "I have no money," Lantz said, but they both shrugged and ran skipping across the street. The running wasn't necessary, because the street was empty. It was, Brenna thought, a typical rainy boulevard outside a little train station in a prosperous little town anywhere in the civilized world of Old Earth. There were some smallish cars, but none moved. The cars sat parked at the curb on either side of the street, following the convention of the steering wheel on the left (as opposed to the Commonwealth and Japanese convention of the driver sitting on the right). This entire little world was detailed down to the least little item, Brenna thought. Still, somehow, it did not feel like Earth. Not exactly. "Something is different," she said carefully, not wanting to say wrong. Something was different, not wrong per se.

"It's a beautiful place," Lantz said as they hurried through the lightly dribbling rain. It was good to feel raindrops on one's forehead, Brenna thought as they ran across the opposite sidewalk and pulled open the heavy, stylish brushed-steel door of what billed itself in pink neon as the Largo Style Shoppe.

Inside, rock music boomed-no vocals, just suggestively throbbing instrumentals. The air was dry and clean. It smelled faintly of cloth and fabric glues. On flat tables they found bolt upon bolt of attractive cloths and fabrics. Cheery summer dresses hung on one carousel rack. Coats for rainy wear stretched twenty feet along a wall closet in all sizes from little girl to adult woman. One corner was filled with shoes, another with lingerie, another with umbrellas and winter coats and scarves. "A little for everybody," Brenna said as she fingered the fine materials and looked for price tags, but found none.

"Look at these hats," Lantz said. She pulled a plastic rain hat over her head with both hands and twirled around laughing. The hat was transparent, with a wide floppy brim, and covered with pastel dots.

"Here is a sweater for you," Brenna said holding up a heavy knit. It was dark blue and looked almost mannish. It had a thick collar and heavy knitted pillar forms running up and down the front and back. "Nice," Lantz said, holding it up in the white light. "Cool," she said, slipping into it. She shivered with pleasure. Brenna turned a word trick, saying: "Warm," and they both laughed.

"Have you been to the ladies' room lately?" Lantz asked.

Brenna shook her head. "No, why, do you have to go?"

"I think so." Lantz looked a trifle uncomfortable. "I almost don't know how."

"Oh, you'll figure it out," Brenna said. She spotted a sign in the back of the store with an icon suggesting the ladies' restroom. "Over there."

Lantz walked off in that direction, idly fingering coats and pants as she went. On one carousel was a display of loud, happy yellow teddy bears. On another it was a pile of stuffed rabbits with reddish glass eyes. She disappeared into the WC and Brenna eagerly sorted through a pile of leather coats looking for something in her size.

Lantz screamed, and Brenna went running. She wished now that they'd gone back for the rifles, if it had been at all possible to find them in the slag. As she ran toward the bathroom, Brenna reflected that all this seemed too good to be true. There must be a catch-like mudmen pouring out of the walls to eat them alive. But it wasn't mudmen that made Lantz scream. It was a puddle of blood on the tiled bathroom floor-her own. "I don't know what happened," she said. She held her hands to her mouth and leaned against the wall in shock. "I walked in thinking I'd go to the loo" (she pointed to a row of stalls) "and all of a sudden this gush came out. It's not a period or anything, Brenna. I'm bleeding inside."

"Do you feel faint?" Brenna felt the raw edges of insanity gnawing around her at that moment as never before, and pushed it all away. She clung to all that there was, which was what was here--nothing else. She put an arm around Lantz's waist to help her.

"Just tired."

"Do you hurt?"

Lantz pulled away from Brenna's embrace and shook her head thoughtfully. "No." She probed her midsection with her palms and reaffirmed: "No pain."

"What is going on?" Brenna said looking at the slick of oily red blood smeared on the floor like a spiral galaxy. Lantz had stepped in her own blood, and now she wiped her shoes on a handful of paper towels torn from a dispenser. "I wonder who maintains all this so neatly, this whole ship and all?" Lantz said.

Brenna wondered too. "Not mudmen, that's for sure. They're too dumb."

The answer presented a moment later as the two women explored this place called Largo. "I'm glad you have a warm sweater," Brenna said as they left the Largo Style Shoppe. They came back into night and rain. "I'm glad too," Lantz said. She wore the plastic hat with the yellow red and green dots on it, and held it by the brim with both hands. "Wow, this is like back on Earth."

Brenna sniffed the air. "Yes. I can smell green things. There must be a park nearby. Smell that kind of tangy rich stuff? That's soil."

"I know soil," Lantz said as if Brenna held her for a dummy. They jostled each other in the ribs. "Race you across the street," Brenna said.

"Wait," Lantz said. "Take a look."

They walked back to the Largo Style Shoppe and looked inside the window. It was dark inside, and the music no longer throbbed. Brenna tried the door but did not force it. "That's an airlock on the edge of the door," she said. She ran a fingertip up and down the sturdy flex material. "You know what? I'll bet the ship sucks all the air out and leaves a near vacuum. That's how things stay so fresh. The minute you go from one place to another, the lights go on and air rushes in. We're walking through a vacuum-sealed museum."

"Oh come on," Lantz said, but her disbelief seemed to fade as they walked along the sidewalk opposite the train station. From here, they could see that the station was pitch-dark inside. "You may be right."

"So figure this," Brenna said. "We look up and we keep see the stars, even through the clouds and the rain. Maybe it's a band of glass running around the ship. Maybe Largo is some sort of giant shopping mall that stretches around the ship under the glass. Maybe it was meant to be for all those people to live in...but they were eaten..." She held her hand over her mouth in horror at the thought.

Lantz did not find the idea amusing either. "I'm not too sure, Brenna. If people were meant to live here, to cruise here everyday, they wouldn't need those vacuum compartments. I think this area has another purpose. Don't ask me what."

Largo proved to be a ghost town in its own right. They wandered in and out of shops and taverns. In one bar, a mechanical bartender mixed drinks and did magical tricks for them while they laughed. He was a fancy brass imitation of a 19th Century saloon bartender. He had the kind of moveable jaw that ventriloquists' dummies had, but there was no ventriloquist to do tricks with him. Brenna leaned over the bar out of curiosity, and saw that he was just a set of leather bellows and articulated steel pistons from the waist down. Lantz laughed. "He mixes a mean margarita though." She walked over to a juke box and pressed buttons. There was no coin slot. The music just started pouring out-no vocals, just a rich, thick paste of rhythmic sound that wrapped pleasantly around them.

"These aren't real margaritas," Brenna said. "We'd be flat on the floor. These are goody-goody drinks with honey and oats and other health stuff in them. That stuff around the rim isn't salt but crystallized vitamin sprinkles."

"It's fun to pretend," Lantz said at her barstool. She sipped while twirling on the stool. "Too bad there aren't any nice-looking guys around."

"I sort of wish Ridge were here," Brenna said.

Lantz spoke around her straw, which was on her lips. "You like him, don't you?"

Brenna nodded. "I was attracted to him from the first moment I saw him. I felt terrible because I thought I was married to Ricardo and had children." She still felt a devouring sense of loss as if part of her soul had been sliced out with a gutting knife.

"I'm so sorry about that," Lantz said. "I was supposedly still single. Maybe because no guy wants to get near a redhead who pumps iron and shoots guns with the best of them."

"That's all a lot of hooey," Brenna said. "They made us from bits and pieces of other people's lives. Now it's up to us to live our own lives."

"That's sort of how life is anyway," Lantz said. "Nobody just pops into the world without a program running. Everyone has one of those player piano sheets written by their parents, their culture, the whole thing."

"Yes," Brenna said, "so now we just have to figure out how to live our lives. I wonder if we could somehow find Tomson and Ridge."

"We could try," Lantz said. She yawned, setting her drink aside. "Aren't you tired at all, Brenna?"

Brenna did feel a certain faraway bone-weariness. "Nothing serious yet. I'm getting there. They must have fed us a bunch of uppers, because I'm still raring to go. But I could close my eyes for a little while."

They walked down the rainy street together, looking into shop windows and noting that same phenomenon that everywhere they went, lights turned on as they approached and shut off as they passed. "That could get annoying," Brenna said after a while.

"The dark scares me a bit," Lantz said. "Say, do you suppose it ever gets to be daylight in here?"

Brenna said: "I imagine if we were orbiting a planet like Earth maybe. You know, a planet that's just bathed in sunshine. Reflected sunshine would light this place up like a million candles."

"I'd like that."

As they strolled along, the shape of Largo became apparent. The city formed a thin ring, maybe 100 feet thick, about a mile around the wider edge of the ship's nose. Imagine drawing a thin blue line around the thick part of a bullet, Brenna thought...the outer wall was either thick glass or, more likely, a reflective and conductive bluish material that gathered an image on the outer hull and transmitted it through the hull, recreating it in pixels on the inner hull surface-Largo's "sky." On either side of the street were shops and other buildings up to three or four stories high. Some reached almost to the hull. Brenna assumed that the band of real estate forming Largo was hemmed in on either side by steel decking and beyond that would be the more normal (though generally spectacular, except where ravaged by time and mudmen) ship's quarters. It still wasn't clear what the purpose of Largo was, if not to serve as a shopping mall and recreational area for the thousands who had been killed while in deep sleep.

"There is a hotel," Brenna pointed out. "Want to find a room and take a bath? Rest a while?"

Lantz rolled up her eyes. "That sounds divine. My God, yes."

They strolled up the ornate gray marble entrance of the Hotel Largo. The entrance was framed in honey-colored marble pillars with Ionic friezes top and bottom and then a little arch carved full of grapevines, cherubs, and wicked satyrs. As they pushed through the heavy double doors, they heard the customary rush of air filling the spaces ahead. Lights came on. They heard faint, very Continental violin music. The lobby was a high, domed affair with a wrought-iron mezzanine drowning in greenish light from more Art Nouveau stained glass. The air was at once light and cozy. Brenna expected to see men in spats and bowler hats, and women with parasols and hoopskirts, but the usual deathly stillness prevailed. "This could become dispiriting," Lantz said as they took a little brass-cage elevator up to the second floor. "Spooky, I mean."

They emerged on a floor carpeted with long Persian runners. The doorways were set back in little alcoves for a look of privacy to offset the closeness of everything here. Brenna jogged up and down the hall throwing doors open and admiring the variety of sumptuous furnishings. Lantz trailed a bit more tiredly, yawning from time to time. She looked pale and drawn. "Look, Brenna," she said pointing into a lavish marble room that contained a yellow-rimmed swimming pool done in green and blue floral tiles. Mirrors decorated the walls, and there were at least six alcoves, each containing its own hot tub. An atmosphere of vapor and camphor scented with lemon and oranges drifted through the air.

Brenna cautiously tested the waters all around and found them temperate. The two women stripped naked and plunged laughing into the large pool. There, Brenna swam laps while Lantz rested in the shallow end. Lantz held her face up to the light and her hands on the yellow tiles along the sides while her trim lower body floated lazily just under the surface. "How do you feel?" Brenna said as she emerged sputtering from a long trawl along the glowing blue bottom. The water was chlorinated and clean, and stung the eyes. It burned pleasantly in Brenna's nose but made her sneeze. Lantz nodded and kept her eyes closed. "I'm listening to the violin music," she said smiling with pleasure. Her freckles looked carroty and her skin as pale as eggshell paper. Brenna swam up and down a few more times. "I'm getting a little tired now too, Lantz. Want to try some of the hot tubs?"

"I'd like that, but I'm too lazy. I'll just float here a while."

"Okay, suit yourself!"

Brenna climbed out. Artificial gravity pulled the water off along the smooth planes of her body and made her feel heavy. She wondered if humans had not been meant to be aquatic animals somehow. Hooting and laughing, she ran in a circle around the pool and then jumped with big splash into a steaming hot tub. At first the heat stunned her. Then she settled back and let the jets of water under the surface massage the aching and abused muscles and bones of her body that had been through so much duress in the past day. "You should try this!" she called out. The floor around the hot tub was dark tile inset with lovely pink and chocolate stones. It slanted lightly inward and drained back all the water she'd splashed out during her jump. "I can't remember when I last ate," she said out loud, hearing her voice echo amid the olive walls with their curving paintings of nymphs and gods and other classical themes right out of a Bad-Nauheim or Mondorf-les-Bains or Tivoli spa. "All we need now is young men in loincloths to bring us more of those fake health margaritas."

After a while, the warmth became more than she wanted to enjoy and she got out. She found a pile of fresh clean white frotte towels on a table in the alcove, and dried herself. The warm moist air kept her warm and comfortable. She knelt by the side of the hot tub and washed her filthy, torn jumpsuit. "I think we'll do some more shopping after you've rested," Brenna said. She wrung her uniform out and hung it over a chair to dry. In this climate it should take a while to dry down to a sort of warm damp condition, and then she'd find a warm spot in the hotel to finish drying it. Maybe while Lantz slept. "We should find the biggest beds in the hotel," she said cheerfully as she rounded the corner, coming back into the main hall with its yellow-framed pool.

"Lantz?" Brenna heard violin music and hurried to her friend's side.

Light poured down from the glass ceiling, an avalanche or chandelier of overly bright bioluminosity that was the lightest of light yellows like lemon ices. Shades of darker greenish light played in there along with streaks of red and blue and gray. The rich light poured down through hanging plants, palm fronds, slowly turning dark fan blades, little Victorian faux Bernini pillars of bronze holding up the mezzanine. The light gleamed off dark lavish surfaces-large brownish Han vases, polished tables, windows inset into the dark oak walls, *Largo* posters with beautiful smiling faces, and more. The light fell down on the aquamarine pool waters that stirred lightly with a chlorine foam over a bright pool bottom decorated with inlays of colored glass beads in the shape of a palm tree.

"Lantz!" Brenna exclaimed and ran to the pool, where she could hear the violin music more clearly than ever. Under cascades of piano music coming from the walls, the redheaded woman lay as Brenna had left her, in the pool with her arms on the yellow ledge. Her head was tilted back as if she were asleep, but her eyes were half open and glazed. Her mouth hung open as if she had taken one last shuddering breath before her heart stopped beating and her lungs stopped rising and falling. Brenna cried out "Oh no!" and ran to her side. Brenna splashed into the water beside Lantz and sought a pulse. Lantz's pale skin was already chilly, and her flesh had a rubbery feel to it. "My God no!" Brenna exclaimed tearfully and held her hands over her face. Stirred by the turbulence of Brenna's legs in the water, Lantz's body slipped gently into the water feet first, all the way to the bottom, and that was where she lay in an attitude of utterly peaceful repose with her arms lightly apart. Her hair came undone and floated like reddish seaweed.

Brenna stood frozen in shock at the pool's edge. The body lay in the water where it had slipped. Lantz's torso lay on the green glasses of the palm fronds.

Abruptly, Brenna ran into the hot tub alcove for her jumpsuit. It was still wet, so she ran back to the poolside and put Lantz's still-dirty clothes on. It didn't matter now. Anything to get away. Her pleasure here was spoiled by the terrible realization that if she did not find Ridge, she would be all alone here. Forever. And that was too terrifying a thought to bear. Sobbing, she ran down the rainy street in the empty night city. Feeling nearly hysterical, she banged on the opaque windows of those odd little cars parked at the curbs. They were empty. One or two lit up faintly, inviting her to get in, but what could they do other than run her around and around Largo?

Then she heard a man's voice. "Lantz? Brenna?"

Ridge?

Confused, she stopped and looked around. Then she realized it was Lantz's collar com. She cupped it in one palm, pulling it close to her chin. "Ridge? Where are you?"

"I'm standing in this train station, wondering where you are."

"Oh God," she said. "Ridge. Hold on, I'm running to you as fast as I can."

"Maybe you'd care to *tango*," he said in a dry voice, as if nothing were wrong. And maybe again for just a little while, nothing was wrong. Brenna ran down the sidewalk. She ignored the rain hitting her face. If only we can have a little time together, she thought. It's not much to ask. Not after we have had so little and lost so much.

Ridge stood waiting on the sidewalk outside the Largo train station. Brenna fled along the sidewalk and splashed through puddles as she flew toward him. Ridge spread his arms and hugged her tightly against his hard, strong frame.

Chapter 15

Y ou can never come back here," Venable said.

Ridge stood in the semidarkness of WorkPod01, wondering about the next clue. What was this Largo? And where? He vaguely remembered from some fragment of music lessons, literally in another life, that the Italian word Largo was notation meaning a slow and solemn musical passage.

"Go," Venable said, "we will speak again elsewhere. Look for me at the police station. Now quickly go before the air is sucked out of WorkPod01 and cleansed and pumped back in. You'll suffocate. It is how we keep both the tiny bugs and the larger contaminants out."

Like the mudmen, Ridge thought as he pressed vainly against the doors. They would not budge. Was he trapped here? He heard a rush of air behind him and turned to look. Another opening had appeared in the wall, this time to a small plain room with a plain wooden bench wrapped around the far side to sit on. The bench was varnished to nearly orange hue. Ridge stepped inside and sat on the hard bench. A thick, riveted metal door like in an ocean liner slipped shut. He was trapped in near complete darkness in this little pod that smelled of varnished wood and painted steel. The compartment was cramped and uncomfortable. He supported himself by pressing his palms on the wooden bench. Abruptly, the compartment jerked into motion. He realized it was a slightly modified version of the message cylinder or whatever in which he and Tomson had been shot out of the ship's bow. Ridge held on as the capsule sped through the bowels of the ship and slowly came to a halt. The door slid open, and he stepped into fresh, rainy night air. He stood in an ornate little hall that looked like an elevator lobby except he was looking at four little compartments in a row, one of which he'd just arrived in. Nice elevator system, he thought. He glanced over the directory of highlights in Largo, noting the location of the police station. It was called Largo Public Safety Office.

His next thought was of safety, and he listened for mudmen sounds, but heard none. His rifle and flame device were on the platform outside WorkPod01. He was unarmed and relatively helpless, wherever this was. He was intrigued by the attractiveness and elegance of his surroundings. They vaguely brought to mind the beautiful marbles inside the ship's nose. He walked out into a fancy sort of little railway station and saw a mosaic sign off to one side: Largo Railway Station. Then he remembered that he should try to reach Lantz or Brenna on his collar mike.

Just minutes later he stood on the rainy sidewalk outside, with Brenna in his arms. He marveled at her, at this little city, and then again at the feel of her in his arms. They kissed long and hard without exchanging explanations or excuses or reasons why or why not. Arm in arm, they strolled up the street. Along the way, he explained how Tomson had died, and she told him how Lantz had died. They came to a lovely hotel entrance, which said Hotel Largo, and she told him: "That's where we were when it happened."

Drawn by a mix of instincts, from morbid curiosity to wanting to know why, they walked into the hotel arm in arm. He let her lead him down a hall of plants and mirrors. She explained about the air getting sucked away and how that preserved everything. Sounded logical, he supposed. Having seen Tomson post mortem, he had no desire to see any more of their kind dead, but he felt it was sort of an obligation. He just wished he were writing their final stories in a notebook or recording it in a camera, for posterity, in case anyone cared. Then again, he and Brenna cared, and maybe that was all that really mattered.

Lantz still lay on the floor of the pool. "I guess," Brenna said, "it means the mudmen don't get in here too much."

"Are we going to just leave her there?" Ridge said as he weighed the pros and cons.

"We can deal with it in the morning," she said. "I want to lie beside you and...just not talk, not run, not be afraid, not feel all this loss."

"I understand," he said, and took her upstairs where they found a quiet little corner room and locked themselves safely in. There, they had a large bed to themselves and they made love while the rain tinkled on the windows above and the wind sighed outside the window and distant violin music drifted through the back courtyards, over the railways, over the fences, over the plate glass or whatever separated them from the whirling galaxy outside.

In the morning, Ridge set out by himself while she slept. It was always night in the city, and he wore a coat he'd found, with a high collar, and deep pockets to put his hands into. He walked several blocks until he came to a building whose green light over the entrance signaled that it was a police station. The sign read Largo Public Safety Office. Like most things in Largo, it was a small version of some larger place back on Old Earth. He pushed his way through the door as the air rushed in and the lights came on. He studied the directory inside, noting the little white bell buttons next to each resident. On the sixth floor was Venable. He pressed that button. "Yes?" came the familiar voice.

"I am here."

"Ah, yes?"

"Why did Tomson and now Lantz die the way they did?"

"Did you have a lovely night with your dear woman?"

"Yes. Not that it's any of your business."

"No, of course not."

"What's the score?"

"You are temps. You only live one day."

"I was afraid of that." Black panic rippled up and down his back, more than at any other time. It was one thing to be terrified of mudmen, thinking you could survive to live a normal human life span. How magnificent 75 or 85 years now seemed. Even ten years. One year. "Can we bargain?"

"I am not in a position to offer you anything. It cannot be changed. It is the way you were made. You and Brenna. Look in the mailbox."

With trembling fingers, he rifled down through the row of battered and rusty mailboxes, each of which had a unique little name tag. When he came to a white stencil that said Venable, he pulled open the little door. A white tissue lay inside. "Take that," Venable said. "If you find you are going first, give it to her. It will make her sleepy and she will go with you."

"Damn this whole operation," Ridge said as he pocketed the pills in their primitive tissue wrapper. He wondered how the packet had gotten there, then peered inside and saw the slot that undoubtedly led to some dispenser in the automated guts of this intricate city.

"You see how it is," Venable said sadly. "Wish I were going with you."

Ridge understood. Venable had years, maybe centuries, but he'd been created a freak more cruelly than anything the engineers and thinkers had done to the mudmen or to the temps. "How do we pull the plug?" he asked Venable wearily.

"I cannot answer. The phages won't let me."

"The what?"

"The phages. Things that eat things. They are in our bloodstreams. They eat poisons, even bad thoughts. Everything is chemistry, Ridge. I thought you understood that."

"If everything is chemistry, then it can be changed. You change the mix, you change the soup."

"I don't know, Ridge. The soup has been this way for centuries. Can you get me a body? I remember what it was like to be young and strong. You don't know that, do you?" His voice changed. It assumed an accent that Ridge needed a few minutes to place. Venable said: "You want to put crackers in the soup, buddy?" He laughed.

"You are crackers, you old hack. Who did this to you?"

"I volunteered. Someone had to take the hit. The other officers were already either dead or dying. When the comets ripped through, we caught a lot of radiation. They all stayed at their stations until the end."

"They are still sitting there waiting for the sun to rise."

"Yes," Venable said. "Waiting for New Earth. We'll never see it, you and I and Brenna. You two will mercifully long be gone, and my usefulness will end when the ship drops into orbit. Then Largo comes to life, and I go bye-bye."

"They could stick you in a new sack of bones."

"Can't be done. Memories that specific can't be cloned. Just generics, snatches, like stray bits of music heard through a window down the street on a rare and perfect spring day. Can't see the player, don't know the context. No beginning, no ending, just the middle. No donut, just the jelly at the center."

"What do I do?"

"Go back and play with her. Keep the pills in case you start going first. Enjoy every minute that you have."

Back at the hotel, Brenna was still asleep. Ridge crept naked into bed beside her and woke her with his passion. After they'd made love again, they lay together on the bed in a sea of green light and listened to music that Brenna chose from a radio on the nightstand. Ridge, for a joke, tried calling on the black telephone, but all he heard was static. They laughed as he hung up. She snuggled close to him, and he held her tightly. "Why do they have Largo?" she muttered into his chest hair.

"It's a city from Old Earth to keep in orbit around the New Earth," he told her. "It's sort of a training wheels place to teach them how to build cities when they find New Earth."

"Will they find New Earth soon?"

"I made a deal with Venable."

"You saw him?"

"Yes. He's not just another pretty face."

"He's not handsome like in the view screen images we saw?"

"You could say that. We're going to orbit a likely looking sun in about 100 years, and if that doesn't pan out then we'll probably hang it up for good."

"We won't be around then to find out."

"Probably not." He rose and went to the window. In this artificial city, it was night all the time on the street, but the biolumes above in the skylights kept a 24 hour cycle that mimicked day and night on Old Earth. "Do you feel rested?"

She yawned. "I could have used another hour or two of sleep."

He felt a distant weariness gathering in his bones. "What do you want to do today? Want to play, or work?"

"Do we have a choice?" She stretched and rolled luxuriantly on the bed. "Is some dreadful work detail going to take us back to those tunnels? I'm spoiled now. I never want to go back there."

"I think we've paid our dues," Ridge said. He sat on the bed beside her and stroked her back.

She closed her eyes and rested her head on her folded arms with a happy expression. "What if we stayed here, Ridge? What if we had a baby or two? Can we do that?"

Ridge felt a stab of hurt, knowing what she did not yet know. "I don't know that it's impossible. We wouldn't know unless we tried."

She turned onto her back suddenly and reached out for him. "Come here. Let's do that wonderful thing some more. We're on vacation." He grinned and crawled onto the bed. He could not get enough of her.

They spent some hours wandering through the city. They found a small carnival and he sipped hot coffee from a stand while she rode alone on a little child's ride of metal airplanes hanging from a revolving arm. As he watched her, he knew she would love more than anything to hold a child on her lap, to go around and around, up and down, gently, and to sing to that child as she had sung long ago to keep peace among her team members. He finished the rest of his coffee, balled up the paper cup, and tossed it into a trash incubator that was perfectly clean and empty, just waiting for the first bit of refuse from daily human life.

Arm in arm, they walked back to the hotel. Along the way, Ridge listened to her chatter and agreed with everything she said, but he kept desperately thinking there had to be some way. They got back to the room and lay on the bed listening to the rain outside. She lay on her back staring up into the skylight, where the light gathered like a waterfall of sunlight. She yawned deeply and turned onto her side, curling up. He covered her with a blanket and stroked her face with the backs of his fingers. She looked so young and pretty, and yet he saw age creeping up the sides of her neck, just the faintest of wrinkles, and she was starting to get hollows around her eyes. He sat up on the bed and fingered the pills, then slipped them back into his pocket for later.

Somewhere, a radio played. Ridge ignored it, while racking his mind, running over and over the events in WorkPod01. Was there some other clue, some other thing he'd missed?

The music began to get his attention. It was *tango*. Ridge recognized the *bandonéon*, an accordion-like instrument, and wondered why he knew that. He pictured a man and a woman moving across a smoky room. He pictured them coming to sudden stops, regarding each other, and then rolling back the other way on another round of life and love. That had been life on Old Earth. Here it was a one-way *tango*, this temp life on *Nebula Express*. Ah, such a bitter pill! No wonder *tango* was filled with melancholy yet passion. The impossible becomes the thing most desired. Love is the most impossible because it is the union of two who cannot ever be one, though they strive against all the laws of the universe. And so the next generation comes, the next *tango*, the next waltz across the floor.

Ridge half-rose in shock when he heard a man start to sing in a Flamenco-like wail. For the first time, a man's voice accompanied the dark and urgent rhythms of the dance. It was a man of Old Earth singing the *cançion* in a rich voice, in the criminal argot of the forbidden classes, *lunfardo*, and to his amazement Ridge understood who else spoke like that. Venable. Ridge went to the window, away from the bed where she might overhear, and spoke into his collar com. "Venable, I know you can hear me. This is Ridge. Ricardo, if you wish."

"I am busy listening to the *cançion*. Do you hear it?"

"I hear it, *compadrito*. Why did you not tell us about Ricardo?"

"She is my daughter, or what is left of her after the cleaners destroyed the dormitories where our people slept."

"Why did the cleaners do this?"

"Time went by. Too much time. There was genetic drift. We lost control of the programming."

"Life on the ship is evolving?" Ridge asked.

"Yes. It is gradually going beyond our control."

"And Ricardo?"

"You are Ricardo, or what is left of him, Ridge."

"That is why she and I had such empathy. You brought us together. Why?"

"I needed to know if memory could be passed on with the tools we have."

"Can it?"

"Not very well. But you did remember each other."

"So we were a start. After we are gone, will you try again?"

"Yes. As often as we must, until we can regain control of the genetic programming and take the ship back from the cleaners."

"That means more Ridges and more Brennas, Venable. More suffering. How can you do this?"

"No choice. You see now I suffer. My very existence is suffering. I am a disembodied soul."

"And the babies? You'll do that to her again? She has mourned for them constantly."

"She was not supposed to find out, so I told her they grew up to live their own lives."

"And that was a lie?"

"I said what was necessary to spare her the pain of knowing the truth. There were no babies. It was part of the pabulum the engineers and thinkers fed you all. You and she did not have long enough together. Just a few nights in the great apartment in the Avenida Boedo before the comets were spotted and we all got ready for this journey. You must not tell her. That would be a worse blow than losing them, never to have had them. She would die a thousand times rather than just once."

"So we were just an experiment," Ridge said bitterly.

"We are all just an experiment, Ridge."

"They made a monster when they made you."

"Think about the eternal rest that is about to come to you. You do not have much longer to suffer, either of you."

Chapter 16

Ridge walked out of the Hotel Largo and into the rain. The streets glistened with water and neon. Ridge's thoughts were saturated with water, which was the universal medium on *Nebula Express* as it had been on Earth.

The brain in Ridge that thought these things was mostly water, as was the man who walked down the street carrying that brain. Water coursed through the ship the way blood ran through the human body, and blood after all was nothing more than oxygen-red water with nutrients and biochemical nanomachines. Likewise, water poured from falls high up in the oxygen-rusty hull of the ship. Water ran through the tubes and pipettes keeping Venable alive, which in turn provided some feeble remaining guidance to the ship's systems. The mudmen inhabited a world of slag and rust soaked and heavy with water. The incubators in WorkPod01 (or WorkPodNN or whatever the iteration of the moment called itself) filled with water, which nurtured a fetus in its wet embrace, and as the temp-fetus grew, it absorbed its amniotic fluid and emerged dry and whole as a human being meant to live no more than one very long day. That human being carried in it all the water and nutrients it would need on its brief mission to add yet one more work-shift to the million work-shifts that would be needed to restore this ark that carried the entire human race in search of a new planetary water-world.

Ridge entered the police station and started rummaging in cabinets and drawers. Lights flicked on as he entered one room after another, and flickered out as he left. He heard the inrush of breathable air before him, and its outrush behind him as the ship sucked the air back into its main atmosphere.

Ridge found what he needed. In a locker he found a collection of matte black weapons and olive-drab military style nylon-weave web gear: belts, bandoliers, pouches, holsters. The equipment still smelled of the factory, preserved in generous amounts of petroleum-based Cosmolene-type preservative grease. He crisscrossed bandoliers of ammunition over his shoulders. He hung a heavy handgun in a holster under each arm. He picked up an assault needler that could fire a thousand tiny rounds of sparking wire that would enter a mudman body and twirl about with deadly randomness before losing momentum. He also slung a grenade launcher over his shoulder, and around his neck hung a fat bandolier with eight rocket-propelled miniature grenades the size and shape of typical dinner-table pepper shakers.

On his way back to the hotel, he had his hands in his pockets. His fingers encountered the small paper packet, and he threw it impulsively into the street. He glanced back and saw it soaking up water and ruining the pills inside that offered a Venable-style solution. Ridge marched all the more stubbornly, rejecting any solution that negated who he and she were...not he and she as generic experiments that could be rebirthed at will without regard for their humanity, but unique, one-time and never-again human beings like any others who had lived from generation to generation during the Holocene Era of Old Earth-the time between the Ice Ages and the departure of mankind to the stars.

As he entered the quiet, lovely atmosphere of the hotel, he held the assault rifle cautiously before him. He stared around corners and looked left and right down hallways before proceeding to the next room or the next level. He took the stairs rather than let himself be trapped in the elevator. If ever Venable needed to do away with him, it was now.

He walked through the steaming swim-room and noted that Lantz's body was no longer in the bottom of the pool. The cleaners must have seen to that during Largo's sleep cycle, when even he and Brenna had dozed. After all, in the final hours of a temp's day, the nutrients started wearing down and temps began to yawn and thinking about lying down to sleep. Temps began to dream about dreaming.

He found Brenna on the bed where he'd left her. She had turned onto her other side. A large stain of yellowish plasma water, inset with a thin puddle of blood, stained the sheet and the pillow on the side where she had been facing when he left. Now she faced the other way. He leaned lovingly over her and used the side of his sleeve to wipe flecks of blood from her lips and chin. "Brenna!"

She moaned in her sleep. Her eyes fluttered partially open. "So tired."

"I know, Brenna. We're going to take a little trip. Come along." He tried to help her up, but she flopped listlessly. He slung the needler over his shoulder so it dangled down his back. He picked her up and carried her on his arms. Her head cradled against his chest, and he kissed her rich umber hair. Her legs dangled to his left, and one arm hung straight down. He was too heavily burdened with the guns and ammo and Brenna to be able to shift her arm up onto her sleeping form.

He carried her down the stairs, through the lobby, and out into the street. The load was heavy, and he walked to one of the small cars by the curb. He slung Brenna over one shoulder and tried to pull the door open. It appeared to be locked. He kicked at the passenger side window, but it wouldn't break. Keeping Brenna over his shoulder, he recovered the assault gun from his back in a twirling motion that brought its barrel up, he stepped back and aimed from an angle to deflect the resulting energy. He fired several bursts. The window exploded in myriad tiny glass crumbles that fanned over the sidewalk in one direction and blew into the car in the other, which couldn't be helped. The glass was designed to shatter without being sharp. He opened the door and gently placed Brenna on the bed of torn upholstery and harmlessly piled glass crumbles. Then he got into the passenger side. There was no key, so he hotwired the electric connections underneath. It was just like driving any car on Old Earth, and he had memories of how to do that. He did a U-turn and drove down the street in a spray of rain. A large fishtail of water cut the moist air behind him as he raced along.

At the train station, he drove directly onto the sidewalk and braked with squealing tires directly before the steps. Wielding his gun and watching on all sides for cleaners, he walked around to the passenger side. He saw no evidence of mudmen or any other life form, but he wanted to take no chances. Carefully, gently, he lifted Brenna from the car. She moaned softly and put her arms around his shoulders. "It's going to be okay," he said, "we are halfway there." In response, she lost consciousness again. Her loose arm dangled once again, while the other was crushed against his stomach. He carried her through the echoing main hall and around to the elevator lobby in back, where he had arrived from WorkPod01.

He gently lowered Brenna onto the floor of the still-open pod in which he had arrived. He unloaded his heavy arsenal onto the floor around her. Keeping one handgun in his hand in case of ambush, he carefully backed into the pod. The rudimentary controls were simple, but he used voice commands. "Close," he said, and the door slid quietly shut.

"WorkPOd01," he said while trying to make her comfortable. He sat down on the rolled-up bandoliers and cradled her head in his lap. He stroked her hair. "Return," he said because the first command had not worked. He shouted: "Venable! I am the only hope for this ship!"

At that, the pod swept into motion, and for a second Ridge thought the Captain meant to dash him to his death. The Captain said nothing. The pod flew through hidden pneumatic shafts in the walls of the bow section and in the hull itself, and then wrenched to an over-torqued stop that pressed Ridge against the wall. He felt his body compress in multiple G-forces and held on to the bench behind him with both hands. Brenna's unconscious weight pressed against him and threatened to suffocate him, but the pod stopped and the deceleration G-forces ended as abruptly as they'd begun.

The door opened without a word from either Ridge or Venable, and Ridge stepped out into WorkPod01. Another team must have just left, because the incubators were newly horizontal and just half-way full of water. Ridge blocked the transit-pod door with his body and with the assault rifle as he lifted Brenna out. With Brenna slung over his shoulder, he pulled his weapons and ammo out. The door slid shut, sealing the transit pod.

Ridge carried Brenna to the incubator whose lid-markings bore the same designation as her jumpsuit collar. He was sure she had been born in this incubator. Ridge pulled at the lid but it wouldn't open. "Venable," he said in a warning voice.

No answer. He laid Brenna on the floor, picked up his assault rifle, and tapped repeatedly, sharply, against the side of the lid. Sweat poured down his face, and his stomach was in knots. "Venable, help me!" He bit his lip with concentration as he tapped again and again. Finally the seal popped with a sigh of wet air, and the lid unlocked. He raised it up. Stripping Brenna naked, he placed her gently in the still rushing, foaming fluid. He gave her one last hug, one last kiss, and she barely seemed to know who he was. He slammed the lid down and saw the seal reform. He looked for a second or two at her sleeping features as she sank into the engulfing waters. More water rushed in over her face, and bubbles floated across her features. She opened her eyes and mouth once-just for a second-in a horrified moment of realization that she was drowning-before she relaxed and sank down into the oxygen-rich liquid. Ridge gasped at his own recklessness. This immersion would either kill her, or save her life. There had been no alternative.

Angrily, he stormed to the wall where he knew the opening into the CP was. "Venable!" He banged on the wall. "Let me in!"

Silence.

Ridge picked up the grenade launcher. "Venable, I'm going to count to three. One way or another, I'm coming in there. I don't really care what happens to you, which is fine because you do not care what happens to me or her."

"You must not do this," came the feeble voice.

"There is no choice and no time." He stepped back as far as he could and released a round. The gun barked in his hand. The air between gun and wall flared in white light. The door blew out in a mass of twisted metal and plastics. All around the opening, tortured and damaged controls sparked. Of the door itself, little more remained than some fine black mesh that hung down as acrid smoke drifted away from the impact and was sucked up by air-conditioning vents.

"Please stop," Venable said.

Ridge climbed into the cramped little CP. As he did so, he laid the launcher down on the doorframe to make sure the ship could not somehow close him in.

"Ridge!" the face of Venable cried out from its tray of fluids. "Please, let's figure this out."

"Right," Ridge said. "Let's do it my way, shall we? We've been doing it your way." He reached behind the tray and yanked on the tubing there. Water splashed all around. Quickly, Ridge used his fingers to sort through the surprisingly flimsy plastic hoses bundled in padded harness-clips. The face in the tray drifted from side to side on wildly patterned ripples with an anguished impression. Ridge figured out which of the nutrient water hoses went to which incubator. Rummaging in drawers of spare parts that looked like the plastics kits at some neighborhood department store, particularly in the garden department, the section he remembered in which one found all the parts for a lawn sprinkler system. In hasty, bitter triumph, he held up a Y-joint with one hand and a can of purplish join-sealer with the other. He had to lean down with his teeth and rip the plastic of the hose going to Brenna's incubator. When that didn't work, he sawed frantically with a little file. The tray with Venable's face and organs in it shifted ever closer to the edge and looked ready to fall off. Venable's mouth moved in panicked gasps for oxygen or attempts to tell Ridge something, and his eyes were large, and finally his eyes started looking glazed and the mouth stopped moving. Ridge saw the edge of a wooden knife handle protruding from the bric-a-brac on the counter under the tray. In a single motion of his arm, he swept the tray away. The tray sailed through the air, twirling, losing its fluids. The tray bounced off wireframe shelving, twirled some more, and hit the wall. The tray bounced off. There was a large shiny wet spot on the wall, and a mass of grayish tissue and purple matter like kidneys dripping down the walls. Rolled up in a mass where it had slid down to come to rest in a dusty, dirty box full of screws and bits of wire and half-empty tubes of this and that was Venable's face, with one blank eyeball staring away at the wall.

Ridge used the newly found knife to sever hoses and hook up new connections. It was a desperate gamble, more likely to fail than succeed, but it was the only hope. Ridge could only pray now that the ship still had enough fuzzy logic or meme programming or fuzzy logic problem solving abilities to make the necessary adjustments after reading the new situation.

Multiple hoses, albeit smaller ones, had fed into Venable's tray and into canisters under the table where his nutrients had been mixed. Ridge disconnected that system and yoked the canisters into the system feeding Brenna's and one other receptacle. When it was all done, when the joints were sealed and the system was bubbling happily and there was nothing else he could think to do, Ridge wiped his hands on a rag and muttered to the ship in general and to Brenna in particular: "Now we'll see if we wake up at all, and if we remember who we were, or if we go to sleep and never wake up and eventually this whole rusting hulk goes sailing, baseball-heads and all, into some blazing sun somewhere that will never even notice that the entire human race just did its final fire dance."

So saying, Ridge went back outside to check briefly on Brenna. She seemed to be sleeping peacefully-or was she dead?-in her incubator awaiting the time a hundred or a thousand years from now when the ship went into orbit around a New Earth, and Largo woke up to a new dawn. Ridge went to his own incubator. Struggling for a few minutes, he managed to raise the lid. He took off his clothing and climbed inside. Water splashed around his naked body parts as he turned over onto his back. He lowered the lid down on himself and went to sleep amid the sweet soft white light and churning air bubbles that saturated the faintly pink broth in which he was about to steep himself.

Chapter 17

Ridge sat at the table in WorkPod01, eating cereal, and reading *The Odyssey* on a digitablet. As he read about the violent and gory battles on primordial Holocene Earth, he was rapt and lost in that world where wind keened through rolling grasslands and cattle lowed on distant hills while warriors clashed and died. He could almost hear the whinny of horses, the crackle of burning walls, the cries of wounded and dying men. A voice speaking nearby pulled him out of that reverie.

Venable, wearing an officer's black Class B jumpsuit, sat across the white tabletop from him. Venable folded his hands on the table. He was a handsome young man in his mid-30s, with dark brown hair cropped close, and dark blue eyes in a lightly tanned skin. "Can you feature all that?"

"What do you mean?" Ridge put a tongue depressor in the book as a mark, closed the book, and put the book on the shelf under the table.

"The sights and smells. Do you relate to them?"

As the two spoke, various crewmembers came and went between their moon doors and the common quarters such as bathrooms, showers, and weight room. They all looked vaguely familiar, though none were from the last iteration except one. There was no Tomson, no Lantz, no Mahaffey. He thought he did see Brenna beyond the rippled glass door of the shower area, combing her hair and singing to herself as she looked into a mirror surrounded by little round light bulbs. Again and again she ran the brush through her thick hair which was deep blood red like autumn leaves.

"It's as if I'm there," Ridge told Venable, thinking of the unpleasantness at Bronze Age Hissarlik.

"Excellent. The ship did a good job putting us together."

Ridge looked around. "This is a broth."

"Yes." Venable looked at him thoughtfully. The faint flicker of his eyes betrayed complex criss-cross considerations, not all happy ones.

"Are you part of this iteration?"

Venable shook his head. "I don't think so." He turned his head to look at, and guide Ridge's gaze to, the open door far off in a corner. Ridge looked at the door with the hint of jumble in the small room, and the yellowish light pouring out. "I go back there."

"I thought I pulled your hoses."

"You did. We're all part of the ship though. You knew that."

"Yes. I didn't mean to terminate you. I figured the ship would take care of you."

"It's not the ship so much," Venable said. "It's about the genetic broth, and the ship's mission. I just want you to understand."

"I understand, or maybe I don't. Why?"

Venable leaned forward. His collar was casually open, revealing stray comma-like hairs against dusky skin. "Ricardo had persuaded Brenna to leave her modeling job in New York City and move to Buenos Aires to marry him. They were happy together and she was pregnant when the comets appeared without warning, coming up at a near perpendicular angle to the solar system ecliptic."

"So there was at least one set of child genes," Ridge said. He lost interest in eating and pushed the cereal bowl aside. With one finger, he idly traced sharp jaggy figures in the bluish milk spilled on finely rippled white plastic. Little bits of soggy cereal were stuck in there; *good detail,* he thought, *nicely done, ship.*

Venable continued: "The angry one was Venable, who had loved Brenna from the first and was determined to steal her from Ridge. The old *gaucho,* Caulfield--"

"Uncle to both Ricardo and Venable," Ridge offered.

"-Exactly. Caulfield owned significant portions of the global economy, including trade, hospitals, blood banks, and shipping, just for example. Caulfield had one huge ship plying the planetary trade run. In fact, Caulfield had a monopoly on the Neptune run. His ship was just arriving in orbit of L5 near Luna when word of the comet swarm first made the news. It was academic that Caulfield would refit *Neptune Express* for a desperate gamble to take a few thousand colonists to the stars. With enough genetic material in racks to furnish unique DNA for a million persons, and the finest wetware including AI, wormware, you name it, Caulfield was the only one who could get a ship ready. With no habitable worlds in the solar system to make a new home, mankind needed to break out into the Milky Way."

"Yes," Ridge said, "and the new ship, *Nebula Express*, set off on a course running counter to the stellar vortex of our galaxy, thereby multiplying her effective speed in searching for the best new world. Have we found it yet?"

"Yes," Venable said. He sat back with his hands in his pockets and looked at Ridge with his chin resting in the deceptive informality of his open collar. "We make orbit in another fifty years, and at that point Venable will be the master of the ship, and Brenna will be at his side. There will be no place for Ridge in that scenario."

"You are telling me this--why?"

Venable grinned and folded his hands between his knees. He leaned over his knees as if he held the secret of fire between them. "I want Ridge to know he lost."

Ridge nodded. "I see. The victory is no good unless the loser knows he is getting creamed. Sort of like Achilles slicing Hector up with his sword."

Brenna came walking out. "Ridge, I thought we were waiting for Largo to come to life." She looked ravishing in her pink slip. Her figure moved like shadowy music against the back-glow of light from the shower. She was still pulling the brush through her hair, and smelled like damp flowers from her morning shower. "Why are we back in this workpod?"

Ridge shrugged. Venable had left, disappeared, gone back into his room, whatever-that distant corner door was closed. "The ship wants to dump our genes, I think. The ship wants to flush us out. I'm supposed to get terminally wiped on this iteration. I don't know what they have in mind for you." A horrible suspicion dawned on him, and he did not want to scare her with it.

She sat down where Venable had just sat. "Darn this hair," she said making a pained face as she pulled on the brush and it only inched through her hair without coming out. "I'd give anything for a decent wash and perm on uptown Santa Fe or Campos."

"I'm sure we will find a decent hairdresser on Largo," Ridge said. "Why don't you go in your cube and lock yourself in? You'll be safe there. Maybe you can skip going out on the job."

"Oh no," she said, "they won't let anyone stay. You know the workpod gets locked up tight as a drum. Now we know why."

Other team members were starting to appear, buttoning uniforms and adjusting hats or carrying web gear in preparation for the day's work. Already, a red light flashed its silent alarm. An image appeared on the view screen near the portal, and the team leader appeared beside it. It was a young, earnest man with short blond hair and sincere Boy Scout eyes. "He knows nothing," Brenna said.

Ridge examined the young leader and the others. "None of them do. Maybe they have a few molecules of Lantz or Mahaffey or Tomson, but they are unique."

She sat holding her brush tightly in her hands on the table, shoulders squeezed narrowly together with the tension of her thoughts. "Each a unique life, engineered to be disposed like a lab rat after 30, 40, 50 hours."

Ridge put a hand over her two hands and brush. "We have to focus. We can't do anything for these people, but we might be able to stop Venable once and for all. I think he's called me out for battle."

"Oh darling," she said with tears in her eyes. She pulled her hands out and caressed his hands in hers. "Please be careful."

"Ready?" said the young leader. Team members crowded around. They looked relaxed, self-assured, courageous.

Captain Venable's image smiled and spoke in the view screen as before. "You have an important mission. A stray space object has hit the ship, and there is considerable damage. Yesterday's workpod team managed to get an important milestone under control, and you can bring us a step closer to ultimate success today."

Ridge whispered to Brenna: "Just another load of food for the mudmen. Watch your step." Brenna put her arm around his back. Her hand squeezed his side with near-painful force, in silent agreement.

"Thank you and God speed!" said Venable with that wide, pleasant grin. The view screen went blank. The light atop the portal winked red-red-red-red...

No bleeding man pounding on the window this time, Ridge thought. Not even a warning for this crew. Venable has made sure of that.

A man and woman with hand-held electronic box controls pushed the sliding doors apart. The work crew walked out onto the platform. The young leader signaled, and the man and woman walked the door shut. As the door slipped closed, and sealed itself with a click and a sigh, the red light stopped winking. A green light started winking in its place. "We are on our way," the young man said proudly. "Let's see what we can do to make the Corporation feel we earn our pay." He raised one arm and signaled to the woman at the controls: "Start us rolling."

Ridge and Brenna both tensed as they noticed what none of the others had any reason to be suspicious of. In the darkness, just beyond the circle of light shining on wet, drippy surfaces, faint red dots moved. Barely visible smudges of gray light-mudmen heads-moved this way and that. Now they heard the first of those low fluting sounds. One mudman uttered a long, soft breath, and another elsewhere replied in the same wistful, melancholy timber.

As the platform gave its first little jerk, and the bicycle chain stretched between pulleys started a greasy rattle, Ridge heard a series of clicking sounds he recognized from some past life. "Down!" he said, and pushed Brenna onto the platform. She did not fight him, but buckled at the knees and fell onto her palms with her terrified face to one side on the dirty steel grating. He threw himself over her, just as the first bullet started to strike the team members clustered helplessly and naively on the platform. Several powerful machine guns opened up, and bullets spattered and ricocheted off the steel walls. White cobwebs marked smashed spots on the heavy windows above, though for the moment the windows and the walls appeared to be holding. The six other work team members did not remain standing long. In seconds their riddled, bleeding bodies lay sprawled in a heap on the grating. Ridge closed his eyes and held Brenna tightly. He could feel the dead bodies around him bucking as more bullets struck them. Ridge did not feel any pain or numbness or ripping impact that suggested he'd been hit. He pressed his face close to Brenna's and felt her regular though terrified breathing. The firing stopped.

"Oh God," Brenna whispered as a pale shadow flitted beneath the platform on the curving, bumpy, wet inside of the hull.

"We've got to run for it," Ridge said. "On my signal, go." He waited for a moment, gathering his energy and staring through the holes in the grating for the best direction to take.

Already, the platform rocked once, twice, three times and more, as mudmen dropped down to finish off the kill. He could smell their mushroom, earthy sweat. He heard the chorus of satisfied breaths as they contemplated how full their stomachs would soon be.

Hearing the first rip of claws through cloth, Ridge wrapped his arm around Brenna. Together, they rolled once, twice, and fell off the platform. He grasped a vertical stanchion as they dropped. He broke their fall and caused them to swing like a pendulum away from the platform first outward then toward the hull. They let go and fell, crashing in a daze, rolled down heaps of sliding slag, and ended up in a soft mound of black stuff like coal dust about 100 feet below. On the platform, mudmen chorused greedily and appeared not to notice.

Ridge and Brenna ran as best they could. They held hands and alternately fell, clambered, and slid on the slippery mass. They could hear the piles of slag groaning softly as the ship turned. Much of the ship's cargo structure had apparently been shattered and then had spent centuries rusting. The ship turned like the body of a concrete mixer, and piles of rusty debris made grinding noises as they slipped along the inner surface an inch at a time.

"There!" Brenna said. She pointed upward. Ridge saw the platform slowly following them. From it hung the arms and torsos of dead team members, and the shadowy bodies of mudmen were hard at work with slashing claws and bloody chewing mouths. Along the forward railing were several figures with machineguns. Ridge exclaimed as he recognized what was at work there. The mudmen-like figures wore black jumpsuits and masks. The masks were tied behind the head with soiled linen ties, like surgical masks, and the faces were all identical: Venable's luminously greedy face and crazed eyes. "Those are a cut above your ordinary mudmen," he told Brenna. "Venable had the ship make those, using uniforms from the officers I saw in the CP that time. They are all mummies, but the ship has their memory soup. Apparently Venable has enough control to be able to tap into the heart of the ship and make it do whatever he wants."

Several weak brownish spotlights now shone down on Ridge and Brenna from the platform. They heard a voice, Venable's. He sounded angry and desperate. "Brenna! You weren't supposed to be on this iteration. Come, and I'll save you!"

Brenna hugged Ridge's arm with both of hers, and pressed against him. "I wanted to come with you. I waited until he was gone, and then I came out of the shower room. I don't ever want to leave you. I love you."

"I love you and that's how it will always be," Ridge said. He squeezed her, then let her go again, just holding her hand. He looked up at the platform. The speaker was one of the black-suited mudmen. The others carried machineguns, but this one did not. Instead, the lead Venable-clone did not even have hands, but instead had twisted bunches of white tubing about a foot long that wiggled like nests of pale snakes when he raised his arms. "Must be something that grew like a tumor on those tubing connections I whipped together," Ridge told Brenna, meaning the speaker above in his entirety. "Somehow, the seams must have leaked and cells got out there, and gene code, and that thing grew slowly over the years. It formed the other mudmen in its image."

"That means Venable creates the mudmen," Brenna said.

"Brenna!" Venable cried in a wailing voice that drifted over the wet slag heaps in that bronzed, doom-ridden light.

Ridge pulled Brenna along all the more forcefully. The platform above made greasy rattling noises as its pulleys turned and the chain propelled it along after them. "What do we do?" Brenna asked as they ran on strong new legs, with fresh lungs and factory-fresh bodies.

"We have to get to Largo," Ridge said. "It's the only place we might be safe." He thought of the police station there, and what was left of its armaments. "We might stand a chance at holding them off."

"And then? We spend our last hours in a hotel room, afraid they'll come bursting in on us?"

Ridge could not answer. He merely pulled her along, and she readily came, holding his hand. Even now, they could not see the lights yet of the nose area, nor the glow of that trolley station into which the platform must inevitably travel. "Let me think a bit."

More machinegun fire punctuated the air. The echoes were deafening. Rusty water splashed up, as did stinging particles. Ridge and Brenna ducked left and right.

"There is the bow section," Brenna said pointing at dim coppery light ahead.

"They're desperate now," Ridge said. One by one, he saw the Venable clones drop down from the platform with their machineguns and clamber down the slag heaps. He said: "They can't catch us quite so easily once we're in the labyrinth of the bow area with all those levels and rooms."

"But it's infested with regular baseball-heads," she said.

They reached the base of the wall separating the bow from the cargo holds. The wall was of riveted steel. It had many odd sections welded on top of one another-circles, squares, oblongs, triangles. Some looked like doors with barlike handles and locks. Steel ladders stretched precipitously up the wall. Here and there glowed indirect light from lanterns hooded by weeping reddish iron casques aimed inward toward the wall. Ridge and Brenna started climbing without a clear goal-anything to escape for yet another minute or another half hour of life.

The Venable clones were running across the dark hills, firing their machineguns. Ridge winced several times as the metal surface near his head rang with an impact. Once or twice, dust kicked up and stung his face. "You okay?" he asked. She replied from directly under him: "So far, so good."

He found a handrail and pulled himself up on a narrow ledge. He leaned down to pull her up. They were dizzyingly high, at least 100 meters. "I see a doorway!" she cried. At that moment, more weak spotlights cut in. Light roved over the tramp-steamer surfaces around them. Shots popped far below, and bullets whizzed and twanged through the air by their heads. The platform blocked most of the shooting. Ridge glanced down and saw small figures climbing while others watched. "I think they may be afraid to climb."

Brenna ran forward and pushed a door open. "We're in!" He followed her into a dimly lit room full of huge pipes and sighing steam. "Some sort of boiler room, maybe for the climate control," she guessed. They clambered among shadows, across girders, and up higher into more shadows. The place smelled of oil and steam, of coal and dead rats, of decay and flowering mushrooms.

They climbed through a less unpleasant warren of dry concrete pens that smelled of potatoes or rags or soured wax. The wan light here came from metal-covered biolumes shaped like eggs. They emerged into a marbled corridor that smelled of fresh wax and glowed with indirect lighting from gilded wall sconces. Nougat-creamy gargoyles and *putti* and lightly draped nymphs floated in the shadows under the ceiling amid Art Nouveau stained glass *oculi* and long, narrow windows. The walls themselves were of fine dark woods. Statues of mythological men and women stood frozen in alcoves. The statues were draped in flowing garments that exposed rippling muscle (the men) or smooth skin (the women) and bore Homeric helmets pushed back over elaborate hair tumbling from under ribbon-ties. "It's a museum," Brenna said. "I remember some of these statues from my childhood. We lived in Buenos Aires and my parents used to visit your parents at the Palacio Colfiriano."

"That's right!" Ridge said. The memories, once a small trickle came loose like wheat in sacks, grew into floods. "Colfirio was my uncle. He adopted both me and Venable, cousins to one another, after our families died in a plane crash. It was a ski trip in the Italian Alps."

Now the paintings, all around as they ran down the corridors, made sense. Some canvases stretched from floor to ceiling. One showed Napoleon on a horse, leading a charge as thousands of heroic Guards overcame impossible odds during the early glory years when the world trembled in the Napoleonic wars.

A sound traveled over the marbled floors: fluting. The mudmen were close! Ridge and Brenna came to a lobby of gilt panels and dimly silvery mirrors. They saw a bank of elevators and pressed all the buttons. "They are closing in on us!" Brenna cried as the fluting tones trembled in the air around them on all sides.

"They are surrounding us," Ridge said. "Seems to be their style. Surround and devour." The doors rumbled open, and they ducked quickly inside a carpeted elevator car. Its gleaming brass doors slid smoothly shut. At the last moment, something slammed against the outer wooden door in the lobby, a mudman claw probably, but they were safe for the moment and on their way up. Ridge remembered the buttons and pressed the one for the executive boardroom at the very nose.

For a moment, they thought they were safe. Brenna looked up and wrinkled her nose. "I smell mushrooms and soil and worms wiggling under damp rocks."

"Mudmen," Ridge said. "They will be waiting for us up there." He pressed the red Stop button. The elevator ground to a halt and hung swaying. Now they heard the frustrated, disappointed wind of the mudmen. They heard the rasp of eager chitinous claws on soft marble. It was a sound that traveled up and down the spine like chalk on a blackboard. Ridge shivered involuntarily and held his palms over his ears. What to do? They were stuck between floors.

"We cannot afford to stay in any one place," Brenna said.

"I know. Let's try this." Ridge stood on a brass rail separating top and bottom of the interior décor. He pushed away the ceiling panel designed for workmen, and pulled himself up. His head emerged in elevator shaft, which appeared to be made of steel beams held together in crisscross patterns by huge bolts. "Wow," he said as his eyes became accustomed to the weak amber light. Brenna clambered up and they both stood on the roof of the elevator beside a bluish greasy coil of cabling around a pulley. Thick cables above and below apparently connected the car to opposite ends of the shaft, in the oddly adapted artificial gravity.

"We are in the structural guts of the bow section," he said.

She added, "this must be how the whole ship looked before the space debris took out the central cargo areas."

The former *Neptune Express*, now called the *Nebula Express*, consisted of a slightly ovoid cylinder with blunted pointy ends. The insides got their structural integrity from a crisscross of riveted steel, like the guts of some spaceborne Eiffel Tower. Now that they were in the heart of the bow section, they saw that everything else was bolted on to that inner structural steel. The floors themselves were steel boxes stacked on top of each other like in a child's toy construction set, for all that the boxes contained all the world's surviving treasures of marble and gold and all sorts of precious materials. It was a giant steel construction set whose cubes, boxes, domes, spheres, pyramids, and polyhedrons contained the history of mankind. Inside were stored the accumulated remnants of Colfirio's avid lifetime collecting: friezes of Mesopotamian kinds hunting lions from chariots; pharaohs wearing the combined crowns of Upper and Lower Egypt; Roman wall paintings from the House of the Mysteries in Pompeii; Chinese vases and Japanese prints; African ceremonial masks; Inca mummies and Aztec gold; greenish-pink Mogul inlays and Hindu elephant gods sitting among Buddha statues; combined warrior and priestly vestments of Crusader priests complete with chain mail and swords; a thousand artifacts, a million texts and images, all stored in this construction resembling Victorian ironware department stores.

"Mudmen," Brenna said, pointing to the mounds and piles of dead husks all around. Ridge nodded. "They breed like moths, apparently, like insects, from larvae. This looks like one enormous hive."

"That means there is a queen somewhere," she said. They walked cautiously among the piled bundles that looked just big enough for each to hatch one mudman. Most had torn sides, where the newly hatched cleaners had chewed their way out. "Cleaners, Venable called them." Ridge scoffed. "It's a long way from creating drones to keep the ship clean, to their getting out of control and evolving into clawed killers."

They saw some larvae with cottony surfaces under which infant mudmen slept. Their eyes were closed in mudmen dreams, and their claws were open and defenseless over their faces. Soon enough, they would emerge from their cocoons as full-sized adult mudmen ready to hunt and kill, to remove corpses from hotel swimming pools, to polish marble corridors until they gleamed, and to eat anything that moved.

Ridge and Brenna found a small door, a small passageway, and crawled through it into a service elevator. They rode this grim, hard metal box upward as far as it would go. The ride ended in a gleaming gallery of blue and white tiled kitchens, whose walls were narrow all around, giving a familiar claustrophobic impression. "The executive suites must be right above us," Brenna whispered. Ridge nodded and held a finger over his lips for her to be quiet. They listened for mudmen songs, but heard only the faint whisper of climate control ducts, and air in elevator shafts. They wandered hand-in-hand through the kitchens, which looked as though crews could come in and start cooking at any moment. By now, Ridge knew who kept everything so sparkling clean. He and Brenna walked through one galley after another. A bar cabinet was stocked with gleaming bottles of white and brown liquors as well as red and yellow wines. The wines had spoiled, Ridge was sure, but the liquor looked pristine. Pots and pans hung from the ceilings. Dishes and cutlery stood at attention in plastic trays. Carving knives, prongs, and soup spoons sat in crocks. Ladles of all sizes and shapes hung among the pots overhead. Rows of mugs hung from hooks. There were tiny points of dissonance, if one looked closely: moths flew in and out of drain pipes in stainless steel sinks that had not seen flowing water in centuries. Refrigerators stood a quarter inch open because their rubber seals had disintegrated and made a pile of gray dust on the floor. Pretty soon, Brenna and Ridge had completed a circle around the entire deck. There wasn't a view screen or porthole anywhere (or what passed for a porthole; likely a viewing surface that transmitted images from outside the hull as if there were a window).

"Look here," Brenna said, pointing to a small ladder leading up to a trapdoor. She said: "Looks like there might have been a way to pass trays of food up that way."

Ridge climbed up the ladder and shook the door. It wouldn't budge. There was a complicated lever with sliding arms, and he pushed that aside. He felt the door pop loose a millimeter or two. He caught a glimpse of the lobby where they had once stood speaking with an image of Venable over the secretarial desk. "We could go up another level," he said. "We want to get to that executive level and see if we can negotiate with Venable, maybe. What else can we do?"

Brenna frowned as she looked up. "Ridge?"

He looked down. "Yes?" As he did so, he saw the growing horror on her face. She started to say: "Mudmen" and at that moment Ridge saw the claw coming through the door. Each of the mudman's hands had one large claw and three small ones in opposition, like a thumb and three fingers. A head like a button mushroom with stitches around the sides, and slitty eyes looked down in mudman glee as it reached out for him. Its claw raked Ridged over the head before he grabbed the arm and twisted. The thing rounded its mouth and wheezed a horrid squeal that started as glee and ended in pain. More mudmen piled on top of it. Ridge punched upward several times, caving its face in while he twisted its arm until the arm came off in his hand with a sour honk of twisting innards and torn mushroom bone. The thing lashed out with its other hand and cut Ridge across the forehead. Ridge ignored the blinding pain and the blood running over his face. He reached up with both hands and hung from the lever. The first mudman died as he crushed it with the door, plus the others were stupidly putting their weight down rather than pulling up. During that moment of mindlessness, Brenna climbed up along Ridge wielding a large kitchen butcher knife and started carving at the mudman. First she sawed off its head, which fell down and spattered on the floor. As sickly, yolky yellow fluid drooled down out of the neck cavity mixed with greenish blood, she carved some more. She carved off its shoulders one by one and they fell on the floor exposing papery muscles and exposed ribs that were a poor genetic imitation of heavier, sturdier human ribs. The mudmen appeared to be quickly, cheaply manufactured (or hatched) life forms of limited usefulness and lifespan. In a way, it was another triumph of Venable cynicism, Ridge thought as he staggered back. Brenna finished sawing the mudman cadaver in half at the waist, and took Ridge's place hanging on the door. Ridge stepped back blindly and fell on the floor. "I've slammed it shut!" she said. She groaned with effort. He heard a click. "I've got it locked."

"Quick," he said, lying on the soft rubbery floor but propping himself up. "Get me a towel, anything to stanch the blood and clear my eyes so we can get going."

She found a box full of sealed packets with wet first-aid wipes and brought that to him. They tore open all the packets and got the blood flow stanched. The wipes had that sharp stinging smell of isopropyl alcohol, and he hoped they would help kill the germs in his wound. She found an old shirt somewhere and brought it to him. She tore it in strips and tied them around his head. His forehead burned and throbbed, and his head hurt a little. He hoped there wasn't some mudmen poison in those claws. He recalled old school warnings about mushrooms and hoped they didn't have some deadly poison that would kill him as he walked. So far so good, he thought as she helped him up and they hurried back the way they'd come.

Three hooting tones sounded all at once in the next room. Brenna and Ridge jumped back as they caught just a glimpse around the corner of three mudmen rising up through the shaft they'd come from. That way was now blocked. "They've got us surrounded," he said. "What to do?"

They looked around, rifling through cabinets, and Brenna found it first: a row of gas canisters lined up in a cabinet under a sort of barbecue stove. Each canister was about the size of a gallon milk bottle and had a fitting that allowed it to be screwed into the receptacle in the stove from which gas was drawn off to burn under food. The lighter lay on the tile counter, and Ridge grabbed it. Brenna handed him a bottle. It wasn't mean to go this way, but he'd have to improvise. He reached over and tore one of her sleeves off. He wrapped the sleeve around the brass fitting. He opened the liquor cabinet, took down a bottle of rum, and smashed its neck off in a sink. With several abortive snaps of the lighter, he managed to get the contraption blazing. Behind him, Brenna tore off her other sleeve and manufactured a similar bomb. Ridge stepped into the doorway of the room where by now a half dozen mudmen were milling around hooting and breathing at each other-apparently they worked in a collective thinking mode, not being very bright individually but being rather fiendishly effective collectively. Ridge was in luck. A second or two later-the mudmen had just begun to turn and raise their clawed hands toward him-the silica based rubber petcock melted off the bottle, and a thick continuous flame gushed out. The flame was a meter long and half was wide in diameter. It was reddish and bluish but white toward the origin, and caused mudman flesh to shrivel. The place filled with a stink like singed plastic, and a sooty, greasy black smoke drifted about. The mudmen shrieked and tried to run, but their fellows blocked the way. A half dozen became quickly incapacitated. Brenna handed him a new bottle as the old one petered out. He rolled the dying bottle across the floor into the crowd, and the surviving mudmen dove back down the hole. Brenna walked about with a meat cleaver, chopping up the remaining mudmen, some of whom still reached up with wide reddish eyes and pleading round mouths-more from hunger than from a dull realization they were in pain and dying. The last mudman down the hole pulled the door shut, and Ridge obliged by standing on the trapdoor.

"This won't do," Brenna said.

"I know," he said. "I have an idea."

"Me too." Together, they gathered all the bottles of liquor. They stacked up the gas bottles, wrapped them in odds and ends of cloth, and soaked them with rum or vodka. Ridge lit the first bottle and stood prepared as he signaled Brenna to pull on the door. As the bottle caught fire with a loud *whoosh*, he nodded to Brenna. She pulled open the door. A number of mudmen, having already forgotten their dreadful lesson, hovered below with round mouths and beseeching eyes and gripping claws reaching up for human flesh. Ridge doused them in flames and they melted back-literally-shriveling in a lot as they fell back. Brenna lit a bottle on fire and dropped it down the hole. It exploded in a ball of flame as the bottle shattered below. This gave them the idea to advance on their enemies, and they descended into the hole throwing more bottles and shooting more gas until the heat and smoke were so bad they had to climb back into the galley and close the door. They could hear alarms going off as the ship realized it was on fire internally. Ridge was so flushed with combat and anger that he didn't care if the ship exploded in space and if he and Brenna and the rest of the human race died at that moment, just so long as these genetic monsters were destroyed.

Klaxons blared, sirens shrilled, alarms warbled. The noise was deafening. The kitchens began to fill with smoke, and when he saw Brenna double over, coughing and choking, Ridge knew they could not survive here in the burning hell they themselves had created. He signaled to Brenna and climbed back up the ladder. They worked in unison, using up the last of the alcohol and gas bottles. She pushed open the trap door in the ceiling, and as mudmen claws streaked down, he turned a withering gas fire on them. The arms shriveled and dropped off. A mudman reared up on fire and staggered away. Its upper body fell off and the lower torso walked another few steps before falling down. Ridge and Brenna forced their way up into the executive lobby. There, they killed another half dozen mudmen before the smoke started to thicken. It was a race for time between the growing smoke and the hard-working exhausts in the climate control system. Decorative plates and collars fell from the ducting, exposing raw silvery accordion ducts that trembled from the maximal exertions of the engines trying to clear smoke out. The system had been designed centuries ago to handle some pretty devastating fires, but the machinery and the material were old and on the verge of failing. "Down!" Ridge yelled. He and Brenna threw themselves on the carpet amid burning pieces of mudmen bodies and embers glowing in the rug fibers. Lying down might buy them another minute or two of life before the smoke overwhelmed them.

Flames licked up as the secretary desk began to burn. The seat behind it smoked thickly. The noise continued unabated, and Ridge noticed that sprinklers had finally begun to weakly start twirling out water once they pushed through all the accumulated moths' nests and other debris in the pipes.

A change seemed to go through the ship, and Ridge wondered if it was about to blow up. That would be the final and irrevocable end of everything, he thought, as he crawled close to Brenna and put his arms around her. She choked and coughed and pressed her face against his chest. He held her closely and stroked her thick hair, thinking this would be as good a way as any, to go together, if go they must.

The lights went out, and the ship shuddered. Then an emergency light came on, and another. The klaxons fell silent, as did the rest of the noise. The ship was at its utmost limit, and conserving power as it struggled to stay alive. If the hull were compromised-if the air and water it had hoarded all along escaped-then the ship would have no way to repair its precious life content. Systems would shut down, and she would become a drifting hulk, a cold cinder, a shattered shell drifting among the galaxies for the rest of time. How many such hulks from how many lost civilizations were even now floating on the luminous tendrils of alien nebulas? So Ridge wondered as he pushed the cloth up out of his eyes, and brushed his blood away with grime-blackened fingers. Brenna's face was pale and composed as she lay in his lap, with her lips turning blue and her eyes gaining shadows as when a brightly orbiting satellite disappears around the cusp of a planet and enters the nightside where sunlight is no more than a weakly reflected silver dream. So he thought as his own eyes started to close.

Even at that moment, he looked up and saw that with the ship's systems failing, the doors to the inner sanctum in the nose of the ship had slipped open. In the dim light of the emergency apparatus, he glimpsed the inside of that room whose ceiling was the small dome inside the very bullet-nose of the entire ship itself. He saw in there a great coffin, like that of a pharaoh or some Maya king buried in jade and gold. The coffin was of a reddish stone with creamy yellow veins. It had a thick glass lid, and through the lid he saw the sleeping face of the *caudillo* himself--Armando Cleator de Colfirio, the billionaire who had built *Nebula Express* out of a planetary cargo vessel during a final frantic year of preparations.

Wrapped around the coffin was a huge mass of mudman material like a tide flowing down from a mountain. Snuggled in the top of the dome itself was a face of sorts, with many slitted eyes that now opened to look down in baleful reddish hate and rage. The Queen, whom Venable had inadvertently created when twisting the genes of the cleaner humanoids to serve his selfish ends. Embedded in her grasp was Venable himself, looking helpless and melancholy. When Venable saw Ridge, Venable's face assumed a mix of fear and fatalistic expectation. His eyes spoke of the colossal evil he had created, in whose lap he now lay as it manipulated him in order to control the entire ship. Apparently, the *caudillo* had succeeded in immuring himself so tightly and thoroughly, probably with redundant and independent support systems, that the Queen had not managed yet to terminate his incubation.

Ridge staggered to his feet. He heard the Queen blow like a ship in her harbor, a thousand mudmen mouths strong. She bellowed defiance and loathing as Ridge staggered into the inner sanctum, the workpod that kept the pharaoh in wait until his afterlife. Ridge lit a pair of canisters and walked in with a flaming ball in each hand. The Queen screamed as he tossed first one, then the other. As he did so, he glimpsed the mechanism by which the mudmen were created. Her great hulk contained a thousand little orifices, which had been closed, but which now fell open as the flames began to kill her. She sweated yellow and bloody fluids, groaning loudly, and from her orifices popped a mass of slithering black things resembling eels. As these things slid out of their holes and wiggled down the slopes of her body, they contacted the air and puffed out into cottony larvae. Still wiggling, they crept away from her body and entered holes in the floor-which had probably been designed long ago with cabling and conduit in mind but had now assumed a biological function. Ridge understood: they dropped down into the hollow spaces in the ship's nose, between floors, where they attached themselves to the steel girders and grew until a mudman ate its way out and commenced its simple life of cleaning and killing, which after all were the same thing in a mudman's feeble and programmed brain.

Venable looked toward Ridge with enormous longing in his eyes, trapped as he was in the webbing of the Queen's cobwebs and pupa weavings. Ridge understood in that moment that Venable had only one thought, and that was: I have lost. I did not win over you, and Brenna remained yours to the end. Emanating a look that said those things, Venable blackened, shriveled, and doubled up on himself. His hands rose up toward his head, and he seemed to tilt his head into his hands, and his sizzling brain fell out even as the entire blackening mass contracted into a shapeless oblong of charred and oily flesh. A white coating of ashes formed, hiding the thing that had been Venable, and in that moment the ship shuddered again. The ship seemed to relax a bit and die just a little bit more.

Ridge fell down and flickered in and out of consciousness. Wondering where Brenna was-hoping to have one last glimpse of her before he died-he raised himself effortfully on his elbows and coughed. He thought he spied her lifeless figure lying several meters away in the center of the reception area.

Flames licked up and the Queen fell silent. The last of her eels fell down and wriggled on the floor, burning to death. The caudillo remained in his coffin, seemingly unscathed. His pale skin and sharp nose glowed red in the firelight, and his white hair looked almost transparent.

A voice spoke, in Argentine-accented English: "Thank you, Ricardo. You and Brenna have done well in ridding us of this monstrosity."

Ridge was on the verge of fading away, when he felt a cool breath of air. Was this death? Was he falling into a pond of fresh cool water where all this grime and pain would be washed away? Was this some peaceful garden where one could lie comfortably and smell blossoms in the night as white nymphs came this way, slipping gossamer garments off pale shoulders even as their feet stepped into a silky pools of water?

"Breathe," said a voice. Ridge recognized the long-ago voice of Colfirio. It was a strong, determined male voice, aging and racked with cigar smoker's debilitations, but still in charge as always.

Several masked faces looked down, and Ridge smelled mushrooms. He was too weak to care, too weak to be afraid for himself. *Brenna?*

"She has a pulse. We can bring her back." It was the voice of the sleeping *caudillo*. Colfirio, or the ship, or both said: "Thank you, Ridge. I am in control again, for the first time since Venable's coup as we passed through the Oort Cloud. Yes, it has been over two thousand years, and we have suffered much, but we are in what you Yanks call the home stretch. Trust me. You will see." With that, the voice in the walls trailed off. The caudillo had said all he needed to, and he was never a man to spend an excess *austral* or an excess *antipodo* or a word too many.

Mudmen wearing the uniforms of ships' officers lifted Ridge. Each of them wore a mask, only now the masks were cloth images of Colfirio. Ridge thought he recognized the uniforms he'd seen on the mummies in the CP. They had that same mushroom odor. They were the genetic ghosts of men long dead, whose courage had kept them at their instrument panels even as they died. They were the essence of men whose memories lingered in the ship's communal database, and now that Venable's corrupt touch was off the hapless cleaners, the mudmen had one last task to perform before breathing their last flute tones. Wearing the uniforms of the mummified officers, they brought oxygen to Ridge and Brenna. Ridge hoped for the best but was resigned to the worst. He hoped if he and Brenna must die that she would go easily and comfortably. In the long, lingering dream that followed, the officers carried Ridge and Brenna back to WorkPod01 and hooked them up to the newly cleansed incubators there. Gone were the temps who came forth about once a week to be little more than food for Venable's mushroom slaves. Gone were the memories of those brief but precious lives.

The officers carried Ridge through the control room and hooked him up to the same special receptacles that held their own DNA and memory broths.

Ridge lay immobile on an improvised bed-an officer's cloak, thrown nobly and casually on the great oak conference table-as he watched Brenna's immobile pale form being lowered into the life-sustaining waters under her new glass lid.

Then the mushroom officers opened another lid and lifted Ridge. Together they stripped him and lifted him off the table.

As they carried him to his own incubator, he floated naked and full of wonderment on their hands, under the many glass windows (or viewing ports) almost as if he were floating in space itself. Before being laid in his bath of waters with the lid lowered, so sleep came over him, Ridge gazed in limitless wonder upon the Eagle Nebula (M16) with its enormous silhouettes of evaporating gas rising up. There, he beheld a wondrous sight—6,500 light-years from Old Earth and about 3,000 light-years from where *Nebula Express* now streaked through space, en route to the New Earth detected not long ago. Looking like figures wearing cloaks, the huge "elephant trunks" reared up from a vast cloud of cold molecular hydrogen. Metaphors did not suffice. One thought of stalagmites rising from a cavern floor, nunnish figures offering mystic mercies, gaseous towers rearing up in defiance, but most importantly, clouds giving birth to infant stars. Torrents of ultraviolet light, from the vigorous blue pinpricks of hotly burning new baby stars, boiled off the clouds from which they stole their fuel. Energy blew off in columns aligned with the mean axes of spin as the stars trembled just under the explosion threshold in their frantic incineration. Many of the pinprick stars were still hulled in glowing clouds of superheated gas. Some had burned themselves free and looked like burning eggs about to hatch in free space-all within the much greater flowing stream of circling energy that was the whirlpool of the Milky Way itself.

Chapter 18

New Earth was a watery world orbiting a sun much like the old, and that was what had taken the expedition so many thousands of years-finding just such a place among a hundred million or more suns in the Milky Way.

Ridge stood on the balcony of the family estate in the hills above Nuevos Aires. He sipped from a glass of sweet, sharp Armagnac on an inlaid table near the window sill. The windows were open, for it was a spring night, and the air was balmy. Both large moons were full and bright-yellow with mottled gray craters among the as yet only budding and still barren black tree limbs. Only one of the two reddish oxidized moons was visible, and that only low over the haze of light surrounding the city. There was one other important object in the sky as Ridge looked out comfortably, adjusting his bow tie by pulling on it with both hands, and as he then brush his tuxedo with both hands. That other object was a faint blue streak, a fine line, which was the viewing area running in a fine band around Largo. It was up to the Old Man now, and he had not made up his mind yet, though time was running out for him to die his final and natural death. All the treasures had been offloaded and were now on display in the House of Humanity on Avenida Plate overlooking the harbor. Should *Nebula Express* be scrapped and sent into the sun? Or should the ancient ship be maintained as a museum, or maybe the core of a new shopping complex, in orbit around New Earth?

"Ridge!" Brenna called.

"Coming!" He picked up his drink and turned away from the window. He crossed the large drawing room of the family *estancia* overlooking the city on one side, and the ocean beyond that (Nuevo Atlantico) and in the other direction the pampas that gleamed in moonlight.

The Old Man, Colfirio, had made some definite adjustments in kicking off the new world some 20 years ago when the ship hove into orbit. As the ship assumed her orbit, and the natural daylight of Nuevo Sol filled the sky above Largo, the first *tangueros* had come dancing down the streets with their *bandonéones*. They were the first reconstituted full men, the ones who prepared the ship for the rest of the men, women, and children. Much of the ship was still a ruined hulk, and the lives lost in the dormitories to Venable's mudmen would never be regained-which made for an eloquent testimonial, in all its irony, to the unique wonder of each human life. However, all the lives stored in codons and aminomemes were soon enough reconstituted in broth incubators and soon enough the stream of men and women dancing *tango* filled the streets of Largo with celebration. Then came the hard work of fine-tuning and terraforming the relatively primitive world whose several giant islands seemed either rocky and volcanic, with appropriate hardy lichens and mosses, or arid deserts dotted with stubbornly water-retentive pickleweed in a whole glorious *organum* of genera and species. At the same time, the Old Man made sure to install equity and democracy in this kingdom for which he had paid in Old Earth *diñero* an eon ago and part of a galaxy away. On each sweet river he ordered a city founded, roads laid out, places for gathering as people had always done, and most importantly universities in which to cultivate the common human memory and avoid dark ages and war. He was old now, and confined to a wheelchair overlooking the city of his dreams. Gentle breezes stirred his white hair and raked his mottled skin as he stared out with vague gray eyes. If he felt he had lost or gained anything during the ordeal in transit, he did not speak of it to anyone.

Today it was no different. The sun shone brightly, and the wrinkled old man smiled without his usual gruff and almost cruel strength. His blue eyes twinkled merrily as he lay wrapped in a russet blanket. In the distant blue harbor, ships lay at anchor. As he had specified in the founding constitution, his heirs would retain a good fortune, but most of the land and property had been turned over to the communities, and the most energetic and gifted men and women could work hard to buy privatized capital to build a new economy within a humane and equitable social framework. The old man's work was just about done, and he sometimes joked he had now become a temp of sorts, albeit with no special work or hardship, but just to enjoy the presence of his grandchildren.

There was to be a great celebration on the twentieth anniversary of the *caudillo*'s first footfall on the planet that might have been named after him, but he refused the honor and instead asked simply that it be called New Earth. By now, there was no record of where Old Earth had been, which might even be rebuilding itself from its incineration under the comets, but there was a plan to one day beam messages in that direction of the galaxy in hope of hearing from some distant cousins. Perhaps a few of the colonists on Triton or Luna or some other corners had survived and rebuilt. One might listen for radio messages from that direction. At the moment, the colonists were too busy laying roads and breaking fields and irrigating the land to wonder about their long-ago home.

Ridge stepped into the grand patio where a group of little school children in their best suits were being marshaled for a choral rendition, Songs of Hope and Faith. So read the little brochure Ridge studied with amusement and pleasure as he crossed the marbled floor. His own children-two boys and two girls-would be singing among them. He and Brenna had been given a late start in this new life. It had taken the new people extra time to find and consolidate the scattered thoughts and memories of those who had suffered most under Venable's ministrations. A generation had grown by before Ridge and Brenna were raised from their tombs. Colfirio had already been hard at work, in a much younger body than that in which he had gone to sleep, and now he was growing old again a second time. He would leave his entire remaining estate to Ridge and Brenna, and everything must be just so. To that end, he'd had the best physicians and biofactors working for years to put together the best of who Ridge and Brenna had been. They'd even retrieved the child with which she'd been pregnant when the comets struck Old Earth, and that child was now a willowy blonde with serious eyes and regal demeanor, named Landa after the red-headed woman from Tacoma who had lived so briefly and had no children, but had died, Ridge hoped, happily in the cascades of warm water and green light and piano music in the Hotel Largo so long ago and far away.

Brenna smiled as she turned, holding up the baby of a sister who was both younger and older than Brenna. The sister, Marta, had been born before Brenna was reborn. It was one of the many wonders of their new life. Sometimes, like now, when he put his arm around his wife and took her aside for a private kiss, he would ask her: "Do you remember much about the trip coming over?"

She would laugh innocently and shake her head. "No, not much at all, and I suspect it's best that way. Do you remember any of those horror stories grandfather sometimes tells late at night when he is tired and giddy, and should go to bed?" She looked more radiant than he could remember, and she was positively aglow over her children. She looked lovely, Ridge thought, with her dark red hair and pale skin, with her serious eyes and bright smile as she stood in the sunshine surrounded by children and with the wind lightly blowing her flowery dress. Ridge would shake his head and say, "Probably not half as much as I could remember, and definitely much more than I wish to remember."

More Info: Worlds of John Argo

John Argo is a writer of Science Fiction, Dark Fantasy, and Science-Horror Fiction (SH, or Dark SF). He lives with his wife and family in Southern California. He is a published poet, as well, which more than anything defines his rich, nuanced style.

Whenever you read a John Argo story or novel, no matter how dark or thrilling, you will find a love story at its core. In these tales, we travel to the far sectors of the human existence, while the characters' search for meaning glows like a lantern in darkness. Trust John Argo as a frequent traveler and tour guide along highways through imaginative space and time.

John Argo is the Web publishing pseudonym of San Diego author Jean-Thomas Cullen, who also goes by John T. Cullen. He has been publishing online since 1996. His webplex includes www.metrowebplex.com (central hub of multiple sites) and johntcullen.com (personal auhor site).

John Argo's web presence is at Clocktower Books (world's first real digital publisher*, online since 1996):

www.johntcullen.com
* * * *

*Clocktower Books was, to our knowledge, the world's first publisher, ever, to publish real digital, proprietary (not public domain), novel-length fiction (books) online in digital format for download. We launched this program in 1996, using an innovative process of publishing weekly serial chapters. Readers who needed to know the outcome, and couldn't stand the suspense, could email for a complete digital text file anywhere in the world. We received raves and kudos from around the globe. We used this serial chapter method to publish three John Argo books over 1996-1996: *This Shoal of Space* and *Pioneers* (both SF); and *Neon Blue*, a suspense novel. All three novels were bestsellers in the earliest e-book forums, including the original Barnes & Noble website in 2000, and other venues including Rocket eBooks.

Publisher's Dedication

(Circa 2007:) **To *Deep Outside SFFH*,** the world's oldest professional web-only magazine of science fiction, fantasy, and horror (speculative & dark fiction), launched April 15, 1998. An archive site is still maintained (www.deepoutside.com). Small but mighty, the magazine was and is an innovator stressing quality over quantity, equally valuing literary and commercial components of short fiction, promoting the particular strengths of digital media without losing what has been great about print media. The magazine continued uninterruptedly publishing online as *Far Sector SFFH* (www.farsector.com/) until January 2007 under the sole proprietorship of John T. Cullen, with help from a team of dedicated authors and editors. Far Sector SFFH has an entry at the online SF Encyclopedia, while Deep Outside SFFH will be featured in Mike Ashley's fourth in a quartet of scholarly books on the history of SF magazines (Liverpool University Press).

Strengths include new modes of distribution that break from the past and work with innovators like Fictionwise (fictionwise.com). *Deep Outside SFFH* (originally *Outside: Speculative & Dark Fiction*) became the first such web-only magazine to be listed in Writer's Market (1999 Edition) alongside the pulps. Founders were John T. Cullen and Brian Callahan. Significant contributors have been A. L. Sirois, John Kenneth Muir, Dennis Latham, and Shaun Farrell, plus of course all the authors we published over a decade. We published many unknown newcomers, as well as established talent. Some of these authors already had won prestigious awards (Pat York, Nebula), while others went on from obscurity to win important awards and nominations (Tim Pratt, Ted Kosmatka, and many others).

Most important, of course, is content. While digital innovations are exciting, there is no substitute for good old-fashioned storytelling from fine authors like Dennis Latham, Pat York, Melanie Tem, Joe Murphy, A. L. Sirois, Joel Best, and many others the magazine has sent to your viewing surface.

Message sent back in time to the Futurians of the 1930s: *"We have landed in the future, which we find to be exhilarating. Maybe 'breathtaking' and 'terrifying' would be better adjectives. Humans are still behaving stupidly, and wantonly killing each other, so we add 'disappointing.' Will send full report soon. Aim your crystal radio sets to the following coordinates..."*

www.ingramcontent.com/pod-product-compliance
Lightning Source LLC
Chambersburg PA
CBHW030332180626
46810CB00003B/1330